nightrise

Praise for the *everafter* series

ForeWord Reviews 2009 Book of the Year Awards Finalist for Horror

everafter

"Stark and Tam have managed to scare the bejesus out of me in their highly skilled effort to introduce Valentine and Alexa, two professional students, who are thrust into the forbidden realm of Vampires and Weres. ...the writing is superb, the characters believable, the plot strong...I have to give these authors kudos."
— *Kissed By Venus*

nevermore

"You will not be able to put this book down once you start. I found it well written and totally interesting and I recommend it to any of you who are interested in the shifter concept."—Amos Lassen, *Literary Pride*

What reviewers say about Nell Stark's fiction

"In this character driven story, the author gives us two very likeable and idealistic women that are without pretense. The growth these two experience from their involvement in an important cause, as well as the friendships that they make throughout the year, is moving and refreshing. Kudos to the author on a very fine book." —*Curve Magazine*

"*Running with the Wind* is a fast-paced read. Stark's characters are richly drawn and interesting. The dialog can be lively and wry and elicited several laughs from this reader. ...the discussions of the nature of sex, love, power, and sexuality are insightful and represent a welcome voice from the view of late-20-something characters today. The love scenes between Corrie and Quinn are erotically charged and sweet."—*Midwest Book Review*

Visit us at www.boldstrokesbooks.com

By Nell Stark and Trinity Tam

everafter

nevermore

nightrise

By Nell Stark

Running With the Wind

Homecoming

nightrise

by
Nell Stark and Trinity Tam

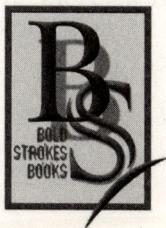

2011

NIGHTRISE

ISBN 10: 1-60282-238-7
ISBN 13: 978-1-60282-238-2

This Trade Paperback Original Is Published By
Bold Strokes Books, Inc.
P.O. Box 249
Valley Falls, NY 12185

First Edition: August 2011

CREDITS
Editor: Cindy Cresap
Production Design: Susan Ramundo
Cover Design By Sheri (graphicartist2020@hotmail.com)

Acknowledgments

We are first and foremost grateful to Cindy Cresap, who has helped us to weave together the many threads of Val and Alexa's story.

We are likewise indebted to Radclyffe for sowing the seed of this idea years ago, for her invaluable feedback on this narrative, and for giving us the opportunity to publish with Bold Strokes Books. We'd like to thank all of the wonderful, hardworking, and selfless people at BSB—Connie, Lori, Lee, Sandy, Paula, Sheri, and others—for helping to put out and market quality product year after year. The members of Team BSB, including our many fellow authors, continue to inspire us and we count you all in our extended family.

Finally, our thanks goes out to each reader who picks up one of our books. This series is, above all, for you, and we hope you enjoy it.

Dedication

For the friends who helped us find our way back
to each other, once upon a time.

alexa

CHAPTER ONE

I woke to the sound of sirens. Shrill and persistent, they reverberated in my ears and echoed my panicked thoughts. *Gone.*

Valentine was gone.

The urge to shift came on strong, and I curled into a ball around my twisted blankets. As the sounds of alarm gradually lengthened and faded, my heartbeat began to slow. I unclenched my fists and rolled onto my back to stare at the spider web of cracks in our ceiling. My ceiling. *Gone.*

And yet she wasn't. I hadn't seen Val in almost two months, but only because of a concerted effort on my part to avoid her. The gossip mill of the wereshifter/vampire Consortium was churning with news of her. Despite my self-imposed isolation, bits and pieces reached me, the flotsam and jetsam that survived each bend and drop of the river. Valentine Darrow had opened a highly exclusive club right underneath the mayor's nose, near Gracie Mansion. Valentine Darrow had signed a lease on a penthouse apartment in Soho that had its own pool. Valentine Darrow was having an affair with Helen Lambros. Valentine Darrow was the woman to see if you were a vampire wanting to secure your financial future in these times of political upheaval.

I hadn't had the strength to investigate any rumor except the last, and I'd been shocked to find it true. Only a week after our separation, apparently, Valentine had dropped out of medical school to take over the management of the smallest and least glamorous of her family's banks. It had been known as Darrow Savings and Loan, a small-time operation that catered mostly to those of the older generation who lived on the porous border of Hell's Kitchen and Midtown. Now, it was called the Bank of Mithras—a reference to the governing body of vampires, of which Val, as the sole survivor of the clan of the Missionary, was a member. Within days of her taking over, the bank had received several substantial deposits. And just like that, the trend had been set. With the Order's endorsement, Val would be making money hand over fist. Maybe the rumor about the pool was true, too.

I turned onto my side for a few moments before finally swinging my legs over the edge of the bed. Late afternoon sunlight filtered through the nearest window to warm my feet as they rested on the floor. I scrubbed my hands over my face and tried to gather myself. I'd slept away the middle part of the day for the third time this week. It was a concession to my feline half, who loved to doze in the warmth of the midday sun. I felt lazy for sleeping while most people had to work, and while the majority of my cohorts studied for the next day of class, but it also felt good to indulge my inner panther. Especially since she was all I had left.

My mouth felt dry, but I bypassed the bathroom in favor of the kitchen sink. I didn't want to interact with a mirror right now, when I could feel the pillow crease on my cheek and the snarls in my hair. I had curled up on my bed immediately after coming home from class, without eating anything for lunch. Or breakfast. Half-heartedly, I put a piece of bread in the toaster and washed the few dishes I'd used last night. A wine glass. A bowl, still partially filled with rice. One pot.

You're not eating enough, babe. I heard the words, the familiar intonations, as clearly as though Valentine were actually behind me, and I wrapped my arms around my middle as the spike of pain in my heart tried to flay me open. Early on in our relationship, Valentine had proclaimed herself my own personal chef. She had experimented tirelessly with my mother's recipes until she had perfected my favorite childhood dishes. And she had always refused to let me skip meals, even when I'd barricaded myself in the library to study for finals.

"Even your ghost is a worrywart, Valentine," I whispered, forcing myself not to turn around. My mind was just playing tricks on me again, as it had so often during these past weeks. Karma had suggested I relocate, and she'd even offered me the second bedroom in her apartment. But I couldn't make myself leave. I couldn't give up this place, not when Val's essence seemed to permeate the very walls. And so I let the memories and sensations of Valentine as she had been—my loyal and loving champion—cascade over and through me despite the pain. She was my soul mate. Or at least, she had been. I wasn't even sure that I believed in the concept of soul mates until Valentine's departure ripped open such a chasm inside me, I didn't ever think I'd be whole again. Maybe her soul truly was haunting me now—now that she was a full vampire.

When she had gotten sick in the late autumn, I hadn't been surprised; each semester always brought with it a new cadre of germs. But instead of shaking off the bug, she'd grown rapidly worse. Val was always a terrible patient, and she'd refused any medical attention. I shouldn't have trusted her judgment. Only when she lapsed into incoherent rambling, her skin fiery to the touch, did I contact the Consortium medical staff. While I waited for their house call, I'd forced a thermometer between her lips and discovered that her fever was pushing 104 degrees.

An echo of remembered terror sliced through me, and I leaned against the kitchen counter, toast forgotten. Harold Clavier himself, the chief Consortium physician, had shown up on our doorstep with a stretcher. As his assistants had worked to secure Val, I'd bombarded him with questions, only to be interrupted.

"You truly do not understand what is happening?" he'd asked in a tone both incredulous and disdainful. "Valentine is on the cusp of her transition. She will be a full vampire within the week."

I should have known, or at least suspected. Val had been increasingly withdrawn in the months leading up to her illness, but I'd attributed her behavior to the stress of her second year of medical school piled on top of the anxiety she was suffering as blood prime—the last surviving member of the clan of the Missionary. Balthasar Brenner, a powerful werewolf alpha bent on overthrowing the Consortium itself, had a price on her head. She had every right to be preoccupied.

What I hadn't known then was that Valentine had stopped drinking exclusively from me. The first time hadn't been her fault; while I was in Africa over the summer, she had been given a blood transfusion against her will. As far as I knew, that transfusion marked the beginning of her downward spiral. Until that point, the vampire parasite that lived in her bloodstream had recognized my blood as a substitute for Val's red cells. But as soon as she'd been exposed to the blood of others, mine stopped having special properties. Once she had emerged from the brief coma that marked her transition to full vampire status, I'd learned that Val had been drinking from other people for months—usually around the time of the full moon, when I made trips into the countryside to allow my panther the freedom to run under the open sky.

Valentine had betrayed me. That's what it felt like. But then again, I was the one who had left New York for the summer, and my absence had been one of the contributing factors that led to her need for a transfusion. Hadn't I betrayed her, in a way?

I shook my head and reached for the piece of toast. It was cool by now. After spreading some jam onto the bread, I took a bite. My stomach churned, but I forced myself to chew and swallow. And then again. I couldn't afford to become weak. Retaining control over my panther demanded concentration and inner fortitude, both of which were in short supply at the moment.

Sometimes, the hardest cross to bear was the knowledge that Valentine still wanted me. She had woken thirsty from her coma, and I'd been there to sustain her. But her mouth had not been gentle on my skin, and her need had not been laced with tender passion. I'd had to struggle not to shift, and the experience of feeding her had left me nauseated instead of satisfied. And then I'd learned about the others from our mutual friend Karma.

A fellow shifter, Karma had been instrumental in helping me to become a Were so I could sustain Valentine forever. When we spoke shortly after Val's transition, Karma admitted to having heard gossip about an increase in Val's appetite, but at the time, she had dismissed the hearsay as rumormongering. I wasn't angry with Karma—in this case, pinning down blame was a useless exercise—but I couldn't help wanting to shake Val until her sharp teeth rattled for hiding the evidence of her deterioration.

Valentine hadn't been apologetic in the slightest. "You've known the strength of my thirst from the beginning," she had said, lips twisting into an incredulous frown when I confronted her. "And it's grown exponentially. You can't honestly expect me to be monogamous now. That's completely unreasonable."

Despite my sorrow, I had been firm. "Those are my conditions. Me and no one else, or this is over."

She had paused, her eyes growing hazy. For a moment, she'd almost reminded me of her former self—soft and open, vulnerable in her desire. "You do taste so damn good. Exquisite, like a bouquet on my tongue. So much better than any—"

And then she'd cut herself off. Her gaze had measured me, both the length of my body and the strength of the steel behind my words. My skin had crawled under her callous appraisal.

"Fine." The word had pierced that silent moment, shattering my hope. She had turned and walked away then. Out of the door and out of my life. I hadn't seen her since. But her declaration had been tinged with petulance, and I knew she wasn't pleased. I knew she still wanted me. Craved me, even.

The knowledge was a comfort colder than my toast. When I realized that I was just staring at the half-eaten piece of bread, I threw it into the trash. Why, why did I have to keep reliving those final moments? Why were my emotions just as raw today as they had been then? Why couldn't I find shelter in reason and reach even the smallest modicum of acceptance?

The phone rang and I answered it quickly, glad of the distraction. It was Karma calling to check up on me. "We're going out tonight," she said without preamble.

I sighed. "Why do we have this conversation every week?" I wandered out into the living room and sank onto the couch, trying not to think about how many times Val had made love to me there, when she couldn't wait the few seconds it would take to reach our bed. "I've told you before: I can't go out. Not yet. I can't see her."

"Tonight is different. It's shifters-only at Luna, so you can be sure you won't run into her."

I had just opened my mouth to take a different tack when the doorbell rang. "You're not going to turn me away now, are you?" Karma sounded rather smug.

For a moment, I thought of doing just that. But as quickly as it had come, the flash of anger at her intrusiveness receded. Despite months of my reticence and solitary confinement, Karma hadn't given up on me. She called every day, coaxing and pleading and cajoling me into conversation. Now she had decided it was time for the next step.

"All right. You win." An unfamiliar smile tugged at my lips as I rose to buzz her in. Brushing some crumbs from my shirtfront, I prepared myself for the gentle chiding I would undoubtedly receive.

"Thank you for humoring me," she said as she stepped inside. The scent of jasmine attended her light embrace, and as I inhaled deeply, I felt my stomach settle.

"Thank you for being persistent." I hung up her coat and gestured for her to join me on the futon. Dressed in brown slacks and a shimmering gold top that matched the flecks of color in her dark eyes, she looked out of place in my shabby apartment. "Something to drink?"

She remained standing. "I'm fine. Let's find you something to wear."

While she went through my closet, I perched on the bed, wishing I could just lie back and let myself fall asleep again. But Karma remained singularly focused on her mission. When she extracted a pair of crimson leather pants and tossed them to me, tears suddenly threatened.

"I was wearing these when I first met Val," I said quietly.

She was at my side in a second. "Oh, sweetie, I'm sorry. I didn't know. Let me put them back."

"No, it's okay." I slid my fingertips over the supple leather and tried to muster a brave face. "Not only are these totally hot, they're also really quite comfortable."

"See how they feel," Karma said, flashing me an encouraging smile.

Suddenly determined, I kicked off my sweats. I was beautiful. I was intelligent. I was strong—stronger even than the grief that had taken root in my heart. And I was going out tonight.

❖

My bravado sputtered out as soon as the taxi pulled away from the curb. Ever intuitive, Karma reached for my hand. For several long, silent minutes, I drew strength from her closeness, but as soon as I could trust my voice again, I pulled away.

"So tell me what you're working on right now." I needed a distraction, and Karma's anecdotes were always good; as a curator for the Egyptian Art exhibit at the Met, she routinely handled items that had survived for millennia, and I enjoyed hearing her stories about both the artifacts in her charge and the history behind them.

"Last week, we got a shipment of artifacts recently excavated from the Nile delta. Some truly remarkable finds."

Her enthusiasm made me smile. "Oh? Will a few join the permanent collection?"

"Absolutely." She reached for her purse as the cab neared Luna, the most upscale and exclusive of the clubs that catered to New York's wereshifter and vampire populations. "We're still in the process of cataloguing, but once we're finished, I might be able to get you an invitation to a private viewing. If you like."

"I'd love to. You wouldn't get into some kind of trouble, though, would you?"

"Only if you stole something." Karma directed the driver to pull over.

"Let me—" But she had handed over the fare before I could protest.

I had no doubt that Karma was perfectly well off financially, but it didn't seem likely that she was as wealthy as I was now. Shortly after Valentine had gotten sick, Constantine had set up a trust fund in my name and refused to hear a word of protest. His sympathy for me, combined with the close call we'd had with Brenner in August, had motivated Constantine to make some provisions in the event of his own death. "You are the closest thing I have to a daughter," he had told me. And he'd also claimed that after a hundred years of investments and interests, the sum he was gifting me was a small fraction of his total wealth.

Sometimes I still felt guilty for accepting his generosity, and I was being very cautious about my own investments. But the security was liberating. Not having to be anxious about how I would repay my student loans or support myself if I couldn't find work as a lawyer freed me to focus on other things. Like my place in the hierarchy of wereshifters, and in the now-endangered Consortium. Like Brenner's plans and movements.

Like Valentine, and whether there was any way in heaven or hell to reverse what had happened to her.

The bouncers recognized us and waved us past the line of people outside the door. Despite Karma's reassurance that there would be no vampires in attendance tonight, I was hyper vigilant. I scanned the dance floor as Karma led me past the staircase that rose sinuously out of the middle of the room, but all I saw were shifters. My panther uncoiled into alertness as she sensed the presence of so many other beasts lying in wait.

We stopped at a table near the bar, around which three other women were already perched on chrome stools. My footsteps lagged as I realized I'd be forced to socialize with strangers, and I shot a quick glare at Karma. Was she trying to set me up? But if she noticed my consternation, she gave no sign, and within moments I was exchanging air-kisses with three of her curator colleagues from museums around the city. It was logical, I supposed, for Weres to be drawn to a profession so richly steeped in history, and I found myself genuinely interested in the news they shared about their work. All questions about myself, I redirected with the caginess I was learning in my Trial Advocacy course.

After an hour passed with no sign of a single vampire, I began to relax a little. Our second round of drinks was hand-delivered by Sebastian Brenner himself, the owner of Luna and one of the most prominent players in the younger generation of shifters. As the estranged son of Balthasar, he had come under recent suspicion. Unlike his father, however, Sebastian embraced his humanity and worked to merge his business and personal interests with those of the mortals who surrounded us. He had proven a valuable ally in the struggle to foil his father's most recent attempt to destroy the Consortium; in fact, I owed him my life. But now I regarded him warily—not because I was afraid of him, but because he had nurtured an attraction to Valentine for a while. He might have seen her recently.

"Hello, Alexa."

When he handed me my drink, I clutched at it for purchase and fought the urge to take a long sip. I didn't want to betray weakness in his presence. "Sebastian. How are you?"

He gestured toward the crowded dance floor. "Business is fine, as you can see. You'd almost think the world had gone back to normal."

I gazed out over the expanse of writhing bodies. "Some of them probably think it has."

His mouth twisted. "Then they're idiots." He was about to say something more when a commotion broke out near the front of the club—a shout, the sound of scuffling, a slamming door. Sebastian's eyes narrowed. One of his bouncers, a heavyset man in a dark blue shirt and gray slacks, hurried across the floor toward us.

Sebastian touched my shoulder. "I'll be right back." He met the bouncer halfway and they conferred, dark heads close together. Sebastian gesticulated sharply, and his employee took half a step backward as though he'd been struck, nodding all the while.

"What is it?" Karma asked.

"I don't know." The man loped back toward the door and Sebastian returned to our table, waving off our concerns before we could voice them.

"Just a group of rowdy vampires, wanting to get in. Apparently, it's someone's coming out party."

My pulse spiked at "vampire," and I had to work at keeping the panic from my expression. There were a lot of vampires in New

York City. What were the odds that Val had come here, tonight, when Luna was off-limits?

"What exactly is a coming out party in this context?" I asked, my head filled with competing visions of GLBT Pride and debutante balls.

Sebastian rolled his eyes. "It's an idiotic tradition created by the human hangers-on. They believe being turned is cause for a bacchanal."

Millions of humans were fascinated by vampires, of course, but only a select few knew of their existence. Usually, they were chosen for their obedience and pliancy. All of them, to my knowledge, hoped one day to be turned. Many died before they ever got the chance, but it was a risk they were willing to take. To someone like Valentine, who had been turned against her will, this tradition must be disgusting. Then again, maybe she felt differently now.

I shook my head, willing the thoughts of her to disperse. There was still some kind of disturbance at the door, and more heads were beginning to turn. I didn't understand the partyers' motivations, and I resented their intrusion now. One look at Sebastian's grim face was proof he shared my feelings.

A different bouncer sought him out, and again he left us. This time, I could hear bits of their conversation. When the man told Sebastian that there were too many in the crowd outside to turn away without risking some kind of incident, Sebastian's jaw muscles flexed ominously.

"Fine. Let them in. But I want them gone as soon as possible. Find reasons, and boot them one by one so they don't have critical mass."

The bouncer was just starting back across the room, when a hush fell over those gathered near the door. And then I heard her voice. It rose in a descant over the heavy industrial throb of the DJ's beat, and I knew I was in hell.

"Sebastian!" She emerged into my field of view a moment later, and my throat went dry. Dressed in white slacks and a matching tank, her bright gold hair set in jagged spikes, Valentine was a living flame. Slender as a whip and as painful, she crossed to where Sebastian stood and kissed him on the mouth.

"Call off your watchdogs. We only want a drink."

Judas. That was all I could think. And her kiss had worked; Sebastian's irritation melted away. He even reached out with one hand to cup Val's waist in a possessive gesture that forced bile into my throat. She didn't lean into the caress, but she didn't pull away either. My panther snarled awake, pushing behind my eyes in search of the danger that had flooded my blood with adrenaline.

I could feel Karma's hand on my knee, but the rest of me was numb. Frozen. I couldn't look away. Sebastian had taken Val's arm and was trying to turn her around. I wondered whether he was worried about what would happen if she saw me. The thought pierced through my numbness, a strange sort of comfort.

Val resisted his pull and sidestepped out of his grasp. And then she went very still as her gaze met mine. How had she known to look? Was it possible that our connection had survived even the death of her soul?

"Alexa." She spoke my name like a prayer, and a jolt went through me, raising the fine hairs on my arms and prickling the skin at the back of my neck. In that moment, I despaired at her ability to still affect me so strongly. For almost two months, I had forced myself to stay out of her path, to concentrate on my studies. Moving on—that's what I'd called it. But I had only been running in place.

She walked slowly toward me, as one might toward a frightened animal. And I was afraid—afraid of the hold she still had on me, and angry that I was granting her such power. Distantly, I felt Karma squeeze my leg, but I couldn't take my eyes off Valentine. Thirst and desire battled for dominance on her face, and the taut muscles of her arms betrayed her tension. She wanted me. Wanted to drink me, wanted to fuck me. Those desires weren't new, and it had been my pleasure to indulge her in them, but always because they had been accompanied by her all-consuming love.

That love was absent now. No softness lit her eyes, no tenderness inflected her movements. She was Thirst incarnate.

The revelation broke my paralysis, and I surged to my feet. Surprise flickered across Val's face, and she paused. We stared at each other, separated only by a few footsteps. Separated by a bottomless chasm.

She cocked her head and looked me up and down. The clinical once-over made me nauseated.

"You look good."

I almost laughed in her face. My Valentine would never have said that. I was far too thin, and I'd had to liberally apply makeup so as not to look like a walking corpse. My Valentine would have been dizzy with worry. My Valentine would have wrapped her arms around me in a loving embrace instead of stalking me like a hunter. My Valentine would have dragged me home—not to gorge herself on my blood, but to cook me a meal and cajole me into eating every bite. My Valentine was dead.

"Stop." The word was steady. Pride filtered through the haze of my pain. "I don't want to hear it."

It was hard to angle my body away from hers, and even harder to walk away. We were connected still, and every step I took seemed to stretch the frail, invisible cord that held me to her. The stretching was pain. By the time I reached the door, my panther was frantic with the need to confront the threat that was causing me such distress. I jostled one of the bouncers in my urgency to get outside and he snarled.

The crisp air knifed down my lungs, bringing with it the jumbled scents of a crowd. I had emerged into the gathering of vampires who were trying to gain access to Luna. Keeping my head down, I shouldered my way through them, desperate to reach open space.

"Alexa? Is that you?"

Kyle Jordan was one of the Consortium's human servants who had been raised knowing the secret of vampires and Weres. He was a loyal source of blood to Helen herself. Or rather, he had been. He had been turned recently, his human scent shot through with the wintry chill I'd learned to associate with vampires. And beneath it all, an echo of Valentine's distinctive fragrance.

The pieces coalesced. Blinded by the hot rush of tears, I stumbled. When he grasped my arm to steady me, I shook him off so violently that he fell to the ground. Kyle smelled like Valentine because she had fed him her blood to turn him. This was his coming out party.

"Alexa!"

Her voice again. The anger pierced me like a knife between the shoulder blades, making it impossible to breathe. My panther clawed her way forward, demanding I shift to face my attacker. I was strong enough to hold her back, but I didn't want to. I wanted nothing more than to lose myself in the elegant simplicity of her animal brain.

With the last of my strength, I spun to face Val. She was standing at the top of the stairs, incandescent against the dark façade of the club. I wanted to slap her inscrutable face. I wanted to kiss her beautiful mouth. I wanted to fall at her feet and beg her to dig down deeper than the parasite that ruled her blood—to find some small scrap of her former self, and return to me.

I kept my fists clenched at my sides. "Stay away from me, Valentine."

As I spoke the words, I let the panther take me. Through my transformation, I kept my eyes on Val, despite the hoarse shouts and panicked cries of the crowd. My ears flickered at the cocking of multiple guns, but I refused to be cowed. A low snarl rumbled deep in my throat as I bared my teeth at the shell of the woman I had loved.

And then I leapt away into the shadows.

CHAPTER TWO

The sun was just barely visible over the East River as I approached Constantine's brownstone. His townhouse was spacious by New York City standards, but it paled in comparison to his former kingdom—the hidden Were city of Telassar, nestled deep in the Atlas Mountains of Morocco. Constantine was living in exile, having been driven out of Telassar by Balthasar Brenner just a few months ago. My jaw clenched at the memory of Brenner, standing outside the walls of the city at the front of his army and demanding Constantine's surrender. The Consortium's forces in Africa had initiated a counter siege last month, but so far their efforts had been ineffective.

As I drew closer, I saw Karma sitting on the steps. She held out a Starbucks cup when I approached her, and I caught the aroma of coffee. Pain flared deep in my chest as I remembered how Valentine had plied me with chai lattes every morning for two weeks while trying to convince me to accompany her on a date. In the first few days after our breakup, the mere scent of chai tea had been a painful reminder of our courtship, and I'd made the decision to return to drinking coffee.

"I am so sorry," Karma said as I took the cup.

Late last night, after finally transforming back to my human self, I had wanted to blame her. But in the intervening hours, as reason began to gain sway, my anger had cooled. "It's not your fault. You were just trying to help. I have terrible luck." I took a tentative sip and found comfort in the bold flavor that slid over my tongue and down my throat. "Thanks for this."

"You're welcome." She smoothed her gloved hands over her slacks in an uncharacteristic show of anxiety. "Any casualties?"

A swell of affection rose in me as I realized that even if I answered in the affirmative, she would have my back. "Not unless you feel a strong affinity to subway rats."

She laughed, clearly relieved. "Were they big ones?"

"The size of housecats." I slid in next to her, shivering as the cold stone of the step seeped through my jeans. "The transit authority should compensate me for getting rid of several."

We sat in silence for a while as the city began to wake up around us. Across the street, a woman in a fuzzy pink bathrobe was letting her dog out to do its morning business. A few doors away, a man in an expensive suit hurried down his front steps and turned toward the nearest subway. Normal people going through their normal routines, but the rhythm of the world still felt alien to me without Valentine at my side. Would I ever adjust?

"I didn't know about Sebastian." Karma rested her palm on my knee as she spoke. "Whatever it is that he's doing with…her…I'm out of the loop."

I closed my eyes against the echo of last night's rage at witnessing Sebastian's hands on Valentine. Their kiss. The only saving grace was the memory of her body language—rigid and aloof in response to his possessiveness. Whatever was going on between them, Sebastian had far more of a vested interest in it than she did. She still wanted *me,* not him. I could cling to that fact until I was strong enough to let her go.

"I'm sorry you're getting caught in the crossfire."

Karma stood and offered me her hand. "If I hear anything relevant, do you want to know?"

I weighed my options. I could remain willfully ignorant of Valentine's actions and lie awake at night imagining every scenario under the sun. Or I could take whatever scraps Karma discovered and lie awake at night mourning the loss of my soul mate. Every day, I told myself that her actions were no longer any of my business, but that was always a lie. Valentine was mine. We had promised each other forever in a way most lovers couldn't.

"I want to know anything. Everything." My gaze never left Karma's as I accepted her outstretched hand. "You'll think I'm crazy, but I haven't given up yet on getting her back."

"I don't think you're crazy. I wouldn't give up either." She squeezed my fingers then gestured toward the door. "It's time. After you."

A few seconds after ringing the bell, we were buzzed in. One of Malcolm's guards stood sentry just inside the door, and I nodded to him as we made our way down the foyer. The hallway opened onto a bright and spacious room populated only sparsely with furniture: a large oak dining table, a matching desk under one of the windows, an armchair near another. Brightly colored shag rugs covered much of the hardwood floor. Contentment radiated from my panther, who loved the airy feel of Constantine's home and felt comforted by her sire's proximity.

While most humans would have hung a large television on one of the walls and arranged couches to face it, Constantine's only wall decorations were landscape paintings, and his guests usually lounged on the floor around a low coffee table. He and Malcolm were already seated, and after peeling off our coats, Karma and I joined them. Soon, the business of the day would begin, and Malcolm and Constantine would join their vampire colleagues at Consortium headquarters. But for now, our select group could discuss shifter politics and strategy without fear of betrayal or interference.

"Good morning," I said, trying to gauge the mood in the room. Neither of them were particularly expressive men, and I couldn't tell whether they were displeased with something or just preoccupied.

Constantine turned his laptop screen toward me. "Explain this."

His browser was open to someone's Twitter feed. I didn't recognize the username, but he or she had last tweeted at two o'clock in the morning. *Just saw a HUGE BLACK CAT run down stairs of 51st street station,* read the update. *A fucking panther in Manhattan, riding the fucking 6 train!*

Torn between apprehension and amusement, I shrugged. "No one will believe it."

"That is not the point." Malcolm's tone reminded me of my father's when I had misbehaved as a young child. "Your control must be better than this. Our situation is far too precarious to risk any kind of exposure."

He dared to accuse me of not knowing the stakes? I wanted to lash out, and my panther snarled as my temper rose. But I held my tongue, and her, in check.

"It's my fault," Karma said.

"It's not." I met Malcolm's gaze. "And it won't happen again."

"I know the past few months have been emotional ones," Constantine said, "and we're all under even more stress than usual—"

As much as I appreciated his sympathy, I wanted to stop talking about last night. Every moment spent reliving it made my chest constrict and my head throb. I held up a hand to forestall him. "Like I said, it won't happen again. Let's move on to the important topics."

Malcolm wasted no time. "The siege of Telassar remains in stalemate. If, as we suspect, traitors in our army are covertly supplying the city, we have yet to determine who the culprits are or how they make their arrangements."

Constantine muttered a string of expletives in French as he ran his fingers through the several inches of curly black hair that crowned his normally-shaven head. He had vowed not to cut a single lock until Telassar had been restored to his command. Now it was my turn to feel sympathy for him; I could only imagine his frustration at remaining in New York while others commanded the forces meant to reinstate him to power.

"More and more fools are flocking to Brenner's banner every day." Malcolm's disgust was palpable. "Karma, you have news on the latest domestic attacks?"

Karma was ready with her smartphone. "Five casualties in a Los Angeles suburb on Friday. Four in Boston on Sunday. And ten in a small town in South Dakota yesterday. All claimed by Weres who profess allegiance to Brenner."

"South Dakota?" These seemingly random acts of terrorism had been cropping up for the past two months, but they had been confined to major metropolitan areas until now.

Karma nodded. "That one was ugly. Six of the ten were humans."

Over the summer, Brenner had released a deadly virus into the shifter community of New York. He had promised the vaccine to any Were who brought him the head of a vampire. Valentine had discovered a cure, and the Consortium had synthesized and distributed it widely. But her breakthrough had only been a momentary setback for Brenner, who launched a campaign of terrorism reinforced by aggressive propagandizing. The peace between Weres and vampires had always been fragile, and as more and more shifters bought into Brenner's rhetoric, the Consortium itself was beginning to fray. Attacks against vampires were at least a weekly occurrence now, and often humans found themselves in the crossfire.

"Three attacks since last week, in addition to the eight thwarted by my team," Constantine mused. "They're escalating." As the chief of tactical operations of the task force charged with countering Brenner's plans, Constantine and his operatives across the country worked to gather intelligence on and neutralize shifter attacks. He turned to me. "What news from the Web?"

I had volunteered to monitor Brenner's public communications, which freed up Malcolm's most trusted people at the Consortium to work on the encrypted messages that passed between Brenner and his lieutenants. "He's continuing to send daily messages across a range of media to his followers. The blog is getting nearly ten thousand hits a day."

Constantine's lip curled. "That fucking blog."

I watched beads of sweat form along his hairline and had to mentally wrestle with my panther as she sensed her sire's distress. Brenner's blog was a particularly sore spot. Full of vitriol and propaganda against Malcolm, Constantine, and other high-profile Weres who persisted in allying with vampires, the blog purported to be a record of "injustices" that were being perpetrated by vampires against Weres. It continued to motivate shifters around the world to abandon the Consortium's founding principles and turn on the vampires.

"We have a new priority," Malcolm announced, snapping me out of my thoughts. "As you know, my analysts routinely track Brenner's known associates, especially those who have remained stateside. Over the past few days, we have noticed hundreds of millions of dollars being funneled through corporate shells into the accounts of several of these individuals."

Karma looked as alarmed as I felt, but from Constantine's grim expression, it was evident that Malcolm had already shared this news with him. My stomach soured as I contemplated the possibilities.

"Do you have any idea what he's planning?"

"No, but I can think of all too many options." Malcolm stood and began to pace. "He could be amassing an army, or building a bomb. Or he may intend to work in more subtle ways."

"Balthasar, subtle?" Constantine's laugh was bitter. "Never. He is going to attack. The only questions are where and when." He glanced at his watch. "And we are not going to learn the answers by sitting around this table."

Karma rose at the clear dismissal. "I'll have my ear to the ground at Luna, as always," she said.

The reminder that she often worked with Sebastian made my panther push for control. Whenever I'd asked what exactly Karma did at Luna, she became evasive. My best guess was that she was under someone's orders to stay close to Sebastian, but given his deep ambivalence toward his father, I couldn't figure out why. He had always struck me as a fairly stereotypical young businessman. Flush with financial success, he cultivated his playboy image surrounded by the social elite and the trappings of luxury.

And now Valentine was part of his coterie.

I stood quickly as the memory of their kiss seared my mind's eye. The panther thrashed again at my flare of emotion, and when Constantine rested one hand on my shoulder, I knew he had noticed my struggle. While many shifters had criticized my arrangement with Valentine, Constantine empathized with my decision to become a Were to help a loved one. He'd made a similar choice long ago, for a brother who had been beyond saving. But as much as I wanted to accept his comfort, my pain was still too raw. I wasn't about to betray any weakness in front of Malcolm.

I took a deep, steadying breath before turning to Karma. "Share another cab with me?"

Constantine saw us all out, and I instinctively turned toward the sun as we emerged onto his stoop. The day's brightness cheered me, despite the chill of the air. Down the street, a construction crew was just beginning its day's work, and the loud beeps of a reversing truck pierced through the city's background noise.

I registered a sharp change in air pressure at the same moment that a tree fell in the distance with a loud crack. But even as the thought crossed my mind, I knew I was wrong. Adrenaline galvanized my heart as the scent of blood filled the air and I whirled to find Malcolm lying on the stone steps, bleeding profusely. Shot. Sniped. A red haze descended over my eyes as my panther struggled furiously to claw her way out, and I dropped to a crouch as I fought for control. I'd never be able to help him if I shifted.

"Inside!" Constantine shouted. Blood slicked my hands as I grasped Malcolm's shoulders and pulled him back through the doorway. Karma was on my heels, already on the phone to Headquarters. Malcolm's guard, who had been one step behind him, was covered in blood spatter and cursing.

Constantine fell to his knees and wrapped his arms around Malcolm's chest, elevating his head so he wouldn't choke. Bright, viscous blood poured from a hole above his left temple, and I could see the white, jagged edges where the bullet had pierced his skull bone. I darted into the bathroom and yanked a towel off its peg, then crouched at Malcolm's side to staunch the bleeding as best I could.

"Why isn't he shifting?" I heard myself ask, feeling oddly disengaged, as though I was watching the flurry of activity from above.

"Maybe he can't." Constantine's words were clipped.

Mind racing, I reached for Malcolm's wrist to track his vital signs. No one really knew what part of the brain regulated a Were's ability to transform, but if that part had been injured or destroyed, it might explain why he remained broken and bleeding in human form.

His pulse stuttered beneath my fingertips, and I looked to Constantine in alarm. "We're losing him."

At that moment, Karma's cell buzzed. "They're coming in through the alley," she reported a moment later, and I left Malcolm's side to unlock Constantine's back door. The medical staff personnel rushed by me without acknowledgement and had strapped Malcolm to a folding gurney within seconds.

"I'm riding with him," Karma said fiercely, though I knew neither of us would protest. As Malcolm's strong right hand, it was her prerogative.

I squeezed her shoulder as she brushed past. "Let me know what I can do."

A hush settled over the house after they left, and I found myself staring at the ribbons and pools of blood that had collected on Constantine's polished hardwood floor. He, too, remained pensive for a long moment before tearing off his bloodied shirt.

"This is madness. Total war. Balthasar is risking our entire community by bringing his battle to the human streets." He kicked off his shoes. "I need to speak with Helen immediately."

Feeling suddenly lost, I moved to wrap my arms around my body only to realize that they, too, were caked in blood. "How can I help?"

He was already halfway up the staircase. "There's nothing you can do right now, Alexa. Go home. Pray."

"I'm not really the praying type," I said, feeling utterly helpless. But if Constantine heard me, he didn't answer.

❖

I showered in his guest bedroom and borrowed an oversized sweatshirt and pants for the trip home. But when I entered my apartment, its stillness and silence felt oppressive. For the hundredth time since exiting the subway, I checked my phone. Still no word.

Fatigue lurked behind my eyes, but I was far too agitated to give in to it. Finally, I decided to attend my afternoon class. It would kill some time while taking my mind off the nightmare I'd just witnessed. Afterward, I would pay a visit to Malcolm and see if there was anything I could do to ease Karma's burden.

As I walked along the south side of Washington Square Park, my phone rang. Eagerly, I looked down at the display…and froze. Olivia Wentworth Lloyd. Olivia was an assistant district attorney, and one of Valentine's childhood friends. Sort of. She and I had met during an NYU career fair last year, but we'd continued to cross paths when she had been attacked by the same vampire who had turned Valentine. While the Missionary had not succeeded in making Olivia a vampire, he had made her suspicious. The last I'd heard, Olivia had fallen for Abigail Lonnquist, a wereshifter who had contracted the same disease that had nearly killed me. Valentine hadn't told Abby's secret, but she had given Olivia a vial containing one dose of the cure for the virus.

Valentine had believed it wouldn't be long before Olivia discovered the full truth about Abby. Was that why she was calling me now? I hadn't heard from or seen her in months.

"Hi, Olivia," I said, trying to sound casual.

"Alexa." She paused so long I thought we might have gotten disconnected, but when I checked my phone's display, the call was still live.

"So…what's up? It's been a while."

I heard her exhale slowly. "Alexa, I know what you are."

Alarm bells clanged wildly in my brain, and my panther woke snarling from her uneasy slumber. "What I am?" I managed to keep my tone light despite the pounding in my chest. "Doomed to be unemployed once I finish school, you mean?"

"Meet me for a drink on Friday night."

"Is that a request or a demand, Counselor?"

There was another long moment of silence, then, and I used it to get my breathing back under control. My panther thrashed behind the doors of my psyche, desperate to confront the unknown threat.

"I don't work at the DA's office anymore," Olivia finally said. "White Star, ten o'clock?"

Now my alarm was compounded by confusion. Olivia had quit her job? I wanted to ask, but it was clear she didn't want to discuss that right now. The real question was whether her invitation was legitimate. My brain suspected some kind of setup, but in my gut, I knew Olivia wouldn't knowingly put me in danger—from the law or anyone else.

"Alexa?"

"Sorry, yes. That's fine. See you at ten on Friday."

When she hung up, I turned away from Vanderbilt Hall and crossed the street. I needed to calm my panther before sitting in class for hours. Even on a blustery winter's day, the spaciousness of the park comforted her.

I sat on a bench and thought about reviewing my notes from yesterday's lecture, but I knew I wouldn't be able to concentrate. Brenner was planning some kind of attack on American soil and had just critically injured—perhaps even killed—the Weremaster of New York. Olivia seemed to have discovered the Consortium's secret. And the love of my life—now a soulless vampire—was somehow involved with Sebastian.

I turned to face the wind rattling the bare branches of the trees and pretended the chill was responsible for the tears that pricked my cyes.

CHAPTER THREE

The rest of the week crawled by. Malcolm remained unresponsive and in critical condition despite several different surgeries and an effort to relieve the pressure on his brain. He was locked in a coma, and neither his human nor leonine consciousness had been able to find its way back. It was rare for a shifter not to heal quickly, and most of the city's Were population was poised to give up hope already. Karma was understandably rattled, but once it became clear that our sitting by Malcolm's bedside would do no one any good, she threw herself back into both of her jobs. By the time Friday arrived, I wanted simply to hole up in my apartment and sleep the weekend away. But breaking my non-date with Olivia wasn't an option; I had to find out what she knew.

White Star only had four tables, but Olivia had managed to grab one near the back of the narrow, dimly-lit space. I paused at the bar to order a drink, wanting another minute to collect my thoughts and my composure. And to ensure that this wasn't some kind of sting operation, with her detectives lying in wait to apprehend me and charge me with…what? Turning into a large cat on a monthly basis? The thought might have been amusing under different circumstances.

When the bartender looked my way, I ordered two fingers of a very fine tequila. White Star was a sipping bar, and if Valentine had been here with me, we would have delighted in the scotches and whiskeys. The delicate absinthe fountain had always enchanted her too, and I could picture her expression of avid concentration as she watched each drop of ice water seduce the cube of sugar into dissolution.

"Here you are." The bartender slid my drink in front of me and as we exchanged bills, I pressed the heel of my free hand against the dip between my breasts. No more daydreams. No more memories. My Valentine's sensual enjoyment of even the smallest of life's details had been replaced by a ruthless appetite that could never be satiated. Resolute, I gripped my glass and threaded my way around tables and patrons to the far corner, alert to anything out of place or suspicious.

As I slid onto the chair across from Olivia, I hoped I wasn't betraying my trepidation. But I could feel my smile falter when she regarded me in silence, her expression accusatory. As though I were a suspect at the interrogation table and not her friend.

"Hi," I said, determined not to let her rile me up. "How are you? It's been too long."

"How do I look?"

At the bitterness of her words, I leaned in to survey her appearance. Her eyes were bloodshot and the skin beneath darkly smudged. She looked haunted.

"As though you haven't slept in a week."

She cupped one hand around her highball glass, as though she were protecting it from me. "I need you to tell me something. To be completely honest." When I nodded, she took a deep breath. "I need to know what you…what you turn into."

I thought about laughing. I thought about lying. I thought about playing dumb. But somehow, Olivia had discovered the secret, and no amount of dissembling on my part would throw her off the scent now. Beneath the tablecloth, I surreptitiously eased my cell phone out of my pocket, intending to send Karma a heads up by text in case the rest of our evening went south and I ended up needing some kind of intervention.

"A panther."

Olivia's expression never changed, but her fingers were trembling when she raised her glass to her lips. I balled my free hand into a fist as my panther, sensing Olivia's threat to us both, made a bid for control. I projected what I hoped was a soothing image: mid-afternoon on the savannah, basking atop a sun-baked rock as the warm breeze riffled our fur. Silently, I urged her to relax into the daydream—to trust that I wouldn't allow Olivia to hurt us.

"A panther." Olivia's voice was hoarse, the words tinged with incredulity.

"How did you know to ask that question?"

She broke eye contact. "You know I was dating Abby, right?"

Valentine had told me that particular bit of gossip during the turmoil following Brenner's attempted destruction of the Consortium. "You *were* dating her?"

"She broke it off a few weeks ago." Her mouth twisted into a grimace of pain. "Said it wasn't me, it was her. Of course. But she seemed upset, and I wondered if someone was controlling her— telling her to stay away from me. So I followed her."

Comprehension dawned. "You saw her shift."

"I tailed her car like some kind of lunatic. For hours." Olivia's laugh sounded strangled. "She drove into the Poconos and parked at one of those scenic outlooks."

"And then she walked into the woods." On impulse, I rested my palm on top of Olivia's hand. Her story was taking me back to my own first sighting of a Were, when Helen's bodyguard Darren had transformed into a large gray wolf before my eyes. That moment had called into question everything I thought I knew. For weeks, the disbelief had felt like a mental splinter, working its way ever deeper into my mind until my entire worldview had been transformed.

"Yes. She walked into the woods." Olivia's eyes were glassy as she relived the memory. "I was trying to go unnoticed, and by the time I realized something was wrong, I was too far away to help. Those seizures…even from a distance, they looked so painful. Like she was possessed."

"In a way, she is."

"Possessed. By a mountain lion. Or some kind of jaguar. I wasn't close enough to tell." Olivia dug her fingernails into the table. "Do you know, I obsessed about the exact species for days afterward. Even went to the store and bought a book on the big cats. But I still don't know what she is."

Moved by the distress in her voice, I smoothed my hand rhythmically over her knuckles. "There was nothing you could have done to help her. And if you'd been any closer, she would have torn you to pieces. After the change, the hunger is unbearable."

"Is it always like that? Always so violent?"

"For most of us, yes." I took another sip from my drink in an effort to quiet my nerves at talking about these kinds of details with Olivia, who was not only a human, but a trained and ruthless prosecutor. But her angst was real, and she deserved answers. Who would give them to her, if not me?

"For you?"

"In the beginning. But I've inherited a greater degree of control over my beast than most, and by now, the pain is minimal."

"Inherited? You were born this way?"

"No."

"Then what happened to you?"

I looked from her to my glass and back again, trying to calm the pounding of my heart and thinking through how much I should say. As distressing as it was to be sitting across from an attorney asking pointed questions about the wereshifter community, it also felt liberating to tell the truth for once.

"I'm not going to answer that question until I know who's asking: Olivia, or the DA's office?"

"I told you, I don't work there anymore."

I sat back and crossed my arms beneath my breasts, determined not to say another word until she decided to be more forthcoming. After staring me down for a full minute, she threw back the rest of her drink and braced her palms on the table.

"Fine. Last month, I was asked to take a leave of absence."

"Why?"

Olivia's eyes narrowed and the small muscles along her jaw flexed. Volatile and uncompromising, she reminded me in that moment of Valentine. They looked nothing alike—Olivia's hair and eyes were dark and her clothing and mannerisms decidedly feminine—but she shared with Val an effortless confidence and seething impatience. I wondered if those qualities had been bred into them by the wealthy and powerful generations of which they were now the scions.

"My superiors thought I was unhealthily preoccupied with an unsolved case," she said when I continued to hold my ground. "Your turn."

What happened to you? There were a dozen ways to answer that question with some semblance of truth, but I found myself wanting Olivia to know everything—for her own protection as much as for my own peace of mind. She was an accomplished investigator, and if she sensed that I was holding back, she would only continue to search for answers. Answers that could get her hurt, or worse.

"When Valentine was turned into a vampire, I had myself deliberately infected with the lycanthropy virus so I could feed her forever. So I could save her soul." As her expression shifted from determination to shock, I allowed myself a bitter smile. "It didn't work."

"Vampires…exist?"

"Is it really so hard to believe, after what you saw?"

"You're seriously trying to tell me that Val is a vampire." Her voice was laced with bravado, but the last word trembled on the air.

"She was turned by the same man who attacked you." When Olivia paled, I reached for her hand again. "Don't worry. You haven't been infected. You were lucky."

In another moment, she had pulled back and was gripping the sides of the table hard enough to whiten her knuckles. "Damn it, Alexa. Start making some sense!"

My temper flared and the panther surged back into the fore of my consciousness. She was always so close to the surface these days, and my fatigue grew stronger as I reined her in yet again.

"I'm sorry," Olivia said, and I wondered whether she had guessed at the nature of my struggle. "I just…"

"It's a lot to take in. I know." I finished off my drink, hoping it would help me relax. The walls of the bar seemed closer now, and I fought off the sense of suffocation that tightened my chest. Not my claustrophobia—the panther's. She wanted to run, despite our spontaneous jag through Central Park last night. Or maybe because of it. Was my control slowly crumbling? Could she sense it?

"So the man who attacked me is a vampire." Olivia stuttered on the last word.

"Was. He's dead now." I had feasted on his corpse without regret, and still felt none.

"Dead?"

"Dead. I swear it." Only then did I realize Olivia had been living in fear of the Missionary all this time. Was he the "unsolved case" she'd been benched for obsessing about? Or had Helen and Malcolm found the influence to derail her career so she would stop poking into their business? Had she been suffering the same nightmares that had plagued Valentine's sleep almost every night until we finally had closure?

She folded her arms on the table and lowered her head to rest against them. The thin wool of her sweater grew taut over her shoulder blades, and I couldn't help but compare her more delicate physique to the tight, prominent muscles of Val's shoulders and back. I was debating whether or not to reach out to her when my phone buzzed. Karma.

"Are you all right?" she said when I answered.

"Yes, fine."

"I need you to come to the museum right now. There's something I have to show you."

I glanced at Olivia; she hadn't moved. She may have brought this shellshock on herself, but I hated to leave her when she clearly felt so vulnerable. "Can it wait?"

"I may have found a way to help Val."

Her words knocked the breath from me. Even my panther was shocked into stillness; poised for flight or battle, her presence trembled on the edge of action. Hope rose from the ashes of my despair to scorch the aching hollow in my chest. "I'll be there as soon as I can get uptown."

Olivia raised her head as I hung up. "You have to go, obviously. But let me buy you breakfast tomorrow. Please. There's still so much I need to know."

Her plea was slightly garbled to my ears, as though she were speaking from behind a waterfall. I nodded dumbly, unable to process anything but Karma's declaration. Everything I had read about full vampires indicated that the transition was irreversible—that whatever part of Val's essential self that had been lost was beyond all recovery. Had Karma managed to discover some way to reverse the vampire parasite's hostile takeover of Val's bloodstream? And more importantly, to restore her soul?

"Alexa?"

"Breakfast. Tomorrow." My tongue felt thick in my mouth. "All right."

"Are you okay? You look like you've seen a ghost."

She wasn't far off the mark, and I willed myself to focus even as the panther paced the circumference of my psyche in agitation. "Just some surprising news."

Olivia started to reach for my hand, but apparently thought the better of it. "I want you to know that I heard about you and Val. And I'm sorry."

"Thanks."

"She's an idiot."

I spun toward the door to hide my reaction. The woman in me was in danger of betraying tears. The panther in me thrashed at the insult to our mate. No matter what Valentine did or said, she would always be rightfully ours. I had impressed that fact as deeply into the psyche of my feline half as she was imprinted into my DNA.

"It's not that simple."

Chapter Four

K arma was waiting outside a nondescript door along the south wall of the Met. I ran across the street, not to avoid traffic but because the burst of activity felt good. As I approached, she swiped her ID card and entered a code at the keypad.

"Hi." I brushed past her and she followed me inside, pausing to double-check that the door had locked.

"Hi." Her eyes glittered in the dim light of the hall, and the fine hairs on my arms rose as I realized just how close to the surface her jackal was. I had never witnessed any kind of breakdown of Karma's control, and the sight was unnerving. My panther shoved hard at the doors of my brain, and I braced one hand against the wall to steady myself under her onslaught. We stood facing each other for several fraught seconds until, with a shuddering sigh, Karma lowered her head.

"What on earth was that?" I asked, hearing the breathlessness in my own voice.

"I'm sorry." Karma moved down the hall, gesturing for me to follow. "I need to carve out some time to meditate. It's been such a crazy week, and I'm especially on edge tonight." She used a key to activate an elevator at the end of the corridor and we stepped inside.

"I know the feeling." As the doors closed behind us, I leaned against the far corner, wanting to give her as much space as possible. "Are you worried about getting in trouble for bringing me up?"

She waved the suggestion away. "That's not it at all. I've been on edge ever since Malcolm, and now…" She closed her eyes briefly before refocusing on me. "Today's discovery has implications. Large ones, for many fields. And people."

I tried to stay calm. Rational. "You found something in the shipment you're cataloging?"

"Yes." She looked me up and down. "I'm glad you're all right. Olivia didn't try to cart you off?"

"The DA's office sidelined her."

Karma's expression turned thoughtful. "I wonder whether Malcolm and Helen had anything to do with that."

"Me, too. But they couldn't shut her up before. What's changed?"

"Foster."

Detective Devon Foster had died trying to apprehend the vampire who had turned Valentine. Or so I'd thought at the time. It had been a shock to discover Foster alive and well as a vampire several months ago. And not just any vampire—the hand-picked head of security for Helen's new task force.

"You think they didn't have someone in the NYPD before?" That possibility seemed unlikely to me. The Consortium had infiltrated most human institutions at least to some degree.

"I think they may not have had someone in the police force who could stand up to Olivia's connections."

When the elevator doors slid open, my next question died on my lips. We were in the most pristine warehouse facility I'd ever seen. The room was organized by dividers into discrete cubes of space, most of which were filled with an assortment of objects. Karma led me down the main avenue that bisected the room, then turned right.

"Here." We entered a spacious enclosure that held a collection of large rectangular stone sculptures. They ringed the space like stoic sentries, and I paused in the doorway to take them all in.

"What are they?"

Karma stood by the leftmost stone and reached toward it, checking her fingers only an inch from the surface. "Ancient Egyptian *stelae*. Boundary markers from the Nile delta." She gestured toward the human figure with a jackal's head that dominated the bas relief. "Anubis, god of the dead."

I wondered if she felt some glimmer of affinity with the deity who shared her beast. "Is that text above and below him?"

"In Hieratic, yes." At my look of confusion, she added, "Adapted hieroglyphs for faster writing. Egyptian cursive."

I moved forward to inspect it. The dusky gold stone was shot through with white highlights, and in some places, the sculptor had used the gleaming veins to artistic effect. I wondered at how the *stelae* must have looked in their natural habitat, rising up out of the earth like the fingers of a god laying claim to the land. Breathtaking, certainly. But Karma hadn't led me here to show off impressive artifacts.

"What do they say?"

"Combined, the inscriptions on these *stelae* create a narrative—one that scholars have believed to be lost. Until today."

"I don't understand. How could it be lost if they knew about its existence?"

Karma gestured in a broad arc encompassing all of the markers. "The story is alluded to in many cultures, much like the 'myth' of werewolves and vampires." She flashed me a wry smile. "But until these stones were discovered, the actual text had never been found."

I squinted at the elaborate spirals and angles of the Egyptian script, as though staring at it hard enough would unlock its secrets. "And this story…it has something to do with Valentine?"

"I think so." She retrieved two small folding chairs from the far corner. "Let's sit. This will take a while."

My panther didn't want to sit; she craved action. But before we could hunt, we had to know our prey. I tried to soothe her with that thought as I settled into the chair facing Karma. Anubis loomed over us, equal parts vigilant and menacing, and I crossed my legs to keep from fidgeting.

"Each major ancient civilization tells the story a different way, but fundamentally—archetypally—it is the same." As she spoke,

Karma half-turned toward the *stelae*, as though they, too, were her audience. "In ancient Egypt, it is told as the tale of Isis and Osiris. Do you know it?"

"I've heard of them, but I don't know the details."

"Isis was the sister-wife of Osiris, a popular and well-beloved king. But Osiris's brother, Set, grew jealous and plotted treason. He had a coffin prepared to fit Osiris precisely and coerced his brother into it under false pretenses. Set then sealed the coffin and threw it into the Nile. Distraught, Isis searched until she found its resting place beneath the roots of a massive tree. She returned it to Egypt for a proper burial, but Set intercepted the coffin and dismembered Osiris's body into fourteen pieces. He scattered the pieces all over the world.

"Isis spent years searching for the pieces of her husband. Whenever she found part of his body, she wept for the space of a day and night. Wherever her tears watered the earth, a beautiful white flower sprang up under the light of the moon, only to wither away at sunrise." Karma leaned forward, holding my gaze. "The legend suggests that the flower has exceptional healing abilities. That consuming it can bring a person back even from death—or perhaps the brink of death. That part of the text is corrupted, and I can't be sure of the exact meaning."

My heart hammered into my throat at the implications. "What are you saying? That this flower can cure Valentine? Restore her... her soul?"

"I don't know. But this is the best lead I've found. The only lead, really."

I battled back the hope that was threatening to override my reason. "Even if the flower would work, and I could preserve it long enough to get it to Valentine, how would we find it?"

The gold flecks that peppered Karma's eyes grew brighter, and again I sensed her jackal near the surface. "That's where these *stelae* come in. They describe thirteen of the resting places of Osiris."

I surged to my feet, no longer able to contain the quivering of my muscles. "The closest." I forced the words through a dry throat. "Where is it?"

Karma shook her head. "These descriptions aren't exactly GPS coordinates. They're more like riddles. Tomorrow, I'll send translations to colleagues around the world to see whether they can identify the locations."

Disappointment lanced through me. Despite the significance of this discovery, there was still nothing I could do but wait and hope. I looked past Karma to the half-ring of *stelae,* absurdly wishing for some kind of Pentecostal miracle. It was agonizing to be in the presence of the location without being able to interpret the text. But I was so much closer than I had been mere hours ago. I had to stay focused on the positive.

"All right. I understand. Will you send the translation to Constantine, too? He might have some thoughts."

"I will." Karma squeezed my shoulder. "We'll figure this out, Alexa. I swear to you."

She couldn't make that promise, but I wanted to believe her. The Consortium's worldwide network would allow her to tap into centuries of lived experience and wisdom. Someone, somewhere would be able to help us connect these puzzle pieces. Even as my rational brain protested that I was allowing emotion to overthrow all logic, I was already planning my next steps. As soon as the first location was discovered, I would travel there immediately and study the plant. Once I had learned enough about its properties, I would return to New York and reclaim my mate. It didn't matter that I couldn't work out any of the details right now. I would make it happen. I had to.

"Shall we go?" Karma turned toward the corridor, but I couldn't seem to pull myself away from the *stelae.*

"What ended up happening to Osiris? Was Isis able to give him a proper burial?"

"Even better. She found thirteen of the fourteen pieces— everything except, of course, his phallus. So she ordered one to be made of gold, and then sang a song around his reconstituted body. Her song was so powerful that it raised him from the dead."

My breath caught at the picture Karma painted. The scene unfolded before my mind's eye: Isis pacing around her husband's bier, distraught but focused on her mission; her long, dark hair moist with the tears she'd wiped away; the rise and fall of her bare breasts as she began to sing—softly at first, then louder and more confidently until even death itself bowed to her will and Osiris raised his head.

I would be that for Valentine. Her Isis. I would search the heights and depths of the world until I discovered the flower and learned to harness its restorative powers. I would return love and joy and compassion to the empty shell of her that prowled the nighttime streets. I would be the one to lead her back into the sunlight.

Whatever it took. I had eternity, after all.

❖

We caught our first break several days later from one of Karma's colleagues in India. The news was also our first major disappointment. Apparently, the fourth location alluded to in the combined text of the *stelae* was a reference to Lohachara Island, located in the Hooghly River between Bangladesh and India. Several years ago, however, Lohachara had sunk into the river, displacing its thousands of residents. Karma and I had debated whether the "Tear of Isis" flower might still bloom beneath the water, but she had convinced me to wait for more information about the other locations before I went haring off on what was probably a fool's errand.

The next morning, I sat across the table from Olivia in the Starbucks on Washington Square, gingerly sipping at my scalding coffee and debating whether to confide in her about the flower. Sharing a breakfast table had become an impromptu tradition ever since the morning after our rendezvous at White Star. On that first day, she had peppered me with questions about wereshifters and vampires, and I'd done my best to answer without giving away too many secrets. I had even told her the truth behind my split with Valentine. Gradually, we had settled into a companionable silence broken only when one or the other of us had a story to share. I would review my class notes and she would read the paper, and whenever I stood to leave for class she would look up at me and ask, "Same time tomorrow?"

And I would say yes. I had no idea what I was doing, but it felt nice. Normal, almost. Healthier, too. For the first time in months, I was regularly eating breakfast. But when my phone buzzed to life displaying Karma's photograph, my appetite disappeared on a surge of adrenaline.

"Any news?" I asked her.

"Yes, but it isn't good."

My stomach soured. "What happened?"

"A sociologist at Columbia identified the tenth location as the slopes of Mount Noshaq, the highest peak in Afghanistan."

I nearly surged to my feet. From the corners of my vision, I caught Olivia staring at me curiously. "I'll book a flight right now. Do you know the nearest airport?"

"Alexa, stop."

"And do you know the elevation? Mountainous terrain will be treacherous this time of year. I should probably—"

"Stop." The quiet vehemence of her monosyllable made me pause.

"What?"

"Al Qaeda is still hiding out in those mountains. The whole region is a minefield. Literally. You can't go over there."

I had to bite my lower lip to keep my temper in check. It was a good thing we were having this conversation by phone. I wasn't sure I could have held my panther back if we'd been face-to-face.

"That's ridiculous. It's not as though I'll be helpless!"

"Think it through," Karma said. "You'd probably be fine as long as you were four-legged. But when you find the flower, you'll need to study it, then gather and transport it. Tasks for two legs."

She had a point, damn it. My sigh came out sounding like a snarl, and Olivia sat back hard in her chair, eyes wide. "What do you want me to do, Karma?"

"I want you to wait. It's been less than a week since I sent out the translation, and we've already gotten two positive identifications. More will come."

I dug my fingernails into a stray napkin on the table and balled it into my palm. My panther stalked behind my eyes, wanting to lash out, and I shared her desire to rip and shred and tear away everything that stood in the path between us and the flower.

"I'll wait. For now. But if we reach a dead end, I'm going."

"That makes sense." Karma's voice was soothing, and I suddenly realized just how demanding a friend I had been lately. Forcing myself to breathe deeply, I tipped my head back to relax the muscles of my neck.

"I'm sorry. You're being a saint."

"We'll get a lead worth following. You'll see."

After promising to call me as soon as she heard any more news, she ended the call and I turned to Olivia. "I suppose you want to know what that was about."

"For a few minutes there, it sounded like you were going on some kind of hiking trip."

"I was on the verge of buying a plane ticket to Afghanistan."

"What?" Alarm flickered across her face. "Why the hell would you travel there right now?"

"You're not going to believe it."

"Try me."

I crossed my arms under my breasts to keep my hands from fidgeting. My panther needed a hunt, and I needed to get out of my own head for a while. "The abbreviated version is that my friend Karma recently discovered an ancient Egyptian inscription about a rare and short-lived flower known as the Tear of Isis. This flower, so the story goes, can bring people back from death's door. We think it might be able to restore Valentine's soul."

To her credit, Olivia didn't so much as blink. "And you can find this flower in Afghanistan?"

"Apparently, yes. The inscription mentions thirteen possible locations, one of which is there."

"But you're not going."

I pinched the bridge of my nose, feeling the onset of a headache. "No. Karma convinced me to wait until we've deciphered some of the other locations."

"This Karma sounds wise. And persuasive. Is she a shifter?"

"A jackal." I watched Olivia's reaction closely, but she didn't seem disgusted or afraid. Only surprised.

"That's exotic."

"Shall I set you up on a date?" I teased her.

She stood and pulled on her coat. "No. Not with her." She brushed her fingers lightly across the back of my neck as she headed for the door. "See you tomorrow."

Her caress ignited a flash of heat low in my abdomen. Startled by my own reaction, I made no reply. It was a relief to feel an emotion that wasn't sorrow or anger, but disconcerting to be stirred by an unfamiliar touch.

CHAPTER FIVE

Bracing myself over the small conference table in Karma's office, I squinted through her magnifying glass at an ancient shard of pottery—the only remnant of a ceremonial urn. Once jagged, its edges had been worn away by the clutches of the soil. An image had been painted on its dusky rose surface, and I leaned closer in an effort to make it out.

"Your colleague is sure this is the flower?" One of Karma's associates at the Met had pointed out this fragment as possibly having a connection to the narrative on the *stelae*.

"As certain as he can be after a brief consultation." Karma stood across the room waiting for the printer to finish its latest job. After gathering up several pages, she stapled them and set the pile next to several others on the windowsill. "He caught me on his way out the door to catch a plane overseas for a conference. He'll do a more thorough examination when he gets back next week."

"And in the meantime, we have homework." I crossed to the window and surveyed the articles that her colleague had recommended. They had all been written by the same person. "What do you know about this Mariano Miralla?"

"Apparently, he spent most of his career researching the folklore and customs of the people who inhabit the region where that clay fragment was discovered. Maybe there will be a connection."

As Karma continued to collate documents from the printer, I skimmed the abstracts of the articles she had gathered. Miralla appeared to have been at his most prolific half a century ago. He had focused almost exclusively on a remote settlement in the shadow of Ojos del Salado, a massive volcano in the Andes mountains that straddled the border between Argentina and Chile.

I hefted one of the thicker documents. "Are you up for burning the midnight oil? You don't have to do this, you know. I can read these through by myself and report back."

Karma reached around me for one of the other stacks of paper before settling onto the small couch perpendicular to her desk. She patted the spot beside her then turned her attention to the text. Clearly, I had my answer.

Four hours and several cartons of Thai food later, I was just about to suggest that we turn in for the night when Karma leaned into my space, her forefinger pressed emphatically to the page.

"This sounds eerily familiar."

The paragraph in question introduced a local legend about a "parched spirit"—an apparition in the form of a beautiful woman who descended from the mountain in times of drought and stole blood from sleeping villagers just as the cloudless sky stole all moisture from the earth.

"It's a vampire myth."

"Yes. But not your normal fare." She turned the page and pointed to where Miralla continued to discuss the legend of the "parched spirit." This ghostly female figure was most frequently sighted on a "haunted" ridge above the crater lake to the east of the volcano. She was regarded as a harbinger of famine, and the villagers considered any person who saw her to be temporarily cursed.

"It definitely sounds like Ojos del Salado has a vampire tenant. Or had as of fifty years ago, at least." I rubbed my gritty eyes. "But what does this have to do with the flower?"

"Look closely. These sightings are during the daytime." Karma reached over to underline several phrases, all of which referenced the sunlight. "The only vampires who can walk under the sun—"

"—are vampires who haven't made the transition." Exhaustion forgotten, I feverishly reread the passage. "Do you think this vampire somehow discovered the flower and its properties?"

"I have no idea. But the Consortium's records go back centuries. If we cross-reference this legend with data in the library, we might be able to learn more about vampire activity in Argentina and Chile over the past few decades."

"I'll go. Right now."

Karma laid a hand on my arm. "It's the middle of the night. If you go now…"

She didn't have to finish the sentence. If I went now, there was a good chance I'd cross paths with Valentine. My stomach churned at the thought. I wasn't ready, especially not after having seen her at Luna. With Sebastian.

Red haze filmed over my vision, and I focused on taking a series of deep breaths. Karma eased off the couch to lean against her desk. With my panther in such turmoil, her jackal had no choice but to respond to a potential threat. My volatility wasn't just affecting me; it was throwing off those around me. Sorrow tempered my anger. Would I ever be ready?

"You're right, of course. I'll wait until morning. And I'm sorry."

Karma lightly shook the pages in her hand. "Just keep your eye on the prize."

❖

"Good morning." Olivia's smile of greeting quickly morphed into a frown. "You look completely exhausted. What's wrong?"

I set my coffee—a red-eye with a double shot of espresso—on the table and slid wearily into the chair across from her. When I'd finally fallen asleep, I had dreamed myself onto a rock-strewn, almost lunar landscape where I pursued a hooded woman who danced over lava floes with impunity.

"It's a long story," I said. "The short version is that I might have to go out of town suddenly."

"To Afghanistan? Alexa—"

"To South America." I took quick sips of the steaming liquid as Olivia digested this new information.

"You think you've found this flower in South America?"

"It's starting to look that way. I'll know more after I have a chance to do some additional research."

Olivia leaned back in her chair and crossed her arms. My attention was drawn to the smooth skin of her forearms—as delicate and elegant as the gold watch that encircled her left wrist. Wholly unlike the taut, coiled strength of Valentine's body.

I let my next sip of coffee burn my tongue. No thoughts of Valentine; not now. If I dwelled too long on the stakes of this project, I risked losing control because pinning down the flower's location was just one step on a long and highly uncertain road. No full vampire had ever been brought back into the sunlight. It might not even be possible, but if I started thinking that way, I'd make myself crazy.

"If this lead pans out, how long will you be gone? What will you do about school?" Olivia sounded accusatory.

"I don't know. And I'll take a leave of absence."

"A leave of absence in your final semester?"

The panther snarled behind my eyes as my temper flared. "Why the third degree, Olivia?"

She looked away. "I just don't want to see you jeopardize your future."

My anger ebbed as I realized that not only was Olivia genuinely concerned, she was also jealous of Valentine and the hold she still had over me. Despite the intervening months, I was willing to drop everything and go on a wild goose chase for the woman who had broken my heart. That had to rankle with Olivia.

But before I could try to explain myself, Karma appeared in my peripheral vision. She was dressed as immaculately as always in a chocolate colored suit, with a matching bag perched on her shoulder, but her eyes were wider and darker than normal. Only another Were would have been able to sense it, but I knew she was on high alert.

I stood. "What's up?"

"Hi. Good morning." She looked to Olivia, who had also gotten to her feet. "Ms. Lloyd, we've never had the pleasure. I'm Karma Rao."

"It's nice to meet you. Alexa speaks of you often." Olivia glanced uncertainly between us, and I knew she had picked up on the tension.

"I'm sorry to have to call you away," Karma said to me. "But there's something I need your opinion on."

"Of course." I turned to Olivia. "See you tomorrow?"

She surprised me by reaching for my hand. "Don't leave town without telling me." She squeezed my fingers tightly. "Promise."

Flustered at the display, I nodded. When she let go, I followed Karma outside. She stepped to the curb and raised her hand for a cab.

"What's going on?"

"Not here. Headquarters."

Her terse reply only ratcheted up my tension, and the panther pushed at the borders of my mind. While Karma kept her attention on her smartphone throughout our cab ride, I fidgeted in my seat, heels tapping a muted staccato against the floor mat. But when we reached Consortium Headquarters, Karma pushed my hand away before I could press the "up" button on the elevator.

"We're not going to your office?"

"Not yet."

Valentine had told me that there were medical facilities in the basement, but the only subterranean level accessible from this elevator was the hunting arena, where Weres who couldn't or didn't want to leave the city indulged the needs of their inner beasts. Lit by scores of sun lamps, the enclosure boasted a thick forest at one end that gradually gave way to a small meadow of prairie grass at the other. Vampire guards watched over the arena from two observation decks. Armed with tranquilizer rifles, their orders were to subdue any Were who turned from hunting prey to hunting peers.

I fixed Karma with a frown. "Why are we here?"

She set her bag down on one of the benches that lined the walls of the foyer leading up to the arena, then removed her jacket. I didn't understand. She was acting as though we were here to hunt, but I didn't want to hunt anything except the flower. And she knew it. As I opened my mouth to demand an explanation, she opened her bag and took out a newspaper. The "Lifestyle" section of the *Times*. She held it out to me, but still wouldn't meet my eyes.

"Page six."

My panther paced in circles, mirroring the spiraling dread in my stomach as I flipped through the pages. Halfway down page six, I saw the headline.

Everything. Stopped.

My nerveless hands would no longer function, and the paper fluttered to the ground, shedding newsprint. The page fell at my feet, facing up. Three simple words knifed into my heart and flayed me open and the panther was coming—she was coming and I didn't even want to stop her and finally I realized why Karma had brought me here. Because she had known this would happen.

Brenner Weds Darrow.

My choked off sob became the panther's growl, and willingly, I surrendered my awareness.

❖

It took me a day and a half to find my way back to human form. This time, I didn't struggle against the panther's will but against my human self. Despair was waiting, and I instinctively shied away from it, taking refuge in the strong and simple desires of my panther's animal brain. Eat. Sleep. Fuck.

Ultimately, it was the urge for sex that roused my human consciousness. I had no interest in satisfying that impulse with another Were feline. I only wanted Valentine, and wanting Valentine was pain.

I woke in the fetal position on a bed of moss beneath an oak tree, my stomach rumbling with hunger pangs. As I stood, a wolf emerged from the surrounding foliage. A wolf, like Sebastian. My panther pushed for dominance again, but this time I forced her back and instead bared my human teeth, releasing a subvocal growl. In a blur of brindle, the wolf turned tail and was gone.

I emerged from the arena to find an envelope with my name on it resting atop a neatly folded pile of clothing. Karma had taken the time to raid my apartment for a change of clothes. I put them on, then opened the note. *Call me.*

But I wanted to know all the details first. Someone had cleaned up the newspaper that my claws had shredded, so I rode the elevator all the way up to the library and sat at one of the public computers. A quick search of the *Times* website yielded the article, and I swallowed down a surge of bile as I read the brief description of Sebastian's and Valentine's biographical details and how they had eloped to Bora Bora.

"She did it for the money," I said, startling a young Were who was reading in a nearby armchair. When our eyes met, he glanced away quickly. Leaning back in the chair, I arched my neck in an effort to ease the taut muscles in my shoulders. My treacherous brain conjured up the image of Valentine and Sebastian kissing on a moonlit beach, platinum rings glinting from their joined hands, and I grit my teeth against the anguished howl that wanted to burst from my throat.

One deep breath and then another. And another. Gradually, my pulse slowed and the panther once again receded from the forefront of my consciousness. Whether Valentine was even capable of love at this point was debatable, but she didn't love Sebastian. I knew that in my bones. She had used him to get to her grandfather's money. If I believed anything else, I would go mad.

A sharp cramp in my stomach reminded me that my hunger wasn't a luxury but an imperative. Shifting back and forth required a great deal of energy, and it had been many hours since I'd caught and killed a hapless rabbit that had been released into the arena by the guards. As I made my way to the restaurant and bar on the top floor, I checked my phone. Olivia had texted three times and called twice. My thumb hovered over the voice mail message she'd left, and I steeled myself. Doubtless, she had heard about Valentine— probably not long after I'd left the Starbucks. A shiver ran through me when I realized just how narrowly I had escaped losing control in a highly public and crowded place. If Olivia had read the paper earlier, or if Karma had arrived later...

Shaking off the hypothetical, I listened to Olivia's message. She vacillated between professions of sympathy and more demands that I not leave the country—at least, not without her.

I sat in a booth near one of the northwest-facing windows so I could have a view of the Empire State Building. After ordering a steak and a very dirty vodka martini—a drink that was "safe" because Valentine regarded any martini not made with gin as an abomination—I called Karma. She picked up on the first ring.

"Alexa." The syllables of my name had never sounded so comforting. Unlike Olivia, Karma didn't have to say anything else to show me exactly what she was feeling.

"Thank you," I said around the lump in my throat. "She…she did it for the money."

If Karma heard the need for reassurance in my voice, she made no indication. "I agree. What do you want to do?"

"I want to find the Tear of Isis. As soon as possible."

"I did some research last night, while you were still four-footed. Most of the vampire activity in Argentina over the past century has occurred in and around Buenos Aires. Many of the most prominent landowners in the late eighteenth and early nineteenth centuries, the *estancieros*, made alliances with a small group of vampires in order to consolidate their political interests in the region."

I drummed my fingernails against the lacquered wooden table top. "But isn't Buenos Aires hundreds of miles from Ojos del Salado?"

"Yes. It will be impossible to tell whether there's a connection unless we investigate."

"I'll book a flight within the hour."

Karma sighed softly. "I can't go with you. Not right now. Not when Malcolm is still in a coma."

I had suspected as much, and oddly, I felt relief. Alone, I could push as hard as I wanted and take as many risks as I needed. No one would be watching my back, but no one would hold me back either.

"I know. You've done so much already, Karma. Please don't feel badly."

"You should have company. Maybe—"

At that moment, the waiter returned and I jumped at the excuse. "My dinner just arrived. I'll call you later."

Part of me felt guilty for brushing her off so quickly, but my conscience quieted as I focused on making travel arrangements in between bites of my steak. By the time I'd finished eating, I had booked an open-return airline reservation to Buenos Aires. My departing flight left in fifteen hours. That didn't give me much time to put my affairs in order and my clothing in a suitcase.

And to drop out of law school.

The thought gave me pause, but only for a moment. I would finish, eventually—once I had brought Valentine back from wherever her soul had fled to or I had exhausted every lead trying. When I did return to school, I could pick up precisely where I had left off. I wouldn't look a day older than I did right now.

I spent the subway ride home daydreaming of racing over the grassy plains between Buenos Aires and the Andes. The earth would be alive and warm under my paws, the air redolent with exotic scents. Crystal clear rivers would assuage my thirst, and the light of unfamiliar stars would guide my path. I would shed the bonds of my grief and glory in the thrill of the hunt.

And then I turned the corner to find Olivia sitting on the stoop of my apartment building. She was hunched over her phone, a steaming cup of coffee from the cafe across the street at her side. She looked freezing.

"How long have you been here?"

Her head jerked up and I watched her take in my appearance. I wondered what she saw when she looked at me—whether my grim resolve showed in the planes of my face, and whether the soul-wrenching sorrow was buried deep enough not to.

"A while. I knew you'd have to come home eventually." She moved her cup so I could sit beside her, but I stayed on my feet.

"Thanks for your message."

"I know you're going to South America. I'm not letting you go alone."

I shook my head. "You'll slow me down. You'll get in my way. And you very well might get hurt."

Her eyes narrowed. "Are you threatening me?"

"I'm being honest." I sat and wrapped my arms around my middle to stave off the chill of the air and stone. "If Karma hadn't come to get me when she did, I would have found out about Valentine and Sebastian while I was in a public place—maybe even our Starbucks. I would have shifted, and I probably would have killed. That's how little control I had in that moment."

Olivia's expression never changed. "When are you leaving?"

My sigh of frustration clouded as soon as it hit the air. "I have no idea what I'll encounter down there. I might be walking into the territory of a very hostile and very powerful vampire."

"All the more reason for you to have backup. What flight did you book?"

For a moment, I thought of lying to her. But if I did, she would discover the truth and come after me anyway. My panther snarled as our daydream of running under the hot Argentinean sun shattered, but the all-too-human part of me felt comforted that I wouldn't be alone in my quest.

"Val brought Abby back from the brink of death," Olivia said. "I owe her. And right now, repaying that debt means helping you."

Tears burned behind my eyes at her words, and I stood quickly, unwilling to let her see the tears fall. "I'll forward you my flight confirmation. Pack lightly."

"Thank you," she called after me as I let myself in the front door.

I was left wondering whether, when this story had played itself out, she would still feel gratitude.

Chapter Six

Olivia and I argued for much of the eleven-hour flight. We had a row to ourselves in first class, and after I filled her in on Karma's findings and the details of Marilla's research, we debated how to proceed once the plane landed. I wanted to get to Ojos del Salado as soon as possible to begin my search for the flower. She wanted to stay in Buenos Aires long enough to determine whether there was some kind of connection between the vampire-sponsored *estanciero* families and the region near the volcano.

"You want us to look for a needle in a haystack," she had said, balling up her cocktail napkin in the palm of her hand.

"*You* want us to drag our feet," I'd shot back. The prospect of cooling our heels in the city, hundreds of miles from where we knew we needed to be, made my panther pace in a tight spiral. She never felt comfortable in claustrophobic airplane cabins, but on this flight, the strain of holding her back had given me a wicked headache.

"With just a little investigation, we might be able to narrow down the search area." Olivia rested her hand on my arm, and I didn't know whether to shy away from her touch or accept it. "I have a contact at the U.S. Embassy. Let me talk to her. She might know someone who could help us."

I pulled back and massaged my temples. Beneath my fingers, I could feel the deep throb of my pulse. My panther was picking up on my ambivalence about Olivia, and her anxiety contributed to the tension in my shoulders and neck. I needed a long, deep massage to coax the tautness from my muscles. Valentine had actually taken a few massage classes, and she could read my body so well that she always used just the right amount of—

"Damn it." My stomach flipped as the memories shattered.

"What?" Olivia's face registered alarm, and I wondered whether she was concerned that I might shift mid-flight.

Unwilling to explain, I shook my head and focused back on our debate. If I needed to give a little ground to gain some peace and quiet, then so be it. "I want us to get to the Andes as soon as possible, but we're going to need provisions. While I find them, you touch base with your contact. But if you don't turn up anything by the time I've secured our supplies, I won't wait."

Olivia opened her mouth to protest but apparently thought better of it. "I hope you do finish school," she grumbled. "You're going to make one hell of a lawyer."

I ignored her and reached for the English to Spanish dictionary I'd brought along. My backwoods Wisconsin upbringing was about to come in useful. We were going to need tents, sleeping bags, dried food, iodine capsules, and canteens. I'd had two years of Spanish in high school, but all I remembered at this point was how to count to twenty and ask for the location of the bathroom. At the very least, I needed to write out a proper shopping list before the plane landed.

❖

We touched down as the sun rose swaddled in wispy clouds the color of cotton candy. I breathed in as I stepped onto the jet bridge, and my panther relaxed ever so slightly at the hint of fresh air. But by the time we had cleared Customs and rented a Jeep, my impatience had returned full-force. When Olivia moved toward the driver's side, I reacted instinctively, narrowing my eyes and releasing the low growl that had been simmering in my throat since boarding the plane in New York.

She stopped in her tracks. "Jesus, Alexa. What the hell?"

"I'm driving."

She didn't speak again until the Buenos Aires skyline filled the view through the windshield. "Why do you keep pushing me away when I'm only trying to help?"

"I didn't ask for your help," I retorted, giving my anger and frustration free rein. To answer her question honestly would mean confessing that she reminded me of Valentine in some ways. And that I found her attractive. Sometimes.

Her jaw tightened and she glanced away. Guilt followed quickly on the heels of my outburst.

"I'm sorry. I'm tired, and my head is throbbing." I reached over to brush my fingertips across her jeans-clad knee. "Look…let's splurge on a hotel, okay? We may as well have one night of luxury before we head for the hills."

A smile flitted over her lips. "What did you have in mind?"

"You're the one with the map."

After a few minutes of study, she raised her head. "The Four Seasons?"

"Why not."

My olive branch seemed to have worked, because between issuing directions, she chatted to me about the Recoleta District, where the hotel was located. It sounded like the Upper East Side: full of high-end boutiques and galleries.

"Have you been here before?" I asked as I turned off the main highway.

"No. I just like to do my homework before I travel."

I didn't reply. It worried me that Olivia was treating this trip like some kind of quasi-vacation. I had no interest in cultural attractions besides the shard of clay that had led us here, and no desire to shop for anything that wouldn't help us survive our wild goose chase.

When we pulled into the semicircular drive, my stomach began to churn. The hotel was a converted turn of the century mansion connected to a modern tower. The ambiance, both outside and within the lavish lobby, was decidedly romantic. Crystal chandeliers hung from the vaulted ceiling, setting the air afire as their light reflected off the polished mosaic floor. Beside me, Olivia was regarding our surroundings with cool appraisal where Valentine would have been exuberant. I could so easily picture Val's broad smile and feel her warm hands clasping my waist as she spun me in an exultant circle. Gritting my teeth against the aching hollowness in my chest, I walked briskly toward the counter.

"How may I help you?" asked the young man behind it, clearly recognizing an American.

"We would like a room for tonight, please. Two beds."

Within minutes, I was pulling aside the blackout curtains over our windows to reveal a stunning view of downtown Buenos Aires, tree-lined streets giving way to the glinting spires of a cluster of skyscrapers.

"Which direction is the ocean?" Olivia mused, hovering at my elbow.

"East."

She rolled her eyes and pushed away from the wall. "No sightseeing. I get it. What's the plan?"

"We'll find a place that sells disposable cell phones and then we'll split up. You go meet with your contact. Check in with me at six unless you discover something earlier."

"You'll be careful?"

"I'll be fine. But that reminds me, if you're going to be vampire bait, then we're going to need to find you a gun."

Disbelief widened her eyes. "Vampire bait? Is that what I'm doing here?"

"Unless they're very new or very stupid, vampires know better than to prey on unwilling shifters. Just be prepared to defend yourself."

"With a gun? Bullets work against them?"

I couldn't help it; I was enjoying her confusion. "They're really quite fragile," I said, patting my pocket for my wallet and room key. Elation swept over me. We were finally on the move. There would be no more waiting now. As I passed Olivia on my way to the door, I found myself smiling. "You shouldn't believe *everything* you read."

❖

The late afternoon sun was hot on the back of my neck as I piled boxes of supplies into the trunk of the Jeep. A dry breeze drove dust devils across the patch of dirt and asphalt that doubled as the parking lot for the warehouse of a local mountaineering company. This facility wasn't in the best of neighborhoods, and I was deliberately allowing my panther to stay close to the surface. The stocky man who had helped me pick out the items on my list had regarded me with a predatory leer until he glimpsed the feline presence behind my eyes. After that, he'd been positively meek.

I had purchased enough provisions to last a month. Dried fruit, nuts, couscous, and rice would be the staples of our diet, which I could supplement by hunting wildlife. We would set up a camp near the base of the volcano and make forays into the mountains from there.

The unfamiliar ringtone of my phone startled me, and the panther nosed her way forward to test the mental walls that held her. I took a long, deep breath before answering.

"How soon can you make it to the National Library? It's in the same neighborhood as our hotel."

"You found something?"

"Possibly. We were able to enlist the help of the Director of Special Collections."

Apprehension shivered down my spine. "We?"

"My contact—a consular officer at the embassy. She has very kindly taken a personal interest in our research project. Apparently, it's a lot more interesting than spending the afternoon processing visas."

Faint laughter emanated through Olivia's mouthpiece—her contact responding to the gibe. I closed the trunk harder than I'd intended. I didn't want other people knowing the details of our mission, not even if they thought it was some kind of academic enterprise. Everyone in New York was preoccupied with Brenner's movements, but I didn't dare relax my guard. Since her transition, Valentine had not only accepted the mantle of the Missionary; she had also claimed her human birthright as the scion of one of the wealthiest families in America. There was little doubt in my mind that Helen would stand in the way of anything that might threaten her perfect protégé. And if this escapade proved fruitful, Val would be mine again. Not hers.

"I can be there within the hour," I said.

Driven by my worry over what clues Olivia might inadvertently drop to her friend, I made it in just under forty minutes. The Biblioteca Nacional de la República Argentina overlooked a verdant courtyard, but I didn't pause to admire the view. When I told the security guard in my halting Spanish that I was looking for two Americans who were in a meeting with the Director, he ushered me down a side hallway and up two flights of stairs before letting me into a windowless room. Three women were clustered at the far end of a large rectangular table. As I stepped into the climate-controlled environment, Olivia smiled broadly. Had she actually found something in a matter of hours?

"Alexa, hi. Allow me to introduce Katrina Mason, my contact at the embassy." She indicated the statuesque brunette to her left, who murmured a hello even as she inspected me shrewdly.

"And this is Dr. Julia Esperanza, who has charge of Special Collections." Olivia gestured to the petite, silver-haired woman to her right. "We've been examining documents that are almost two hundred years old. Apparently, the *estancieros* left detailed property records to avoid inheritance disputes."

Dr. Esperanza looked to Katrina, who spoke a string of Spanish words that I assumed to be a translation of Olivia's speech. She nodded once before replying.

"Dr. Esperanza has spent the past few hours glancing over the wills and deeds belonging to the six greatest *estanciero* families in the hopes of connecting their landholdings to the region discussed by Señor Marilla," Katrina translated. "The likeliest prospect seems to be the Carrizo family. Their last surviving will makes mention of a substantial holding in the foothills of Ojos del Salado, north of the town of Fiambala."

When Dr. Esperanza spoke again, faint frown lines materialized across Katrina's forehead. "This may prove especially interesting for your research. Dr. Esperanza has just informed me that this particular family is...cursed."

"Cursed?" I worked to school my expression in the hopes that everyone would attribute my reaction to American naiveté. A legend of some kind of curse could easily point to vampire or shifter involvement.

"The story is told in one of the deeds of the Vargas family, who annexed most of the Carrizo property in the late nineteenth century. Apparently, some kind of 'monster' or 'ghost'—both words are used in the text—slaughtered almost the entire family in their villa."

I braced my palms on the table to disguise the surge of adrenaline that had set my hands to shaking. "Almost the entire family? Someone survived?"

Katrina relayed the question and Dr. Esperanza bent over a tattered document for several long moments. The anticipation was excruciating.

"One woman may have survived—the family matriarch, a woman named Solana, whose body was never recovered," Katrina said. "The other families conducted a search for Solana, but it was fruitless."

"Was it unusual for a family to have a woman at its head?" Olivia asked.

"Very. As far as Dr. Esperanza knows, Solana Carrizo is the only documented female *estanciero*."

"So maybe this crime was perpetuated by one of the other families," Olivia said. "Because they didn't like a woman being in a position of power."

I nodded, not because I believed that interpretation of events, but because I wanted to steer the conversation away from monsters and ghosts. It seemed far more likely to me that this Solana Carrizo had run afoul of the vampire who sponsored her family.

"The piece of property in the mountains is called 'Rancho del Sombra,'" Katrina translated as she looked at the text over Dr. Esperanza's shoulder.

"Shadow Ranch." Even I could translate that phrase. The name had probably been a reference to the ranch's location in the shadow of the volcano, but the ominous connotation seemed especially fitting now.

"You're really planning to pay it a visit?" said Katrina. "You do realize that the trip will take days. The roads here are nothing like the highways that crisscross the States."

I kept my gaze and voice steady. "We are. And I know."

"We aren't risking any kind of legal sanctions from the government, are we?" asked Olivia.

"As long as you're not excavating, you'll be fine. But if you do discover something, please report it right away."

"Of course." I turned to Dr. Esperanza, who was still hunched over the fragments of frayed parchment. "Gracias, señora."

After Olivia and Katrina had made their farewells, the three of us headed for the exit. "Thank you for serving as our interpreter, Katrina," I said as we walked down the stairs.

"I'm glad I could help. I really did need an afternoon off, and your project sounds fascinating."

As we emerged onto the ground floor, Olivia spun to face us. "Let's all go out for a celebratory dinner. Trina should choose the place." Her color was high, and the light flush painted across her cheekbones set off her dark eyes. She was stunning in her triumph, and I had to look away.

"You two go ahead. I'm going to turn in early."

"Alexa—" When Olivia touched my shoulder, I was hard-pressed not to shrug off her grip. There wasn't a damn thing wrong with feeling a twinge of arousal around her. It was natural. To be expected. And my guilt was wholly out of place. I was a single woman, after all.

"I won't leave without you, Liv," I said lightly. "Promise. Have a good time."

Before she could protest again, I forged through the double doors and into the rising night.

Chapter Seven

We pulled out of the hotel parking garage under a pearl-gray sky. As I turned the car onto the nearly deserted boulevard that would lead us out of Buenos Aires, I smiled in satisfaction. Beside me, Olivia curled into herself and rested her forehead against the cool windowpane. She had returned to the hotel room late, and I hadn't needed the keen senses of a shifter to know she'd been drinking. I'd been able to resume only a fitful doze before my alarm had woken me well before dawn, but I didn't feel fatigued—only energized for the hunt to come.

When I pulled over three hours later for gas and coffee, Olivia woke. She would have drunk from one of our canteens if I hadn't glared at her and pointed to the small store next to the pumps.

"Ojos del Salado isn't all that far from the driest desert in the world. Water is going to be a precious commodity."

She gave me a baleful look and stalked toward the store. After hooking up the pump, I did a few stretches to limber up my stiff shoulders and hamstrings. Olivia emerged with two bottles of water while I was bent over with my palms nearly touching the dust. She whistled, and I couldn't fight the blush that crept up my neck.

"You're feeling better, I take it?" I said, not meeting her eyes.

"Last night was worth a little headache. You should have come with us. We drank some amazing wine." She unwrapped a candy bar as I pulled back onto the road. "Trina had heard that the Fiambala area is known for its vineyards, so we sampled a few bottles."

"And?"

I caught her teasing smile in my peripheral vision. "And I thought this trip was all about business to you. Suddenly you care about wine?"

"I was making conversation to be polite. Do you even remember how?"

She laughed. "You know my last name. Politeness is hardwired into our genes."

I couldn't help but think of Valentine, whose parents had chosen the company of so-called polite society over accepting their own daughter. "Did your family…how did they react, when you came out?"

Olivia blinked at the sudden change in topic. "Ah, there was some grumbling. Mostly on the part of my grandparents and one of my uncles. But my mother and father have never been anything but supportive." She shot me a sympathetic look. "Val didn't have it easy, did she?"

"Never. She fought them tooth and nail. Until…"

"What about you?" Olivia asked quickly. "And your family?"

"They sound a lot like yours—on the tolerance count, anyway. I'm lucky."

"We both are."

We settled into a comfortable silence, and for the first time since we had left New York, I found myself unambiguously glad that Olivia had insisted on accompanying me. The journey would have been long and lonely otherwise. And I wouldn't have learned about Shadow Ranch.

"Solana Carrizo." Only at Olivia's curious glance did I realize I'd said the words aloud. "It's a beautiful name, don't you think?"

"She must have been quite the woman to have bucked tradition and taken over the leadership of her family."

"Maybe she didn't have a choice."

Olivia drummed her fingers on the dashboard. "You think one of her family members forced her into it?"

"Or maybe a vampire did. If they were sponsoring the *estancieros*, then she might have been caught in the middle of a turf war."

"Do you have any idea what they were doing in Argentina?" Olivia asked.

"No." But as the miles of rolling plains passed under our tires, I carefully considered her question. "I wonder if historically, it's been easier for vampires—and for shifters, to a degree—to live in places undergoing some kind of social or political upheaval."

"That makes sense, I suppose. In times of turmoil, people who deviate from the norm don't stand out as much."

"Are you calling me abnormal?" At Olivia's obvious chagrin, I smiled. "Relax. I was just teasing."

"Who knew you still had it in you," she muttered. But then her expression turned thoughtful. "In a way, though, the question of 'normalcy' is legitimate, isn't it? You call yourself a shifter, but what does that mean?"

"It's up for debate," I said, remembering back to several long conversations with Delacourte over the summer. A momentary twinge of grief made my chest constrict. "I'm not sure anyone knows how we evolved, or how long ago. Whether we're different species, or sub-species of humans, or just…diseased."

"But you can reproduce, can't you?"

"Shifters can," I said automatically, then clamped my jaw shut, wishing I could take the words back. There were some secrets that shouldn't be entrusted to anyone outside the community.

"Not vampires?"

When I remained silent, Olivia settled back in her seat. "Okay, fine. I understand. Let's talk about something else, like what we're going to do when we get to Fiambala. We still don't exactly have GPS coordinates for Shadow Ranch, and neither of us knows enough Spanish to go sleuthing."

I smiled. "That shouldn't be a problem."

"Oh?"

"While you were carousing last night, I did some research online. There's a famous mountaineering store in Fiambala that supplies hikers from around the world for treks up Ojos del Salado. I'm betting someone there speaks English, and they may even have heard of Shadow Ranch."

When I glanced at Olivia, she actually seemed impressed. "You've got it all figured out, don't you?"

Not wanting to jinx us, I didn't reply.

❖

We crossed over the city limits of Fiambala just after noon the next day. Olivia navigated us through the narrow streets with a map we'd purchased at a gas station at the edge of town, and within only a few minutes, we pulled into the parking lot behind the store. It was packed with other Jeeps, pickups of all sizes, and even some ATVs.

Inside, a fair-haired couple were surveying rucksacks hanging on the wall and conversing in a Scandinavian-sounding language. I headed straight for the counter, where a tanned youth slouched on a stool. He looked me up and down as I approached, and grinned.

I managed to resist rolling my eyes. "Could you give us some directions, please?"

"Where to, señorita?"

"A place called Shadow Ranch. Somewhere to the north of here."

He flexed his biceps and smoothed one finger over the patchy mustache he'd doubtless cultivated for weeks. "You ever hear 'mi casa es su casa?'"

Olivia brushed the back of her knuckles against my cheek as she joined me at the counter. The boy's eyes bugged at her caress. "Thanks, but no thanks," she said. "Now, how about those directions?"

He blinked at us, said a word in Spanish that I didn't recognize, and disappeared into the back of the store. Olivia's smile was broad.

"You're welcome."

I bumped her shoulder lightly with mine. "I could have handled it."

"I didn't want the poor boy to get his head ripped off. He was only flirting with a beautiful woman."

Thankfully, I didn't have to come up with a response. A middle-aged man emerged from the back with the teen in tow and greeted us with the sandpaper voice of a lifetime smoker. He wore a tight gray T-shirt that accentuated the corded muscles of his arms, and his face was dark and weathered like the crags of the mountains that loomed above us.

"Good afternoon," he said in careful English. "I am Emilio. How can I help?"

"We're doing some hiking around the volcano," I said. "We've heard of a place called Shadow Ranch, and we'd like to go there. Do you know it?"

His eyes narrowed ever so slightly. "You want the…the *casa encantada*, eh? The ghost house?"

"Haunted house," Olivia said. "Yes, we want to see it."

"You see it, the ghost might see you."

"We're not worried," I said. "How do we get there?"

He shrugged and picked up a black marker from its perch on the cash register, then turned over a colorful flyer for one of the local motels and began to draw. As the map took shape, he explained that the path to the ranch had fallen out of use long ago and was easy to miss from the main road.

"Can I drive my Jeep? Or will we have to walk?"

He shook his head. "I do not know."

"You've never been there?"

His brows angled in a frown. "The land is cursed."

I stuffed several bills into the tip jar on the counter. "Thank you for your help."

He said nothing, and as we left the store, I wondered whether he would keep the money. Or whether, simply by virtue of being associated with the haunted house, Emilio would consider it too to be cursed.

❖

We drove past the head of the trail three times before finally noticing the two distinct ruts still visible through gaps in the foliage. But our success was short-lived. Less than a hundred yards down the path, we were forced to abandon the Jeep before a massive fallen tree.

"Man or nature?" Olivia asked as we stood over the decomposing trunk. It was already an inextricable part of the landscape, new plants having taken root in and around the tree's carcass.

"I think someone did this," I said. "Look at the ninety-degree angle with the path. That's not haphazard."

Beyond the obstacle, the trail curved up and to the northwest before disappearing into a dense stand of trees. I returned to the Jeep and hefted the large pack that held our camping supplies, then directed Olivia to take a smaller bag filled with dried food.

"Why do you get to be the macho one?" she said as she watched me adjust the thick straps so the pack's weight was concentrated more on my hips than on my back.

"Because I'm the one with superpowers."

I had been trying to make a joke, but Olivia blinked in surprise. "Your panther makes you stronger when you're human, too?"

"I'm not human," I corrected her. "I just look like one sometimes. And the answer to your question is yes." I could have told her more—how my healing ability and senses were also enhanced—but she already knew too much. Besides, my panther was on high alert now that we were in the wild. She wanted to hunt, and her seething impatience was bleeding into me.

"How many hours do we have until dark?" Olivia asked as she clambered over the tree after me.

"Sunset's at eight twenty-five." Not wanting to be caught unprepared at nightfall, I had looked it up this morning. Of course, if my theory about the vampire presence here was correct, he or she was not confined to the darkness and could surprise us at any time. Not exactly a comforting thought, but I tried to soothe my inner beast by reminding her of our significant physical advantage over vampires.

The trail grew worse as we traveled further from the main road, and Olivia soon abandoned any other attempts at conversation. I let my panther ride close to the surface, allowing her instincts to monitor our surroundings. She scented deer a few times, and once even a bear, but never did she detect anything amiss.

And then, as the afternoon light began to dim and the air grew cooler, we stepped into a large clearing. In the distance, across a hundred yards of tall, unruly grass, sat a white stone house set into the hillside. A two-tiered terrace led down to the field, bordered by a barn on one side and a corral on the other. Behind the house, the land rose sharply, sweeping up and back to form one flank of the mountain.

"Shadow Ranch," said Olivia.

I accepted the canteen she handed me and drank deeply. "Shall we go see who's home?"

Olivia drew her gun and examined it closely, then thumbed off the safety. "Ready when you are."

But when she would have moved forward, I stopped her with my hand on her wrist. "If something happens and I shift, there are two things you should know." She paled slightly at the thought, and I found myself stroking her forearm in reassurance. "I'll have control of the panther. It's always a fight, but I won't hurt you, and I'll be able to understand anything you say."

She nodded once. "What's the second thing?"

"I'll be ravenous. Shifting takes a lot of energy, and I'll need to hunt and eat before I can return to human form."

Her laugh was shaky. "Just as long as I'm not your quarry."

"I told you, I won't hurt you." I made her the promise with a newfound confidence—born, ironically, of that disastrous night at Luna when I'd run into Valentine. I hadn't been able to keep from shifting, but I'd managed to avoid causing any human casualties. After maintaining control through that emotional crucible, I felt reasonably certain that I would only ever surrender to my panther's predatory instincts on my own terms.

"I trust you," Olivia said.

I turned to face the ranch. There was no way to conceal our approach short of crawling through the grass, and if someone were watching from the elevated house, they would see us regardless. There was no sense in stowing the packs here and trying to be sneaky. We were going to have to walk in the open. I took a steadying breath and then moved forward, sticking to the shelter of the trees as long as possible before finally turning into the meadow. My panther wanted to be the one doing the stalking, and I grimaced at the effort of holding her back.

We reached the edge of the terrace without mishap and turned onto the gravel path that wound up to the front door. Dirt and leaves mingled with round, white stones. It was clear that this walkway, at least, had not been rigorously maintained for many years. As we walked, I peered up into the large front windows but couldn't see anything past the glare.

The front door was large and made of oak. Wood grains showed through the burnished gold paint in several places. A fresh coat was long overdue. I glanced at Olivia, who simply shrugged and tightened her fingers on the grip of her gun.

"Here goes nothing," I said before raising the heavy knocker and letting it fall once, twice, three times. I leaned forward in expectation, confident that my amplified hearing would alert me to any movement. But aside from the soft skittering of mice in the walls, I heard nothing.

"Now what?" Olivia asked once it became obvious that no one would be greeting us. She palmed the door handle, but it didn't move. "Shall I shoot the lock?"

"And alert everyone within a mile? I don't think so." I brushed her hand away, gripped the elaborate pewter knob, and twisted sharply as I pushed with preternatural strength. There was the sound of wood splintering, and then the door swung inward.

I glanced over my shoulder at Olivia, who looked equal parts surprised and impressed, and gestured for her to follow me. The interior of the house was dim, and I paused just inside the door to give my eyes a chance to adjust. To our left was a parlor, complete with several armchairs and a chaise lounge. Across the hall, the dining room took up the remaining width of the house. The long table was covered with a sheet, but thick gilt legs made of a dark wood stuck out from beneath the coverlet.

The rooms were deserted. I held my breath to listen, but the house was still. Silent. Even so, my arms and neck prickled in warning, and I shrugged off the pack to gain a greater range of motion. If someone tried to steal it, I would hear their movements.

I beckoned Olivia forward, and we made our way down the hall until it ended at the foot of a spiral staircase. Two rooms branched off from the corridor. To the right, the coppery tiles of the spacious kitchen gleamed in counterpoint to its pale wooden cupboards. To the left, dust motes danced in the sunlight filtering into a room bordered with floor-to-ceiling bookshelves. My attention was drawn to an ornate wooden desk and the artwork that hung above it—a watercolor rendition of the ranch, poised like a bright pearl set deep into the maw of the volcanic ridge.

Wanting to examine the painting, I stepped over the threshold... only to gasp as my panther thrashed wildly. Her desperation punched the breath from my lungs, and I reached out blindly for the doorframe. But my hand closed on air as I was suddenly shoved to the side, and I cried out as my assailant pinned my arm behind my back. My attacker swept my legs out from under me, and for an instant, I was falling.

"Uje!" I gasped. And then my panther was on me.

Chapter Eight

Olivia was shouting something, but her words were lost to me in my bone-wrenching slide into feline form. The disorientation faded as quickly as it had come, and I flattened myself to the ground, haunches coiled to spring. Olivia was pointing her gun at a woman, who was in turn pointing her gun at me. The stranger's wavy dark hair framed a grim expression. She wore form-fitting dark green cargo pants and a matching vest over a beige blouse, and her hand wavered as she debated the focus of her revolver.

"Drop your weapon." Olivia's voice was pitched higher than usual, but her words were steady.

As soon as the stranger's arm began to pivot, I sprang, knocking her to the floor. But as she fell, the sharp report of her pistol pierced my ears. Olivia's cry of pain and the tang of blood in the air drove me wild. Hunger twisted in my belly like a writhing snake, compounded by the wholly feline desire to tear my assailant apart. She struggled, and I pressed harder on her shoulders, piercing her fragile flesh with my claws. I wanted her blood in my mouth and her bones between my jaws. Snarling into her ashen face, I bared my teeth and tensed for the lunge that would tear out her throat.

"Alexa, no!" Olivia cried. She was alive, her words breathless but strong. I paused, saliva dripping onto the woman's neck. Olivia was slumped against the wall, one hand covering her left shoulder. Blood seeped slowly between her fingertips. "It's not serious. I'm okay. I'm okay. Don't hurt her."

My panther's every instinct warred against retreat. She wanted to finish the job, and in so doing, to satiate herself. It was an effort to pull her back from the stranger and into a wary crouch. Tail lashing, I watched as Olivia rose slowly, then took possession of the stranger's gun and ordered her to sit with her back to the wall.

"I did not intentionally fire at you," the woman said. Her accent was an intriguing combination of British and Argentinean, her voice remarkably steady for a woman who had been on the cusp of a gory death. "My gun discharged as I fell. Is your wound serious?"

"I'll live." With a practiced movement, Olivia ejected the stranger's clip and tucked the pistol into her waistband. Blood trickled down her arm, but she paid it no mind. She wasn't losing it quickly enough to risk fainting right away, but that meant the bullet was probably still inside her body. She would need surgery. "Who are you?"

The woman swept her hair back from her face, looking far more regal than she had any right to under the circumstances. "My name is Solana Carrizo, and this home has been in my family for generations. You are the interlopers here. Who are *you*?"

Olivia's jaw dropped and a low whine escaped my throat. Solana Carrizo? The female *estanciero*, who had been born over a century ago? If so, she had to be a vampire. I edged closer to her and inhaled, but her scent was wholly unfamiliar: not pungent like a human's, nor musky like a shifter's, nor the sharp chill of a snowbound winter morning that I'd always associated with vampires.

"Solana Carrizo? But…but how old are you?"

Solana's stare was coolly defiant. "Why should I answer your questions?"

She was toying with us while Olivia was injured. Baring my teeth, I growled and took a menacing step closer in an attempt to show her exactly why she should be cooperative.

"Alexa. Stop."

Solana's thin eyebrows arched. "The cat—she is under your control?"

Olivia shook her head, then winced as the movement agitated her injury. "She's under her own control."

Solana regarded me pensively, then turned back to Olivia. "What is your business here? Why have you trespassed on my land?"

Olivia didn't have an immediate reply, and I could practically feel her trying to sort out how much information to give this woman—or whatever she was. Bending awkwardly, she reached for one of the scraps from my shirt that I'd shredded during my shift and pressed it against her shoulder. The flow of blood had slowed, but as the adrenaline wore off, her pain would only increase. And that bullet had to come out.

"My name is Olivia," she said finally. "Alexa and I—we're searching for something. Something that could save the life of…of a friend. We were told that this place has been deserted for years." She managed a chuckle. "That it was haunted."

"Haunted." Solana's gaze was unfocused, as though the object of her scrutiny was far off in the distance. "In a manner of speaking." She rose to her feet and Olivia cursed, fumbling for her gun. In an instant, I stood between them, snarling.

She waved me away. "Stop this. That wound needs tending to. I know of a skilled *curandero*—a healer—in a nearby village. Let me take you there."

"We have a Jeep just off the highway." Olivia sounded as doubtful of her proposition as I felt. "I can get medical attention in Fiambala."

"Your vehicle is hours away on foot, and dusk is almost upon us. We can be in the village of which I speak by sunset."

"How will we get there?"

"I have a car concealed nearby. The cat—Alexa, you call her? She can follow us."

Olivia looked conflicted, but the right decision seemed clear to me—though I didn't like it. If Solana was a vampire, she had excellent control over her bloodlust. She could, of course, be harmful even if she wasn't, but her words and mannerisms felt genuine to me. It might seem foolish to take such a risk on intuition, but Solana was right; our options were slim. Olivia's condition would only deteriorate, and the longer she went without medical care, the greater the probability of infection became.

Once I hunted, I would be able to follow their trail closely. Depending on the quality of the road to this village, I might even be able to keep pace with Solana's car. Olivia still had her weapon and the strength to use it; she wouldn't be unprotected. Besides, Solana's offer gave us the excuse to stay close to her. She could be the "parched spirit" of Miralla's translated anecdotes, and I wasn't about to let her get away.

"What do you think?" Olivia asked me, fully meeting my gaze for the first time since my shift. It wasn't an easy thing for a human to do. I could tell that the pain was beginning to register; her eyes were hazy and her cheeks had lost their flush.

I paced close to her and brushed against her thigh, then dipped my head and nosed gently at her legs, propelling her in Solana's direction.

"She, at least, believes I can be trusted." Solana sounded bemused, but when she glanced my way, I silently bared my teeth. Her answering nod was proof that she understood the stakes.

If any more harm came to Olivia, Solana's life was forfeit.

❖

As Solana pulled out of the barn, I let my panther's instincts take over. Within minutes, I had flushed out, caught, and devoured a brown hare from the nearby woods. As the hunger waned, my control and concentration improved. I was soon following the fresh tire tracks north and east over a steep rise and along a sparsely forested ridge. Several miles later, the tracks made a switch-backed descent into a narrow ravine that opened into a small box canyon. I scented the village before I could see it, but my panther balked at walking into what she considered to be a trap. The canyon walls were sheer, and the path in was also the only way out.

I abandoned the tracks and clung to the thin cover available from the sparsely distributed trees and undergrowth. The village was a cluster of whitewashed buildings, but most of the rooftops glinted silver from the presence of solar panels. Somehow, clean energy had found this remote community. I wove in and out of the shadows in as wide a circle as the steep canyon walls would allow, until Solana's melodic voice reached my ears. The sound of her conversation was emanating not from one of the buildings, but from a stone structure near the back wall of the canyon. A now-crumbling fortress had been built into the rock at some point in the distant past, but the thin tendril of smoke emerging from one of the more intact chambers signaled that someone had co-opted the ruins for current use. I crouched low, belly pressing against the dusty earth, and slunk up the broken stone stairs.

Solana was speaking rapidly in Spanish. When she paused, a deep male voice interjected a question. As I drew closer, I caught Olivia's scent under the pungent aroma of a large collection of herbs. After listening for several minutes, however, I still hadn't heard her speak or even move and had no way of knowing whether she was silent because she couldn't understand the conversation or if she was somehow in trouble. I crept forward, hoping to catch a glimpse inside the room, but my paws slipped on shale and loose stone crumbled down the steps. The voices inside the room stopped.

In the next moment, Solana was outside the door, regarding me with her hands on her hips. She had moved more quickly than a human could, but the dying rays of sunlight played over her face without inciting a conflagration.

"Your friend Olivia is fine. Miguel removed the bullet, and she is resting. If you return to two legs, you can see her."

As much as I wanted the power of my own voice, I wasn't ready to trust her. When I shifted back, I would be naked and vulnerable. I didn't want to be trapped in a small room where I would be easily overpowered.

At the sound of my rumbling growl, Solana sighed. "You require proof? Very well then. Come inside as you are and see that I've kept my word."

She disappeared, and I cautiously padded after her through an elaborately beaded curtain and into a small square room. The floor was covered with brightly colored woven mats, and herbs hung from the patched roof like alien icicles.

The man whose voice I'd heard was crouched next to a pile of blankets on which Olivia lay supine, the white cloth of a bandage peeking out from under the collar of her sweater. Miguel seemed unfazed by my approach, but I ignored him until I had reassured myself that she was breathing. When I finally looked up, he wordlessly held out a blanket. Apparently, he knew what to expect.

I stretched into the shift, but my panther's will to remain four-legged was strong; she felt ill at ease and wanted the protection of her own teeth and claws. Her reluctance made the transformation more painful than it had to be, and I leaned hard against the wall to catch my breath as bright shards of agony seared up my legs and along the length of my spine.

Solana had taken the blanket from Miguel, and she wrapped it around my shoulders. I examined her through my own eyes for the first time and found her beautiful. She was petite of stature, her delicate frame at odds with the imposing air that surrounded her. High cheekbones framed her hazel eyes, made darker by the pallor of her features.

"Impressive," she said. "I've never seen it done with such speed."

I wasn't about to confess that at my best, I could shift much more quickly. Clutching the blanket close, I turned so that my back was no longer against the wall. "What are you?"

"What do I look like?"

I didn't want to play these games with her, but I also didn't really have a choice. "You move like a vampire." Her patronizing smile confirmed my suspicions. "But your scent isn't right. If you are really Solana Carrizo the *estanciera*, you must have been turned near the beginning of the twentieth century. You shouldn't be able to walk in the sun because you must have made the transition long ago. Unless, that is, you've discovered a way to stop it." I glanced at Miguel, then up at his collection of herbs. If my hunch was correct, the flower might be among them. "Or reverse it."

The smile faded as first surprise and then fear flashed across her features. In another moment, all emotion was hidden behind a grim mask. "Olivia claimed you were on some sort of quest, but she wouldn't tell me the object. What are you looking for?"

It was time to lay all of my cards on the table, and I had to suppress a shiver at the adrenaline rush that spiked my blood. "We came here in search of a plant—a flower—with the ability to restore a vampire's soul."

Her lips thinned, but she gave no other sign that my words had affected her. "That's quite a bit of power to ascribe to a simple flower."

"I can't be sure of how or if it will work, but I have to try." I paused, searching her impassive eyes for some sign of connection or compassion. "Do you have any information that might help me?"

She regarded me silently then turned and asked Miguel a question. When he responded in the affirmative, she indicated the thicker rugs before the crude stone hearth. "Miguel has offered us the use of this chamber while Olivia recovers. Shall we sit?"

"When will she wake up?"

Solana exchanged a few words with Miguel. "Soon. He gave her an herbal tincture to render her unconscious while he removed the bullet, and it should wear off within the hour."

"Gracias," I told him, wishing I had better words to express my gratitude. He nodded, then left the room. I joined Solana at the hearth.

"I am curious about your motives," she said. "Most vampires would never wish to give up the power they have gained in exchange for freedom from the darkness."

"Are you speaking from personal experience?"

She turned her gaze on me and settled back against the blankets. "Tell me your story, and I will tell you mine."

My story. As I considered where to begin, I felt a sense of vertigo, as though I were teetering on the edge of a great mental chasm. My story. Here, now, I was sitting next to a vampire in a tiny Andes village thousands of miles from the city I called home, which was itself a thousand miles from the provincial hospital where my mother had first taken me from the arms of a nurse and smiled and called me "Alexa." That moment and this would have been worlds apart if not for Valentine. She connected the woman in me to the werepanther. She was my past, and I would fight to make her my future.

"My lover and I had been together for almost a year when she was turned by the Missionary," I began. "At first, she tried to convince me that we should no longer be together—that she was too dangerous to me. My blood was powerful enough to stop her transition, but she was afraid that in a moment of weakness, she might take too much."

Solana's sigh would have been inaudible to human ears, but it wasn't to mine. I glanced at her just in time to see a flash of pain twist her lips. "And did she?"

"We had one very close call. After that, I started looking for a way to better sustain her. Ultimately, I decided to become a Were. It took a while before I was able to control my panther while Valentine fed from me, but eventually I was successful."

I pressed the heel of one hand to the hollow space that ached between my breasts whenever the guilt resurfaced. "But then we spent some time apart. Not because of a disagreement, but because I had been invited to spend the summer in Telassar. Are you familiar with it?"

Solana inclined her head. "As familiar as someone who is not of your kind can be."

"I knew that us being apart was hard on her, but I didn't realize just how hard. And then the whole world went mad, when Balthasar Brenner destroyed Sybaris and besieged Telassar and released a shifter virus in New York. My return was delayed."

An echo of the fear and anxiety that had been my constant companions in those days must have shown on my face, because Solana fleetingly rested her hand on my knee. "And so your lover… grew distant."

"I got home before it happened, but I was too late to stop it." Leaning forward, I held her unblinking gaze and willingly let down my guard. "At first, I believed that bringing her back would be impossible. But I think there's a way, and that you know what it is. I'll do anything. Whatever it takes. Please help me."

She turned away, the tiny muscles along her jaw line twitching as she stared into the flames. "To understand what you are asking," she said finally, "requires me to tell a story that no one else except

Miguel has ever heard—Miguel and his father before him, and his father before him. And now you.

"I was born in 1881 into a family of powerful landowners just outside Buenos Aires. My parents had no sons, and my father passed away before his time. He should have named one of my male cousins his successor, but instead, he named me. One of his last acts was to write me a letter in which he described the bargain that our family and others like us had made with a group of vampires. They protected us and furthered our interests in exchange for blood. We gave them our undesirables—our thieves and our murderers. It was, as my father put it, a devil's bargain. And I inherited it.

"The vampire to whom I answered was named Romero. One of his younger associates, Helen, saved my life when the head of one of the other families sought to have me killed, simply for being a woman. Despite my better judgment, I fell in love with her."

The air stuttered in my lungs as surprise stole my breath. "Helen? Helen Lambros?"

"Yes. She has control of the Consortium in New York City now, or so I've heard."

My brain spun wildly. "She does. I know her fairly well. She was the one who turned you?"

The corners of Solana's mouth tightened. "No. But she believed she had killed me." At my look of confusion, Solana rose and began to pace before the fire. "We were happy together for almost five years. And then, one night, she simply took too much. I will never know what, if anything, made that night different from any other. She thought I was dead, but I was only unconscious. When I woke, Helen was gone. I tried to find her, but overexerted myself and fainted again. The next thing I can remember is the taste of blood in my throat and a vampire named Hector standing over me. Hector was the patron of the powerful Vargas family. He may have saved my life by turning me, but he should have let me die."

This was an argument I'd heard from Valentine in the days soon after she had become a vampire, and I reacted viscerally to it. "Why would you say a thing like that?"

Solana remained calm. "Because it is true. In the throes of my early bloodlust, I killed my mother and the elder of my two sisters."

She was watching me closely, expecting a reaction of horror or disgust or both, but I ruthlessly schooled my expression. "I'm so very sorry."

"I am the only one to blame."

Despite having heard only a fraction of the full story, I doubted that. But I wasn't about to argue with her—not when we barely knew each other.

"I fled Argentina then and traveled to England in an attempt to find Helen. She had owned property there at one time, but I could find no trace of her and had no way of discovering where she had gone. After a decade, I stopped looking. After two, I finally returned home, only to find that Hector had taken control of my family's property and had merged our assets with those of the Vargas family. What's more, he had indentured my remaining relatives. They were little better than slaves.

"Hector was powerful and far more experienced than I. When he almost caught me attempting to free them, I fled to these mountains to regroup and plan. One day, I was unwise enough to attempt to feed from Miguel's grandfather, Rudolpho, who was gathering herbs in the nearby forest. The *curanderos* of this region are very powerful, and he was able to subdue me. Eventually, I told him my story and he pledged to help me—a promise he fulfilled, though not as I expected."

She stopped speaking then and looked over my shoulder. Olivia was stirring. As we watched, she raised herself up on one elbow, eyes wide. "Alexa?"

I moved to her bedside and knelt so she didn't have to crane her neck. "Hey, Liv. How are you feeling?"

"A little out of it. Shoulder hurts a bit."

I smoothed her dark hair back from her forehead and reached down to squeeze her hand. "You're doing great. You're going to be just fine. Miguel took the bullet out."

"What did he give me?"

"Passion flower extract," said Solana. "A natural sedative. You should feel completely alert within a few hours."

The anxiety drained from her face, and she relaxed into the blankets. "Thank you."

"Can you fall back to sleep?" I asked.

"I might." Olivia opened her eyes just a sliver, as though her lids were heavy. "You'll fill me in later?"

I brushed my knuckles across her forehead. "Promise. You rest."

When her breathing became even, I returned to the hearth. Solana held out a steaming cup of liquid to me. "Maté tea. A stimulant, though not quite as strong as coffee."

I took a tentative sip, then another. It tasted like a stronger, more pungent form of green tea. I looked up at the plants hanging from the ceiling, wondering which one this was. "You seem to know quite a bit about these herbs."

She raised her own cup to her mouth and breathed in the steam before drinking. "Miguel and his ancestors have taught me well."

A sudden hunch pushed my heartbeat into overdrive and I looked up again, squinting into the dark rafters. "Did they give you the flower? Is it here?"

Solana's silence was as good as an affirmative. "Tell me," I said. "I'll keep your secret. I swear it." I was a hair's breadth from begging, but my pride had long since ceased to matter.

"Yes," she finally said. "They gave it to me, and it is nearby." She held up her hand. "Let me finish my story, and you will have your answers.

"When I had secured a promise from Rudolpho to help me free my family from Hector's tyranny, I expected him to help me raise an army. Instead, he took me on a perilous journey to the shore of the lake beneath the volcano's summit. We camped there for several days, until the full moon. As it rose, a plant emerged from the ground within minutes. It flowered once the moon was free of the horizon. Miguel's grandfather pulled it from the ground, broke off its roots, and commanded me to eat it."

I was barely breathing. "What happened? What did it do to you?"

"I fell into a coma for several days," Solana said. "When I woke, I was terribly thirsty, but I could bear the sunlight."

"My God," I whispered. "It reversed your transition."

"Yes. Every full moon since that day, I have eaten the roots. I've been able to walk under the sun for almost seventy years."

My euphoria burst. If Solana needed the roots every month, none would be left over for Valentine. "What about the stem and the petals—do they have any of the same properties?"

"They do, to a minor extent. Miguel uses them to create poultices for several of the ailing members of his community."

"But can they do what the roots are capable of?"

Solana's face was troubled as she shook her head. "I don't believe so. Miguel will be able to tell us for certain. Perhaps he can think of a way to extend or duplicate the active ingredient in the roots."

I nodded slowly, fighting not to lose hope. Solana shouldn't have to give up the flower, but to have come so far—to have actually found the object of my search only to be thwarted by its singular nature—seemed cruel beyond measure. Still, Solana had not said that she would withhold the flower from me, and her willingness to help seemed genuine. There had to be a way to save Valentine without damning Solana. I refused to believe anything else.

"Then maybe it's time to have a talk with Miguel."

CHAPTER NINE

While Solana went to find Miguel and fill him in on our discussion, I retrieved my pack from her car and changed into proper clothes. The night was clear and cool, and the darkness rivaled that of Telassar. In the absence of light pollution, the sky was salted with stars in such abundance that it would not have been difficult to pick out familiar constellations if I had known what to look for. This hemisphere was utterly foreign to me, and without the comforting anchor of Polaris pointing north, I felt strangely adrift.

A smear of light near the western lip of the canyon's edge heralded the arrival of the waxing moon. It would be full in five days. We didn't have much time, and I had to consider what I would do if Solana ultimately refused to let me take the flower's root to Valentine. Just how far was I willing to go? Even if I could somehow get to the flower first and steal it away, would I be capable of risking Solana's soul to save Val's?

I shrugged the pack over my shoulders and began the walk back to the ruins. No. If we couldn't come up with a solution, I would have to go back to square one—to wait until Karma's contacts discovered another of the flower's locations. Despair threatened at the corners of my brain like storm clouds on the horizon, and I quickened my pace in response. There had to be something we could do, but even if this was a dead end, I had far from exhausted all of the search possibilities. I needed to be patient.

When I slipped inside the stone chamber, Miguel and Solana were conversing quietly near the hearth and Olivia was propped up against several pillows eating soup from a ceramic bowl. I set the pack in the corner and crouched next to her.

"How are you feeling?"

She tried to raise her left hand and grimaced. "Sore. But my head feels a lot clearer. I guess passion flower extract is potent."

Guilt reverberated in my chest. "Olivia, I am so sorry."

She set down her spoon and gripped my hand. "Shut up. I knew the risks. And you warned me, remember?"

"Even so, I should have been able to protect you."

"It was an accident. I really believe that. And I'll be fine." She glanced over to Solana and Miguel, who were still deep in conversation. "So what did you find out?"

I brought her up to speed quickly. "If we can't figure out a solution," I concluded, "I think we're going to have to start over."

Olivia frowned. "Even supposing we do find a way, if this flower is so delicate, how do we preserve it with enough time to get it to Val?"

I hadn't thought of that possible complication and was just about to tell her so when Solana joined us. "Miguel has an idea, but his proposal is risky on several levels."

"Tell us."

"The day after tomorrow, you, Miguel, and I will ascend the mountain to the place where the flower blooms. When it does, Miguel will harvest the stem and petals as usual, but he will implant the root under your skin."

My panther sprang into action at Solana's pronouncement, and I clutched a fistful of blankets for purchase as I mentally held her off. Olivia's spoon clattered in the bowl as she pushed herself upright.

"He's going to do what?" she said.

"Miguel has told me that the flower will flourish until the next full moon if it is nourished with blood. He believes that by planting the roots beneath your skin, he will accomplish two things: the flower will survive, and your blood will absorb its properties."

"Its healing properties?" When she nodded, elation swept over me. "So all I'd have to do is convince Valentine to drink from me?"

"Yes. But while the roots are inside you, you would have to keep yourself from shifting. Your transformation would destroy the flower."

My panther snarled, but I silently reminded her that we had endured much worse. "What about you? How will you get what you need?"

"For years, Miguel has been encouraging me to test whether I truly need the flower every month. It may be necessary, but we have no way of knowing until I stop taking it."

My head spun with all the possibilities. "And you're willing to do that?" I couldn't help but feel suspicious. "For someone you've never even met? Why?"

She looked at me steadily. "I can never repay my debt to Miguel's grandfather, but there are ways in which I can honor his memory. For years, I've protected this village and helped its inhabitants to develop and thrive. Now I have the chance to do for your Valentine what Rudolpho did for me."

"I will always be in your debt," I said, awed by the magnitude of her gift.

She waved away my words. "That's not what I want. But I do wish to return with you to New York."

"Because of Helen?"

To my surprise, she flushed and looked away. "In part. But also because I have been a hermit too long. Battle lines have been drawn and a conflict is imminent. If there was ever a time for me to return to the world, it is now."

For a while, all was silent as I reflected on her reasoning and she brewed tea over the fire. But soon enough, my thoughts spiraled back to the flower and its properties.

"Does Miguel think the roots' effects on my blood will be temporary?" I asked. "Or will having the flower inside me for a few days change my blood permanently?"

As Solana conferred with Miguel, Olivia grasped my shoulder. "I don't know about this. That plan is sketchy, and the word 'blood' has come up too many times."

"My blood regenerates when I transform. I'm not worried about losing a little."

"That makes one of—"

Solana's exclamation—a string of Spanish words that seemed to be invoking a saint—cut Olivia off. She hurried toward us. "Miguel believes that your Were physiology might magnify the effects of the flower."

"Magnify it how?"

"One of two ways. Because your blood already bestows some measure of regenerative ability to a vampire, it's possible that when the flower's essence enters your vessels it will transform your circulatory system. In that case, Valentine would be able to keep her soul with a steady infusion of your blood.

"The other possibility is that the combination will affect her circulatory system. In that case she could become permanently ensouled—beyond the risk of transforming back into a full vampire."

Unable to believe what I was hearing, I leaned back against the wall. There was a chance that this strange procedure could change Valentine forever? If her bloodlust became an indulgence rather than a necessity, she would never again have to feel guilt about feeding from me.

Firmly, I reined in my hyperbolic thoughts. "Is there also a possibility that this might fail? That the roots might not survive even on my blood, or that Valentine won't be affected at all?"

Solana nodded. "Miguel knows nothing for certain. He is extrapolating possibilities based on his understanding of the flower."

"I still don't like this," Olivia murmured. "Too many variables. But I know you're going to do it anyway."

"You're right." Standing, I met Solana's eyes. "When do we leave?"

❖

For the second time since we had left Solana's Jeep at the base of one of the trailheads leading up to the lake, the trail led us over rocks so steep they had to be climbed. Pitons—metal pins used by rock climbers—had been driven into cracks in the rock faces to assist our ascent. Solana had said this was the least popular hiking trail, and I could understand why. She scrambled up nimbly and I followed her, Miguel bringing up the rear. Olivia had refused to remain in the village, choosing instead to stay with the car and within radio distance.

I crested the last rock to find Solana waiting just over the lip. She handed me a canteen and I drank deeply. The shadows were growing as dusk fell; Miguel had switched on his headlamp, and I felt fortunate that my eyes could adjust so completely to the darkness.

"Not far now," Solana said. "A kilometer or so."

I unclipped the radio from my belt. "Olivia, do you read?"

"Loud and clear. Still no hikers behind you. Are you there?"

"Getting close. I'll call again when we've reached the spot."

As she signed off, I reached down to help Miguel over the lip of the cliff. This part of the trail was much more reasonable—a switchback rather than a sheer climb. Ahead of me, Solana moved confidently. The trail must have been as familiar to her as my daily walk to Washington Square.

Not for the first time, I wondered whether her trip to New York would result in some kind of confrontation with Helen. Was Solana planning to see her? Did Helen even know she was still alive— that in her panic so many decades ago, she had made a mistake by leaving? I tried to imagine how I would feel if I were in Solana's place. It wasn't difficult. Valentine had almost pulled a Romeo when she had believed me dead at her hands, but what if she had left instead? I couldn't imagine a reality in which I wasn't inexorably drawn to Val. What had changed in the intervening decades to make Solana keep her distance from Helen, even after she learned where to find her?

After a series of switches, we scrabbled up one final vertiginous ascent before emerging onto a narrow ridge. Below us, the surface of the crater lake gleamed in the dying light, its waters as dark as an oil slick. The trail continued along the ridge toward the summit, but Solana led us away into a cluster of pockmarked boulders. She pointed, and as I peered over her shoulder, I saw that the rocks formed a rough circle. In the middle, the earth lay fallow. Not so much as a strand of alpine grass grew.

"It will bloom there," she said.

Miguel squeezed into the clearing and removed several items from a small woven bag: a knife, a trowel, and several small jars. He called to Solana, and as they conversed, I scouted around the periphery of the rocks to get the lay of the land. When the full moon rose, I would shift and hunt as was my biological imperative. But instead of remaining on four legs until moonset, I would return to my human form and rejoin Solana and Miguel. He would harvest the flower and implant the roots, at which point we would immediately return to the car. Miguel would drive us to Fiambala, where a chartered plane waited to take us to Buenos Aires. If all went well, we would be in New York within twenty-four hours.

My panther was the wild card. I had no way of knowing how she would react to the flower's invasion of my body and how difficult it would be to hold her in check. Just the thought of our long return flight was enough to spike my anxiety, and I focused on taking deep, steadying breaths.

"Are you all right?" Solana asked. It was a measure of my preoccupation that I hadn't heard her approach.

"A little anxious."

She nodded. In silence, we watched Miguel make his preparations as night fell over the Andes. Behind the doors of my mind, the panther paced incessantly, eager to be free. With Constantine's help, I had gotten better at managing these hours just before moonrise when her agitation was greatest and my patience was thin. But tonight, my trepidation about what the next few hours might bring made me restless and jittery.

"You never told me the end of your story," I said to Solana, hoping to distract myself. "Did you ever have your revenge on Hector?"

She settled to the ground with her back to stone still warm from the sun, and I did the same. "I did. But first, I remained with Rudolpho for many months, readjusting to life in the sunlight and learning about the village and its customs. The Tear of Isis is at the heart of its healing culture; Miguel's family has been the flower's guardians since time immemorial. I swore to him that I would protect his people for as many generations as I lived, and he pledged that his family would sustain me."

"Do the villagers have many enemies?"

"Not any longer," Solana said. "But before solar energy arrived, firewood became scarce in this area—particularly on the Chilean side of the mountain. There were raids and skirmishes for control of forested terrain." Her smile was tight and fleeting. "We always prevailed."

I had no doubt that she could be a formidable weapon. "Did they help you to free your family?"

"No. It was my responsibility alone. I used my ability to move in the sunlight to infiltrate Hector's household, and then I killed him. My younger sister and several cousins returned to the village with me and lived out their lives in peace."

As happy an ending as possible, under the circumstances. But before I could respond, an electric charge shot through me, as though I had touched a live wire. I was on my feet without having consciously moved. From the ground, Solana regarded me warily.

"Soon." I choked out the word as my panther gathered herself. The western horizon was growing lighter each passing second, the moon calling to my blood as she called to the tides. Solana joined Miguel in the middle of the clearing while I stood poised at the edge.

A low hum in my ears, a rush of heat along my spine. My panther was almost upon me, but wanting to see the flower bloom, I held her off as long as I could. I felt the moon spring free even as my pupils registered the increase in light—and in that last instant of total lucidity, I watched the Tear of Isis rise and unfold from the earth as though it were a production of time-lapse photography.

The hunger overwhelmed me as my paws found purchase on the shale, but I turned away from the two humans in the clearing and scented down the mountain. I ran toward the lake, effortlessly leaping from boulders to outcroppings, and paused only when I scented prey. Something canine. Sebastian's features flashed before my mind's eye, and I growled. Yes, I was more than ready to hunt something canine.

I began to track the creature, quickly at first, then more slowly as the scent grew fresher. When I crested a slight rise overlooking the lakeshore, I caught sight of my prey: a small fox that had descended to the lake for water. I approached it as quietly as I could, belly brushing the smooth stones. Only when my crawl scattered an unstable mound of pebbles did the fox show any sign of alarm. In another instant, the chase was on; it darted along the coastline before making a break for the cover of foliage beyond. I unleashed the full power of my sprint and was on top of my prey within moments. With one toss of my head, I broke its neck and then gorged myself on its carcass.

The hunger receded just enough for clarity to return. My feline instincts urged me to make another kill—to satiate the dull throb in my belly—but now I was capable of fully asserting my will. I had to get back to Solana and Miguel.

I leapt from rock to rock, balancing myself easily despite the precipitous climb. For several minutes, I gloried in the power of this body—so swift, so strong, so keenly attuned to the natural world. The breeze carried unfamiliar scents I yearned to discover, and the unblinking moon urged me to the quest. When I finally slipped into the clearing, it was with a sense of near-disappointment. Until I caught the aroma of the flower.

Its scent carried a delicate sweetness, warm and comforting. Almost, I imagined, the way light might smell. Solana and Miguel looked wary as I approached, but I paid them no mind. As I crept closer to the flower, its fragrance enveloped me and a rumbling purr rose from my throat. The petals were an indefinable shade between gold and white, and I wanted to touch them—to feel whether their texture was as soft as it appeared.

I let that urge carry me into my shift until I was crouched before the flower on two legs instead of four. Gently, I brushed one of its petals with my index finger. As smooth as satin and soft as cashmere.

"It's heavenly," I breathed, surprising myself at the adjective. Valentine was the one given to hyperbole, not me.

"Perhaps." Solana seemed to have seriously considered the notion that the flower had a divine origin. "It is certainly exquisite to every human sense."

Once I had dressed, I turned to Miguel. "I'm ready. How do we do this?"

Solana stepped forward and rolled up my left sleeve past the elbow while he dug a wide circle around the flower with the trowel. "He will plant the root here," she said, tracing her finger along the long, blue vein that ran along the length of my forearm.

I nodded, fighting back a surge of apprehension by focusing on my breathing pattern in an exercise Constantine had taught me over the summer. By the time Miguel beckoned to me, I felt calm again. Mostly. He looked at me as he spoke, and I waited for Solana's translation.

"Miguel is going to make the incision and collect some of your blood to aid in transplanting the root."

"Fine." I had shed blood for Valentine almost every day when we had been together; a few more drops shouldn't matter. But my panther protested otherwise. She had come to understand and accept Val's bite as an expression of possessiveness—as an assertion of her rightful claim as our mate. Miguel's knife, on the other hand, was very clearly a threat.

He gestured for me to kneel on the ground across from him just outside the circle he had made around the flower. He set an open jar carefully on the ground, and his grasp was gentle as he positioned my arm above it. With the knife poised against my skin, his eyes met mine. I nodded.

The knife scored my flesh cleanly, opening a two-inch gash parallel to my wrist. My panther surged forward at the searing pain, and I held her back with all my might as Miguel turned my arm so the dark blood could drip into the jar. I kept my breathing slow and steady despite the feline thrashing wildly behind my eyes. The moon called to her still, and she craved the use of her claws and teeth against this danger.

To distract myself and her, I focused on following Miguel's every movement. Even as my blood continued to trickle into the jar, he plunged his trowel into the ground with one hand while grasping the flower's stem with the other. It came up quickly, as though its hold on this world was tenuous at best. The dry earth of the mountain dislodged easily from the shallow root system, the circumference of which was barely as large as a half dollar coin. With one blow of the knife, he stripped the stem from the roots and plunged the latter into the bloodied jar.

The gash had already begun to heal; I could feel and even see my skin knitting back together hundreds of times faster than a human's would have done. After setting aside the stem and petals, Miguel lifted the dripping root from the jar and ruthlessly pushed it between the lips of my wound. I clenched my teeth against a scream at the foreign invasion, and my vision wavered as the panther furiously pushed for control.

But then Solana's arms came around my waist, and her cool cheek pressed against mine, and she whispered soothing words into my ear while Miguel held the incision closed. Gradually, the panther's ferocity subsided until her discontent was only a background murmur, like the dull throb of my scar. It was a thick raised line, hot to the touch, at the halfway point between my elbow and wrist. The sole blemish on my body, all others having been purged in the conflagration of my shift.

"M-my God," I stammered suddenly. "I can feel it. It—it's moving." In horrified fascination, I stared down at the writhing skin of my arm, comforted only by the fact that I could still transform if necessary.

"That's a good sign." Solana released me and bent to lift the light pack I had carried up the mountain. She briefly conferred with Miguel. "The movement likely means that it is settling—that it has accepted your blood as nourishment."

In awe, I watched until the rippling motion had stopped. My entire body felt like an active fault line on the brink of slippage. I had to keep my eye on the prize; by this time tomorrow, I would be back in New York. Perhaps even in the same room as Valentine. Nothing would stand in my way.

"We should go," I said.

Miguel had already gathered up his supplies, leaving only a dark circle of recently upturned earth behind him. Solana carried my pack and her own canteen. There was nothing left for me to do than lead the way down the mountain.

Soon, I would be in Solana's car, where I could rest until we reached Fiambala. From there, we would fly to Buenos Aires and then on to New York. New York, New York—the syllables hummed in my ears. Valentine would not be difficult to find. For any other woman, she might be difficult to seduce.

But Val had always been defenseless against me. And I was counting on precisely that to save her.

valentine

CHAPTER TEN

The chamber felt like the prow of a buried ship jutting out into subterranean darkness. From my seat at the head of the conference table, I looked down at the mass of bodies writhing in time to a beat only they could hear. The soundproofing of this room, poised three full stories above the dance floor, was complete. As was its opacity—while I could observe the crowd below in exquisite detail, the glass windows and floor of my sanctuary were mirrored so that patrons saw only distorted reflections of themselves.

Of all the many purchases I'd made over the past few months, this club was the crown jewel. I had named it *Tartarus*—the Hell of the Greeks, but to me it was a heaven. Built into an abandoned subway shaft set deep below Gracie Mansion, the residence of New York City's oblivious mayor, Tartarus existed far beyond the reach of the sun. It was both my fortress and my oubliette. Here in my inner sanctum, I entertained business partners and culled human prey from the crowd below.

But tonight, the woman of my choice was not a human. She had caught my eye from the moment of her entrance. Red hair flowed down her back like spun copper, and she moved with feline power and grace that belied her animal half. My throat pulsed greedily. Weres did not usually offer their blood because most of them didn't have enough self-control to overrule the objections of their beasts. Perhaps this one was different. She had set foot in Tartarus, after all, and most shifters avoided this place like the plague. Here in my underworld, they tended to feel claustrophobic and disconnected from the elements. Unless, of course, they craved the experience that only my kind could give them.

"Everything appears to be in order." The vampire seated to my right extracted a fountain pen from his jacket pocket and signed the contract he had been perusing for the past several minutes.

I exhaled softly. The endorsement of my bank by the Sunrunners, the largest and most powerful of the seven vampire clans, was no small accomplishment. I stood, crossed to the bar, and poured two glasses of Armagnac.

"I appreciate your mistress's business, Bai."

His grin was sharp. "You say that now. She will make you work for it."

I saluted him with my glass. "I'm not afraid of work."

He moved to the lush divan against the back wall and sat, casting his arms out wide as though to embrace the masses below. "Oh? What is it that you fear then, Valentine?"

I sipped at the rich liquid and regarded him impassively. He had been trying to ferret out personal information all night, doubtless at the behest of his mistress. Tian, blood prime of the Sunrunners, was very old and very cunning, but she was also a recluse. Even Helen, who presided over the Order of Mithras and was a Sunrunner herself, had never met Tian.

"I fear nothing."

He cocked his head. "Not even Balthasar Brenner?"

I laughed. "Brenner is a megalomaniac."

"Who razed Sybaris to the ground. That, at least, must command your respect."

I watched the redhead reject the attentions of a tall, dark-haired man. She sipped at her drink, then turned her face up as though she could sense my scrutiny. I wondered whether the gravity-defying architecture of my sanctuary impressed her, or whether she was too experienced to feel awe any longer.

"Not especially," I said. "Valois should never have made his clan so ripe for the pickings."

Bai let out a low whistle. "You've just gravely insulted your predecessor."

"He's dead. Maybe he deserves it."

Bai fell silent, and I wondered what he would report back about me to Tian. He probably considered my bad-mouthing the former blood prime of the clan of the Missionary to be in bad taste, but I doubted he had any idea how little I actually cared about my affiliation. My status within the vampire community was just one of many tools at my disposal and nothing more.

"Those with nothing to fear have nothing to lose," was all he said.

At his words, the image of Alexa flashed across my mind's eye and an echo of her incomparable taste tickled the back of my throat. I swallowed convulsively, but the sensation was gone as quickly as it had come. Suddenly piqued, I threw back the rest of my glass in one burning gulp. Alexa was in South America somewhere right now with Olivia Wentworth Lloyd. My operatives had been unable to determine the reason for their trip, and they had reported that Alexa and Olivia's relationship remained platonic. Still, the thought of them together agitated me. I hadn't yet decided what—if anything—to do upon their return.

Across the room, the two black and tan Doberman pinschers flanking the door suddenly rose to their feet. They did not bark or growl but stood at the ready, ears flicking as they awaited my command.

I turned toward Bai, who was watching them curiously. "We have a visitor." When my phone buzzed, I connected the call. "Darrow."

"Courier for you, Missionary," said my secretary. "From Consortium Headquarters."

"Who is it?" In the past few months, I had lived through several assassination attempts. While I would never let Brenner or his cronies push me to paranoia, I'd learned to be cautious.

"Her name is Giselle."

I smiled. Giselle was one of the human receptionists at Headquarters, and also, I suspected, one of Helen's spies. Helen had sent her to me once in the early days just after I'd turned, ostensibly as an offering of sustenance. Giselle had been a temptation, but at the time, I had rejected her, preferring instead to bridle my thirst and drink only from Alexa.

At the sound of the chime, I moved toward the door. "Stand down," I told the dogs, and they immediately settled back onto the floor—still attentive, but no longer menacing. I pressed a button on the wall panel, and the door slid aside with a soft hiss to reveal the epitome of conventional beauty. Tall, blonde, and painfully slender, Giselle stood outside the door in a low-cut black dress that hugged her body like a second skin. A silver fur coat was slung over one arm, and in her other hand, she held a manila envelope. Her eyes darkened as she took in my appearance—charcoal slacks and a crimson tuxedo shirt, its sleeves fastened with golden teardrop cuff links.

Her painted lips curved in a sensuous smile. "Hello, Valentine."

"Giselle." When I reached for the envelope, she made certain to brush her fingers over mine as she relinquished it. Flames flared in my throat. I had yet to taste her, and on a different evening, when such an intriguing quarry did not await me below, I might have indulged.

I sliced open the envelope and unfolded the single bone-colored sheet of paper within. It was watermarked with the crest of the Sunrunners and embossed with Helen's personal sigil. The letter requested my presence in Helen's office for a brief meeting tomorrow evening. The agenda was unspecified, and I could think of several possibilities. Refusal to join her, however, was unthinkable. Even now, any "request" of Helen's was nothing more than a polite demand.

When I looked up, Giselle was watching me, one thin eyebrow arched. "Ms. Lambros asked me to wait for your reply."

"Tell Helen I'll be delighted to accept her invitation," I said, injecting the words with a sarcastic joviality. Giselle's laugh was a pleasant sound, low and rich. "And please feel free to have a drink downstairs. On the house."

"Sadly, it's all work and no play for me tonight." She turned, granting me a view of the smooth, pale skin of her back and the enticing flare of her ass, then looked over her shoulder. "But come and find me some other time."

I watched her sashay down the corridor, high heels clicking provocatively. From behind me, I caught the sound of Bai's slow exhale. "If you want her, I'll call her back."

He joined me in front of the door. "No. I was merely appreciating."

The planes of his face were sharper than they'd been a moment ago, as if some internal drawstring had tightened. "Are you thirsty, Bai?"

"Always."

I swept my arm through the air, indicating the crush of humanity in the pit beneath our feet. "Then let us quench that thirst."

❖

The private elevator from my quarters to the dance floor descended along a lattice of external cables, its walls reflecting the multicolored spotlights of the club like a prismatic jewel. When the doors finally opened, every head was turned toward us. I ignored all of them but one.

The shifter wore a dark, low-cut blouse with long, ruffled sleeves. Slacks of matching hue melded to her slender thighs. She smiled as I approached—the smile of a confident woman comfortable in the presence of power. I sensed no anxiety from her, which I found truly remarkable under the circumstances. Even Sebastian, on the rare occasion when he joined me here, could never quite curb his instinctual discomfort at being caged so far underground.

I stopped just before our bodies could touch. She was on my turf, but she too was a predator. This would be a more subtle dance than usual.

"Let me get you another drink," I said.

"I'd like that."

Her words were accented lightly; French, I thought. I gestured for her to follow and slipped through the crowd to one of the gates in the bar. When the staff opened it for me, surprise momentarily crossed the elegant planes of her face.

"What's your name?" I asked as I assembled ingredients onto the black marble surface.

"Marcelle."

I watched her watch my hands as I poured first absinthe, then gin, then simple syrup over ice. Lemon juice and an egg white followed. I shook the mix harder than a human could have, and when I strained it into a chilled goblet, the cocktail frothed merrily.

"A Parisian Sour."

She sipped once, then again. "Exquisite. Thank you."

Her throat bobbed as she swallowed, and my gaze was drawn to blue cord of her jugular pulsing just beneath the skin. Would she taste anything like Alexa? No one had come close so far, but I had yet to sample another cat-Were. Anticipation rose in me, a storm brewing just beyond the horizon.

"Do you tend bar often?" Marcelle asked as I returned to her side.

"Only when inspired." I wanted to close the inches between our bodies but forced myself to remain aloof. To betray the depth of my thirst would grant her more power than I was willing to give. "Tell me what brings you here tonight."

"You."

Her answer wasn't surprising; many of the club's patrons were trying to attract my attention. The others just wanted a good party. "And am I what you expected?"

She bridged the gap between us and plucked at the collar of my shirt with her free hand. "I haven't decided yet."

Even her glancing touch was enough to spike both my thirst and my desire. "If I ask you to dance, will that help you make up your mind?"

"It might."

I plucked the drink from her hand and set it on the bar, then led her out onto the floor where the DJ spun a darkly throbbing beat. Guiding her arms around my neck, I wedged one thigh between hers and smiled at her sharp intake of breath. She wanted me already, but I wasn't going to show any mercy until she begged.

We danced for what felt like hours, as I lost myself to the pounding rhythm of the music and the hot pressure of Marcelle's body against mine. The fire in my throat echoed in my groin, fraying the threads of my self-control. Thirst warred with caution in my brain; I needed to taste her, but provoking her beast in such a crowded place would be folly.

When she finally pressed her lips to my neck, I grabbed a fistful of her thick, wavy hair and jerked her head away. "Tell me what you want."

The blue of her irises was nearly eclipsed by black. "Your teeth," she panted. "In me. Please."

I yanked hard, baring her throat to my gaze, and scraped the delicate vessels with my pointed canines. Her pulse hammered at my lips, and caution fled. When I finally struck, her blood filled my mouth as her cry filled the air, only to be lost amidst the cacophony of the crowd.

I drank deeply and knew disappointment. Her blood was musky and rich, but she tasted nothing like the sunburst of ecstasy that was the distinctive essence of Alexa. An unpleasant aftertaste lingered on my tongue, reminiscent of a cocktail mixed with too many bitters. Wolfsbane. Marcelle must have taken a small dosage of the herb to help keep her beast at bay. She had come prepared.

Despite my disappointment, her offering was what my starving cells craved. I drank deeply of her, and within moments, the world leapt into sharp relief. Every sound was more nuanced, every detail crisper. Even my sense of touch was magnified, as though thousands of new nerve endings had suddenly blossomed beneath my skin.

Marcelle tensed, and I wondered whether her inner beast was successfully fighting off the wolfsbane. But when I would have pulled away, she drew me closer with her right arm while her left hand trailed the length of my torso. Her palm brushed the side of my breast, and I shivered in the thrall of desire.

And then I felt it—the almost imperceptible sensation of her body tightening one more notch, like a bowstring on the cusp of release. As her feet shifted position ever so slightly, the pieces fell into place. A feline Were who bore a superficial resemblance to Alexa. Her blunt response to my question about her presence in Tartarus. She hadn't been lying; she had come here to find me. But not because she wanted my bite or my body. Marcelle had come here to seduce me and then to kill me.

The world slowed to a crawl as my instincts shifted into overdrive. I jerked backward, and her knife blade grazed my left bicep instead of plunging into my chest. The blade scattered the light from the strobe, and in that instant, I realized how she'd been able to smuggle it past the metal detectors. Glass.

Snarling, she darted forward and executed a leg sweep designed to take me to the floor. She was fast, but thanks to her potent blood, I was faster. I spun away, reaching for the gun concealed at the small of my back, then drew and fired in the same fluid movement. The bullet hit her between the eyes and she crumpled to the floor.

Several of the human women screamed. The DJ cut the music. Someone nearby vomited. My security guards began to converge on my position, but when I raised my hand, they hung back. Bai stepped into the ring that had formed around me and Marcelle's body.

"You're wounded."

Blood trickled down my arm, but any pain had been momentarily eclipsed by the tide of adrenaline that swept through my veins like a flash flood. "It's superficial."

Bai prodded Marcelle's side with a booted foot. "One of Brenner's?"

"No doubt."

"Do you still think so little of him?"

I laughed. "He failed, didn't he? For the third time in three months." A sudden swell of fury blazed in my chest, and I leaned over to spit on the corpse. "Though he's never made it so personal."

Bai seemed confused, but I didn't bother to clarify. In this latest attack, Brenner had done me a service by showing me where I was still vulnerable. Alexa. He had purposefully sent someone who would remind me of her in certain ways—someone who would move with an echo of her grace and confidence. Someone who would compel me to let my guard down, if only for a moment.

A stinging pain finally filtered into my consciousness, and I beckoned to the guards who waited to attend me. Only a few stitches would be needed to close the gash. If I fed well tonight, the wound would be fully healed within days.

Soon enough, the scar wouldn't even be visible.

Chapter Eleven

While the club's physician sutured the gash in my arm, my chief of security got a call from Sebastian. Someone had tipped him off about the assassination attempt, and he was insistent that I come "home." To him, home was a brownstone on the Upper West Side that I had nicknamed "the mausoleum" for its marble floors, copious sculptures, and Spartan aesthetic. To me, "home" was a penthouse in Soho with its own swimming pool. Sebastian didn't have a key.

Ultimately, it was his promise of new intel on Brenner's recent financial transactions that made me accept his offer of a car. When it pulled up to the curb, he rose from the stoop. Backlit by the porch light, he cut an imposing figure. Tall and broad-shouldered, Sebastian wore his hair in a dark, shaggy mane and cultivated a persistent five o'clock shadow. He looked the part of a Harlequin romantic hero—a part I had yet to allow him to play.

He grasped my shoulders and looked me up and down. "Thank God you're all right."

"I'm fine. She just scratched me."

"I told you that place was a death trap."

Annoyed, I broke his hold. "Only for would-be assassins, apparently." As I started up the steps, the door opened from within. I passed one of Sebastian's guards and headed directly upstairs.

"Where are you going?" Sebastian called after me.

"Shower." I shrugged off my coat as I walked, refusing to wince at the twinge of pain from my arm. I turned into the guest room and shucked off the sweater I'd put on after throwing my ruined shirt into the garbage. Sebastian paused at the threshold.

"Why aren't you using our room?"

My temples began to throb at his proprietary tone. "Because it's not our room. It's yours."

I walked into the bathroom, finished disrobing, and stepped into the shower. The sting of the water on my wound was quickly eclipsed by the sensation of the hot spray raining down on my tense shoulders. But even over the drumbeat of the water, Sebastian's restless pacing outside the door was audible.

"Tell me about this information you have on your father," I called. "And by the way, he owes me a new tuxedo shirt."

"Well, he could buy you thousands with the amount of money he's just transferred out of one of his shell corporations in Poland."

I frowned. "What's odd about that? He has shells everywhere."

"But if he's not shuffling money between them, he always invests in Were-owned companies. Always. This is the first exception."

Surprise made me pause, hand poised over the soap. Balthasar Brenner had several inviolable rules—or so I'd thought. One was not to patronize any company that was not run by shifters. "Where did he move the money?"

"A corporation called Solarium with ties to Christopher Blaine."

I'd heard that name on the news recently. "The politician? The one who just announced his candidacy for the presidential race?"

"Yes. My father seems to be taking a strong interest in Blaine, for some reason. His investment in Solarium was huge. I have the numbers in a spreadsheet if you want to see them."

"Copy it onto a flash drive for me."

His pacing stopped. "Do you need any help with your arm? I could—"

"No."

If his injured sigh was meant to make me feel guilty, it didn't work. When he stalked out of the room, the knot between my shoulder blades loosened. His misplaced possessiveness was grating, and it was getting worse. For the first few weeks of our so-called marriage, he had accepted my distance without complaint.

Maybe he had thought that if he just gave me space, I'd settle in and assume some vaguely domestic role in his life.

Tipping my head back, I let the water pound over my face and trickle between my lips. My throat burned for a hotter and more viscous liquid. Once I'd gotten the information from Sebastian, I would seek out some willing human. Giselle's image flashed before my mind's eye—the flawless slope of her neck, the pale perfection of her skin—and I exhaled sharply as my thirst and desire merged. Galvanized, I stepped out of the shower, dried off cursorily, and returned to the bedroom…only to find Sebastian seated on the bed. His eyes went wide, then darkened.

I reached for my clothes. "You're acting like you've never seen a naked woman."

His upper lip curled in a snarl. "I've seen plenty, though none of them have ever been my *wife*."

I let my slacks fall back to the bed and squared off with him. We needed to have this out. Now. "And?"

"And?" The pulse in his neck pounded against olive-toned skin. "And most husbands get to do a hell of a lot more than look, Val."

My laughter was incredulous. "Oh yes, there's nothing unconventional about this marriage."

Sebastian stood. He was tall enough to loom over me—something most men couldn't do. "I've done nothing but try to make you happy, damn it, and your only response is this antagonism!"

"Happy?" My amusement faded. "I don't want you to make me happy. Our marriage doesn't mean a damn thing, except that because of it, I finally have access to my fucking inheritance. This is a marriage of convenience—a business arrangement. Those were *your* words when you came to me."

Sebastian's breaths were shallow and the tendons in his neck stood out sharply against his blue oxford shirt. His wolf was close to the surface, and out of the corner of my eye, I double-checked that my gun was still on the dresser where I'd left it.

"It doesn't have to be," he said tightly. "We could have more."

"More." Frustration joined the arousal and thirst already churning in my depths, a braided whip that lashed me into action. I let my gaze sweep down his body—from his chiseled jaw, past his muscular torso, to the bulge in his trousers. Sebastian was aroused. I would never let him inside me, but if he wanted me badly enough, he would play by my rules. And I would show him exactly who called the shots in this farce of a relationship.

I grabbed my bag off the floor and pointed to the four-poster. "Fine. Take off your clothes and lie on the damn bed. Face down."

I turned away, but not before watching his jaw go slack and his eyes glaze. He had no idea what was coming, and that was exactly how I wanted it. When I returned to the bathroom, I pulled out my harness and dildo. Many women—especially the straight ones—wanted to be fucked while I drank from them. This cock was eight inches long, and as thick as the circle made by my middle finger and thumb. It matched the shade of my eyes precisely, and I loved the way it glistened as I rhythmically pumped it in and out of my prey.

Once I had adjusted the harness, I liberally coated the dildo with lube, then turned to admire my reflection. My cock stood out proudly from the thick black straps. It curved slightly toward my stomach, calling attention to my rippled abdominal muscles. I smoothed one hand across my breasts, then down to the juncture of silicone and leather. I pressed in lightly and watched my own eyes grow hazy.

"Val?"

The uncertainty in Sebastian's voice brought a sharp grin to my lips. When I stepped into the bedroom, I saw that he had mostly obeyed me; he was naked and on the bed, but lying on his side with a clear view of the bathroom door. I paused for a moment to examine him with a clinical eye. He was a fine specimen, I supposed, for those who liked their men rugged. Dark hair dusted his legs and abdomen—a finer coat than I'd anticipated. His penis was fully erect, long and thick and glistening.

"What the hell?" Surprise and anger warred on his patrician features.

I held his gaze without flinching. "This, or nothing."

The spasmodic working of his jaw, the bob of his Adam's apple—I watched his body betray desire while his mind rebelled.

But his internal struggle was gratifyingly brief. When he remained silent, I knew. And I smiled.

Sebastian watched my approach, craning his neck to keep me in his sightline as I ascended the bed. I gripped his waist and pulled him up onto his knees, then grasped the back of his neck with one hand. Adrenaline sang through my veins at his submissive posture—at the swiftness of his pulse against my fingertips and the quiver that ran through him when my cock brushed against his thigh. I steadied it against him, waiting for his control to break. When I dug my blunt nails into the skin just above his collarbone, a guttural sound rose from his throat.

I thrust my hips forward even as I pulled him flush against my pelvis. His shout was strangled as my cock slid deep inside; his body jerked, but I held him fast. Obscenities spilled from his lips and grew louder as I twined his hair around my fingers. I yanked, bringing his head up off the mattress. In one smooth movement, I withdrew almost completely, then surged forward again. He groaned, fingers scrabbling for purchase on the blanket.

I set up a steady rhythm and worked my cock in and out of him slowly, precisely. He grunted with every thrust and moaned when I scraped my nails down his back. The power I held over him was intoxicating, and pleasure skittered beneath my skin like showers of sparks.

"Do you like being fucked by your *wife*, Sebastian? Is this what you wanted? I don't think it is, but you're damn good at taking it from me."

"Fuck. You. Val," he managed, the words escaping between tightly clenched teeth.

I laughed. "Sadly, you'll never get the chance."

I sped up then, until his body was quivering beneath me. He was close, but he probably couldn't come this way and I wanted to make him lose control completely. I leaned over him until my lips nearly touched his ear.

"Go ahead. Jerk yourself off."

The moment he touched himself, his back arched like a bow. He hung poised there, taut and trembling, for one glorious moment—

then released with an agonized roar. I sank my teeth into the muscle between his neck and shoulder, nearly coming myself when his blood filled my mouth. He tasted like musk and wood smoke, and I drank deeply as he climaxed.

Spent, he pitched forward onto the bed, limbs twitching. There wasn't much time before the inevitable happened, and I had to move quickly. I unbuckled the harness and let it fall to the floor, then gathered up my clothing and grabbed my gun and the flash drive from the dresser. Slinging my bag over one shoulder, I spun toward the door. Sebastian's harsh breaths had already morphed into snarls. I had summoned the beast with my bite and there was nothing he could do to prevent his wolf from ascending.

As the seizures began to flay him apart, I stepped naked into the hall. I paused just long enough to pull on my clothes before swiftly descending into the foyer.

"You have a problem in the guest room," I told the guard who stood just inside the front door. Whether he blanched at the sight of my blood-stained lips or the unearthly howl that suddenly erupted above our heads, I couldn't be certain. Cursing, he ran up the stairs, calling into his wrist mic for backup.

I stepped out into the wintry air, arm already raised for a cab. The night was still young, and I had work to do.

Chapter Twelve

I instructed the cabbie to drop me off at the side door of the Bank of Mithras. Floodlights illuminated its gleaming marble edifice, but the small lobby was dark—closed, by all appearances, when in fact the bank's underground level was open to business for our nocturnal clientele. We maintained a fully operational storefront during the daylight hours, but vampire customers now overwhelmingly outnumbered the humans. Even some shifters had decided to open accounts, though they were few and far between now that Balthasar Brenner had rekindled the tension between our species.

The side door was monitored by a keypad, and only vampire clients and staff had the clearance to enter. Once inside, I rode an elevator down to the heart of the bank. I could have entered my office suite directly from the street via a service entrance at the back of the building, but I wanted to put in an appearance on the subterranean lobby floor. It was good for clients and employees alike to see me taking an active interest in daily business, especially since word of the attack at Tartarus would have gotten out by now.

When the doors opened, I stepped out onto the polished floor and was greeted by a smattering of applause. I allowed myself a faint smile, but didn't linger. To the right of the tellers, Kyle sat at a large desk that guarded the first of several doors to my office. He leapt to his feet when he saw me, but at my warning glance he said nothing.

I gestured for him to follow and led him into the antechamber where visitors who required my personal attention waited before I called them into my office. The room was empty, and as soon as the door closed behind us, Kyle freaked out.

"Oh my God, Val, are you all right? What happened? Everyone is saying Balthasar Brenner sent a team of assassins to the club and you took them out like—"

I cut him off before he could launch into whatever elaborate simile the rumor mill had concocted. "There was one. She's dead. I'm fine, and we have work to do."

His mouth closed with a click. "How can I help?"

Kyle's puppy-like loyalty was his best attribute. I was gratified to see that he hadn't lost it upon being turned, though it might well disappear when he became a full vampire. But that was still months away.

"I want to know everything there is to know about Christopher Blaine's personal life. Dig, and come back with what you've found well before sunrise. I don't want to have to stay here all day."

He paled at the magnitude of my order but only nodded. "One other thing," I said as he turned to leave. "Tell McMahon I want to see her immediately."

Two years ago, Bridget McMahon, buy-side analyst for Goldman Sachs, had been out celebrating the magnitude of her bonus check when she had stumbled into the wrong club and been turned. Last month, I had hired her to head up the Bank of Mithras's research department. I wanted the bank to move beyond its humble beginnings as a simple savings and loan operation, and Bridget's guidance would be instrumental.

After informing her that I needed a preliminary report on the status and operations of Solarium before my meeting with Helen tomorrow night, I dismissed her and turned to my latest project: raising enough capital to create Mithras Brokerage Services—a separate wing of the bank devoted to investment banking. Vampires whose lives spanned centuries shouldn't, I argued to would-be investors, feel at the mercy of human investment strategies. By studying long-term market trends with Bridget, I had already begun to draw conclusions about how to most effectively invest my clients' substantial funds for the long haul.

Sunrise was just over two hours away when Kyle returned brandishing a flash drive. Within moments, I was looking at a photograph of Christopher Blaine, seeming every inch the corporate mogul turned slick politician as he addressed a large crowd at a charity benefit. Kyle ran me through the facts: his single mother, his Harvard education, his early positions within the business development branch of a now-defunct pharmaceutical company, his rapid ascent up the promotional ladder when his employer was bought out by Solarium. The *New York Post* had named Blaine one of the "most eligible bachelors" of last year, but otherwise, his personal life was a black box. Kyle had found vague rumors of a supermodel girlfriend, but the only available photographs of Blaine pictured him with his immediate family. Kyle was scrolling through them when I recognized one of the faces.

"Stop!" Palms planted on my desk, I rose to my feet and leaned forward to scrutinize the face of a blond woman, probably in her mid-thirties, wearing a cap and gown. The stole around her neck indicated some kind of graduate degree. Blaine was the only other person in the picture; his hand rested on her shoulder.

I recognized the woman because Balthasar Brenner was her father. She was one of over a dozen shifters whom Helen had imprisoned at Consortium Headquarters during the virus outbreak in August. I had never learned her name.

"Who is that?"

Kyle riffled through his notes. "Her name is Annabel Surrey. Blaine's sister."

"Half-sister?"

"I don't know. He's twelve years older than her, so that seems likely."

I sat and gestured for Kyle to do the same. "And you found no evidence that he's a shifter?"

Kyle looked startled. "No, but that wouldn't exactly be a matter of public record."

"Is his mother alive?"

"No. She died in a car accident two years ago."

I propped my feet on the desk and leaned back in my chair. I wouldn't have pegged Balthasar Brenner as the kind of person to care about the half-sibling of one of his many whelps, but perhaps Annabel had persuaded him to invest in her brother's company. Then again, the last time I'd spoken with Annabel, she had called her father a "megalomaniacal tyrant." She could have been posturing, but her vehemence had seemed quite genuine.

"Nice work," I told Kyle. "I need to call Sebastian and then I'll be home for the day."

Once he had left the room, I dialed Sebastian's cell. When he didn't pick up, I tried his office at Luna and was greeted by his secretary—a young werewolf who clearly had the hots for him and not-so-subtly disapproved of our marriage. That was probably why I liked her.

"Hello, Christina."

"Ms. Darrow, Mr. Brenner has instructed me not to put you through to him today," she said haughtily.

I laughed. "Well, isn't that mature? You tell him that when he's done throwing a tantrum he should call me back. I have information about a person of interest."

"I'll most certainly let him know." She sounded like a stuck-up automaton, and I could practically see her expression of distaste simply at having to exchange words with me.

"You have an excellent day, Christina," I said, but she had already hung up.

Perhaps I should have told her exactly how much her boss had enjoyed himself earlier this evening, but that would have been cruel, and I wasn't given to schadenfreude. Emotional displays were self-indulgent. Expedience was my only governing principle now.

❖

An hour later, I had just arrived home and was about to wade into my hot tub when a call came in from the concierge of my building. When he announced that Pritchard Darrow was there to see me, I scowled and retied my terrycloth robe.

"Fine, let him up."

While I waited, I mixed a very strong martini. Civil conversation with the most arrogant of my cousins always required a drink. Pritchard was like a small splinter—irritating but not dangerous—and he'd been beneath my skin ever since I'd come out as a lesbian. After years of being on the receiving end of his gibes, insults, and practical jokes, I wanted nothing to do with him. But ever since I'd taken over Darrow Savings and Loan, he had been pestering me in a different way. I'd been staving off his requests for an appointment for several weeks now, and apparently he had decided to take matters into his own hands.

Three months ago, my father had given Pritchard a nascent hedge fund like other uncles might give their favorite nephew season tickets. Pritchard's braggadocio had tripled even as he immediately began to run the fund into the ground. Sloppy research led him to choose terrible investments that nearly always went south. The company was barely keeping its head above water, and I suspected he wanted some kind of a loan from me.

"Oh, how the high-and-mighty hath fallen," I muttered at the chime of the doorbell.

Pritchard was one of those almost-handsome, ex-football players who wore an obviously expensive suit that failed to hide his growing gut. He blinked in consternation when I greeted him in just my robe, but dutifully followed me into the kitchen when I offered him a drink. Apparently, breakfast martinis were par for the course.

"Fuck, it's gloomy in here," he said as he awkwardly perched on one of the bar stools. "How about cracking a curtain or something?"

"I'd rather not." Even the suggestion of sunlight sent a chill through me, but I carefully modulated my voice to mask my anxiety. "Headache."

He leered at me. "Rough night?"

"Nothing I couldn't handle."

When I handed over his martini—made with my third best gin—he swigged half of it down in one uncouth gulp. "So I'm glad I finally caught you. I have a proposition."

I waited for his pitch speech, struggling not to roll my eyes as he chugged the rest of the drink.

"BlueFin has made some exciting investments recently, but they're going to take a few years to really pay off. As a result of recent market downturns, we're struggling at the moment." He took a deep breath and looked me—his carpet-munching cousin—in the eyes. "I'd like you to consider coming on board."

I almost laughed in his face. He wanted a bailout but was couching it in terms of a stake. I pretended to ponder his request, when really I was trying to figure out whether I could pull off a takeover. It wasn't easy to arrange a coup on a hedge fund, but it could be done. As far as I was concerned, why should I buy *into* BlueFin when I could simply buy it?

"Send your proposal to my analyst," I said, grabbing one of my business cards and writing Bridget's name on the back. "She and I will look it over together."

Only when relief suffused Pritchard's face did I realize just how anxious he'd been. BlueFin's situation must be worse than I suspected.

"I'll do that right away, Val," he said, already moving toward the door. "You take care. I'll be in touch."

When he let himself out, I wondered whether I was throwing off some kind of frightening predator vibe that made him want to keep his distance. Then again, maybe he was just worried about catching the gay. Or maybe he found me disconcertingly hot in only my bathrobe. God only knew. I was just glad to be rid of him.

I sent Bridget a quick message telling her to expect Pritchard's files, then untied my robe and let it fall where I stood. As I eased myself into the hot tub, I only noticed the sting of my wound as an afterthought. Even that small infusion of Sebastian's blood had galvanized my healing process.

I leaned back against the edge and submerged myself up to my chin, feeling the night's tension slowly drain from my neck. Of course, if I had been able to drink from Alexa I would be whole by now. Feeding from Sebastian may have taken the edge off, but Alexa had always fully satisfied me.

As I gazed at the shadowed ceiling, I wondered where she was right now, and whether she ever regretted her choice. My craving for her blood and her body had never diminished, but now, I was strong enough not to need her. The old Valentine had been weak and pitiful, desperate and needy. Afraid of her thirst—afraid that in letting Alexa see her need, she would drive her away.

I felt only contempt for my old self. Now, I feared nothing. Now, my thirst had no power because it had no chains.

Now, when I wanted something, I took it.

Chapter Thirteen

When I walked into Consortium headquarters the following evening, Giselle was sitting at the front desk. As I approached to say hello, I couldn't help but appreciate her low-cut and nearly sheer blouse. She caught me looking.

"Do you like it? I wore it for you."

"I'm willing to bet you say that to all your admirers."

She arched one thinly-plucked eyebrow. "Is that what you are? My admirer?"

I flashed my sharpened teeth in a smile and walked toward the bank of elevators. When I reached Helen's office, Constantine Bellande and Karma Rao were just leaving. Constantine's eyes narrowed when he saw me, the muscles along his jaw line bunching ominously. The last time I'd been in his presence, before my split with Alexa, he had greeted me with cheek kisses and a handclasp. His changed demeanor was interesting. I knew he and Alexa had grown close, but I hadn't realized that he felt so protective of her. Karma, on the other hand, showed no emotion—but that was itself indicative of her disapproval.

"Hello, Valentine," she said coolly.

"Karma. Constantine. How is Malcolm?"

"No change." She brushed past me. "We're running late to another appointment. If you'll excuse us."

Unperturbed by their chilly reception, I passed through the open door of Helen's antechamber to find her seated at her desk, framed by the glittering skyline of Long Island City. Unlike most of the windows in this building, Helen's were not equipped with voluminous blackout curtains. Her windows had been painstakingly treated with a complex mixture of chemicals that not only blocked the sun's UV rays, but also filtered the visible spectrum in certain ways. I didn't fully understand the physics of it, but the end result was that Helen could sit in this office during the day. What I hadn't realized until recently was that the window treatment alone did not give her that ability. Members of the Sunrunner clan, I had learned while researching them prior to my talks with Bai, possessed an increased resistance to the damaging effects of the sun.

The sub-species of parasite that had transformed my circulatory system gave me a greater degree of strength and speed, but no such resistance. If I walked out into the sunlight tomorrow morning, I would develop gamma radiation burns within a matter of seconds and my internal organs would liquefy shortly thereafter. If I took a meeting in Helen's office during broad daylight, on the other hand, I would be able to last for several minutes before developing severe sunburn and nausea.

The Sunrunners' increased resistance made them valuable ambassadors and spies, and they cultivated an air of superiority at being "evolutionarily superior." But I gloried in the physical power and precision granted by my parasite and wouldn't have traded those abilities away for the world.

Helen embraced me lightly. "I hear congratulations are in order," she said, gesturing for me to sit as she closed the door. In a double-breasted charcoal jacket and matching skirt, she was even more formally attired than usual. "I met with Tian's delegation a few hours ago, and Bai informed me of your mutual success in closing a deal. He seemed particularly impressed with you."

In the not-so-distant past, a meeting with Helen Lambros—Master vampire of New York and head of the Order of Mithras—would have made me nervous. Now, I relaxed into the leather chair and crossed one leg over the other.

"Was he more impressed by my financial proposal or my marksmanship?"

Her smile twisted, and for one fleeting moment I caught a glimpse of the fiery rage that churned beneath her composed exterior. Balthasar Brenner's guerilla tactics were the thorn in her side; in a matter of months, he had destabilized the alliance she had so carefully cultivated over decades. Unable to ferret out his location, all she could do was anticipate his attacks and react when they occurred. Such forced passivity had to rankle with her.

"We are all relieved that you were able to neutralize last night's threat so quickly," she said. "Bai mentioned your injury. How is your arm?"

I flexed my biceps and felt only a twinge. "Almost fully healed."

"Good."

Before she could steer the conversation to her reason for calling me in, I took the initiative. "Are you familiar with Christopher Blaine?"

If the non sequitur confused her, she didn't let on. "The human politician?"

"That's actually my question. Is he human, or a shifter?"

Helen seemed genuinely taken aback, which was extraordinary. "Do you have a compelling reason to suspect that he is a Were?"

I briefly summarized the information Sebastian had discovered about his father's recent financial transactions. "And Blaine's sister is one of Brenner's children. She was among those interrogated last summer. Blaine is significantly older than her, so I suspect she's a half-sister from after their mother was turned, but that's still just a theory."

"Find the truth," Helen said. "And keep an eye on Blaine. If you need Leon's people, let him know."

Leon Summers was the head of her intelligence force. Even if I had wanted to involve him, I wouldn't have. He had far too much on his plate right now. After Brenner had nearly succeeded in assassinating Malcolm, Helen's safety had become even more critical. In conjunction with Devon Foster, Helen's head of security, Summers had been spending every waking moment identifying and neutralizing threats while also trying to track down Brenner's precise whereabouts.

"I'm glad you brought this to my attention," Helen continued, "but I invited you here to discuss another matter: your Missionary work."

"Oh?" I kept my tone casual but mentally prepared myself for a dressing-down. Helen didn't use words like "invited" or "discuss" in a conversation with one of her underlings unless she was about to take them to task.

"I don't think I have to tell you, Valentine, just how important it is that your clan survive. Balthasar went to great lengths to eradicate the Missionary's line, and it is imperative that we actively work to regain what we lost in the razing of Sybaris."

Her use of "we" made me want to laugh in her face. As both the Missionary and the blood prime—roles that had defaulted to me as the only surviving member of my clan—I was expected to go on some kind of crusade to turn as many humans as possible. Instead, I had been highly selective about whom I'd "converted" over the past few months.

"Your clan is on the verge of extinction. We must choose strong and powerful targets for your efforts if we are to rebuild effectively." She slid a sealed manila envelope toward me. "Enclosed are some recommendations."

I opened the envelope. Inside, a single sheet of paper contained over a dozen names and addresses. Many of them were my peers— the young, well-connected potential movers and shakers of the next generation. And suddenly, I saw this scene as it must have looked two years ago—my hulking predecessor sitting in this very chair, perusing Helen's list of recommendations. My name had been on that list. I knew that now. My name and Olivia's name.

Once, I would have flown into a rage. Now, I forced myself to betray no emotion despite the thundering of my heart and the red haze that had fallen over my vision. In the months since I had become the Missionary, I had turned exactly two people: Kyle and Tonya, both of whom were humans who worked at Consortium headquarters and had routinely offered their blood as nourishment. Their most fervent wish had been to one day become vampires themselves, and I had obliged them. I had no intention of ever turning anyone who was unwilling.

"I'll see what I can do," was all I said.

Helen held my gaze silently, her eyes searching mine. She wouldn't find any answers there. I had buried my fury deep. Perhaps she had preferred me when I was more volatile, more malleable, but I would never let her control me again.

"Good." She stood and I followed suit. "Take care of yourself, Valentine."

"And you."

The effort of reining in my temper made me restless, and my throat pulsed with a matching fire. Wanting to burn off some energy, I took the stairs all the way down to the lobby. When I emerged near the front desk, Giselle turned at the sound of the stairwell door.

"Is something wrong with the elevators?"

"No. I needed the exercise."

She looked me up and down, her gaze openly lascivious. "I don't think so."

I laughed and, miraculously, the tension in my chest eased. "That's not how I meant it."

"Oh?"

She was a captivating sight; her golden hair shone in the lamplight, and her lustrous ruby lips were parted in anticipation of my reply. Lust joined the thirst that parched my mouth. I no longer had any reason to resist my own needs, and I was not going to let Helen dictate my choices. Giselle was not on Helen's precious list, but tonight, she would join the ranks of the ageless if she so desired.

I moved close enough to edge one hip up on the desk. "I want you to have dinner with me."

Her smile was triumphant. "Where?"

If it might be her last human supper, I wanted it to be one of the best. "Jean Georges. When can you leave?"

"Soon. I just need to call for a replacement here."

I settled into one of the chairs in the nearby reception area. "I'll be waiting."

❖

Hours later, Giselle lit a cluster of candles at her bedside while I drew the curtains across her window. Her apartment was small but elegantly decorated—a far nicer place than most receptionists in this city could afford. I wondered if it felt like a gilded cage, and whether she wanted her freedom.

I sat on the bed and she sashayed forward to stand between my legs. But when she began to undo my shirt buttons, I stilled her hands.

"What has Helen promised you?"

Giselle slipped her fingertips beneath my collar and stroked lightly. "She promised to make me one of you, in exchange for my loyal services."

Just as I'd suspected. "Did she give you a time frame?"

Her fingers stilled. "I never dared to ask."

I touched her then, cupping her waist and sliding my thumbs along the flat plane of her stomach. Beneath the silken fabric of her dress, I felt her tremble.

"If you had the power to decide, when would you choose?"

A tiny frown line materialized on the bridge of her nose as she searched my face. "Now. I would choose now."

"Why?"

She pulled back and walked to her window. Drawing the curtain, she stared out at the small slice of cityscape in her view.

"I'm young. I'm beautiful. Isn't it every woman's dream to freeze herself at this moment?"

I kicked off my shoes and reclined on the bed. "Not when the price for doing so is eternal darkness and unquenchable thirst."

She turned to face me. "I'm not some naïve human who thinks vampires are a pretty myth. I've been on the other side of that thirst enough times to understand it."

"You can never understand it," I said softly, "until you've felt it yourself."

"Then let me. I'm ready. I want this—more than I've wanted anything."

She sat on the bed and I propped myself up against the pillows. I traced my thumb along the line of her jaw until I reached the corner of her mouth. When her tongue flicked against my skin, I inhaled sharply. She smiled.

"Helen will be angry with you," she said.

"It won't be the first time."

She sucked the tip of my thumb into her mouth and swirled her tongue. I shuddered, desire pulsing between my thighs in time with the thirst that pulsed in my throat. But I had to keep a clear head for a few moments longer.

"If you do this for me," Giselle said, "I'll serve you forever."

"That's not how it works." I pulled away just enough to cup her face. "You won't ever be a servant. But you will come and work for me at the bank—or anywhere else I might need you."

She rose onto her knees and moved until she was straddling my lap, then guided my hands to her breasts. When I stroked her ever so gently, her body quickened beneath my touch.

"I will be loyal to you," she pledged breathlessly. "Always. I swear it."

I leaned forward to kiss her, sealing her words between us. When I made my touch firmer, she gasped into my mouth. Within moments, her dress was on the floor, and my shirt and slacks followed soon after.

I laid her back on the cool sheets and covered her body with my own, exulting in the softness and heat of her skin against mine. I stirred her passion with deep kisses even as I drove her relentlessly toward climax with my touch. For minutes, I held her on the edge of abandon and teased the racing pulse in her neck with my tongue. And then, when her begging became incoherent, I claimed her.

Giselle's blood was reminiscent of sweet vermouth, and I drank until my world was sparkling clear and hers went dark. As soon as I felt the slackness in her muscles that belied her slip into unconsciousness, I withdrew my teeth and set them to my own wrist. My skin to hers, my blood joining her veins, my parasite colonizing her cells.

Once I had ensured the mingling of our blood, I got to my feet and went in search of my phone. I prided myself on being adept at walking the line between leaving my so-called victims strong enough to fight off the parasite, and draining them to the point of death. Still, to be safe, I wanted Giselle to have medical attention tonight.

After arranging for one of the Consortium physicians to transport her to the hospital wing of Headquarters, I dressed both myself and her limp body. Her pulse remained slow and steady, but I monitored her closely as I waited for the emergency team to arrive. Giselle's surrender to my touch and my teeth had temporarily sated my thirst and my desire, and now that I could think clearly again, I turned my mind to the intricacies of how I might yank Pritchard's hedge fund out from under him.

Within the hour, I was sitting in my office with Bridget where she and I began the process of scrutinizing the spreadsheets Pritchard had sent over that morning. After projecting them onto the plasma screen, she and I combed through his numbers and debated a course of action.

"There's no way he can survive for another month on his own," Bridget concluded. "What do you think of his deal?"

Pritchard had taken the liberty of including a proposal with his data—a deal to bring me in as a thirty-percent partner of his earnings in exchange for a loan that would allow him to meet his next two quarters' worth of client payouts.

"I think I don't want thirty percent. I want one hundred."

Bridget pushed her glasses up on her nose, a small bit of body language that I had learned meant she was deep in thought. She didn't need the glasses, of course. All vampires had perfect vision. But she claimed that wearing them made her better able to concentrate—some sort of Pavlovian association from her days as a human.

"We could play stall ball," she said. "While reaching out to his investors behind his back."

I leaned back in my chair and considered her plan. If we pretended to go along with Pritchard's proposal but deliberately threw up roadblocks to the deal's closure, we could drag out the proceedings for at least a month. In the meantime, we could contact Pritchard's investors—all of whom were wealthy individuals who would not enjoy being associated with a bankrupt hedge fund—and persuade them to force Pritchard out of power.

"I like that idea."

When she took off her glasses and smiled, Bridget looked more like the dangerous predator she truly was. "I thought you might."

"So tomorrow," I began, plotting our next moves as though I were sitting before a chess board, "you'll call Pritchard and propose a counter-offer."

"Of course." Bridget's eyes twinkled. "The negotiations could take days and days."

"Wouldn't that be a shame."

After she left, I decided a celebration was in order. I had likely succeeded in turning Giselle, which would send a message to Helen about just how little I appreciated her interference in my affairs. Now, I had a solid game plan for acquiring a hedge fund while simultaneously avenging myself on my bully of a cousin. Not a bad day's work. But as I was pouring myself a glass of Macallan 30, Sebastian called.

"I'm returning your message from yesterday," he said tersely.

"How very kind of you."

He ignored my mocking tone. "What do you have on Blaine?"

"His sister is Annabel Surrey," I said, wondering whether he would make the connection.

"That can't be right. Annabel Surrey is one of my half-siblings. We met in—"

"In August at the Consortium. I know. Apparently, Blaine is her older brother, twelve years her senior."

"How is that possible? He's not a Were."

"Are you sure?" I shot back. "In any case, I'm looking into it. I'll let you know if I find anything of interest."

"Fine. Good."

At the beep in my ear, I glanced down at my phone's display to find Helen's name blinking at me. Was she already calling to berate me for turning Giselle?

"I have a call on the other line," I said, and before he could protest, I had switched over. "Hello, Helen."

"Valentine." Her voice was taut, fairly vibrating with tension. "Are Bai and the rest of the delegation with you?"

The unexpected question drove any calculated replies from my head. "With me here at the bank? No."

"Very well. Thank—"

"Tell me what's happened," I said before she could disconnect the call.

"They haven't checked in with their driver, who was supposed to pick them up half an hour ago, and I can't reach any of them by phone."

She did hang up then, and I was left to speculate about their fate to myself. All I could be sure of was that if foul play was involved, so was Balthasar Brenner. Immediately, I called in my head of security, a vampire named Caleb Lee who had been Sebastian's head vampire bouncer at Luna prior to coming to work for me. As a human, Caleb had been a federal marshal, and he was well connected as a result. Sebastian had let him go with regret after Caleb himself had pointed out that the recent resurgence in tension between Weres and vampires meant that his presence as club security was putting most of Sebastian's clientele on edge instead of making them feel safe.

Unlike his shifter counterparts, Caleb was slender and of average height—not the kind of person traditionally associated with security work. But he had five different kinds of black belts, and he moved faster than anyone I'd ever seen—including myself. As he sat in the chair Bridget had vacated, I slid a photograph of Christopher Blaine across my desk.

"I need you to put tails on this man. They have to be invisible and unshakeable."

"Christopher Blaine." If Caleb was surprised, he didn't sound it. "He'll be well-protected. How close do you want me to get?"

"Close. I have reason to believe that Balthasar Brenner might try to get in touch with him, and if that happens, we might finally be able to get a drop on the bastard."

Caleb's expression never changed, but a telltale flush rose along his neck. He wanted Brenner's head, and I didn't blame him. Every vampire felt that way, ever since he had nearly extinguished an entire clan and tried to turn the shifter population against us.

"This might get expensive," was all Caleb said.

I leaned back in my chair and smiled for the first time since Helen's call. "Then it's a good thing I own a bank."

CHAPTER FOURTEEN

T hree nights later, I was in a follow-up meeting with Bridget about the status of her negotiations when Kyle called from the front desk with the news that Caleb needed to see me. Urgently. When I greeted him at the door, his smile was grim and his eyes glittered like mica chips.

"We've got him," he said as soon as we were alone in the privacy of my office.

"Brenner? You've located him already?" I had never expected a payoff this soon.

Beneath his triumph, Caleb seemed as incredulous as I was. "In a matter of days, we've done what Summers has been unable to do for months. How the hell did you know to watch Blaine?"

"A hunch. Where are they?"

Caleb flipped open the file folder he'd carried in under his arm to reveal a photograph of Blaine dining with a tall, distinguished-looking man who appeared to be in his early forties but was actually ten times that age. In every other picture I'd seen of Balthasar Brenner, his long dark hair had been pulled back from his face. In this photo, his hair was loose in a wavy mane brushing the shoulders of a gray suit jacket that managed to look expensive despite the graininess of the image.

"They're eating at a very exclusive French restaurant in Georgetown," Caleb said.

I looked at the time stamp on the photograph: ten minutes ago. "You'll shift your tails to Brenner?"

"Yes. Do you still want anyone on Blaine?"

"Only if you have someone to spare." My brain had jumped into hyperdrive. Brenner's location was almost as much of a Holy Grail as Brenner's head.

"I do," said Caleb. "Who knows? He might lead us to something else of interest."

"He might." Perhaps Caleb's people would be able to discover for certain whether Blaine was human or Were.

"Any word on the delegation?"

Like every other vampire with whom I'd spoken in the past few days, Caleb was concerned about the fate of the missing Sunrunners. They seemed to have suddenly disappeared from the face of the earth. The news had spread quickly, with rumors cropping up in its wake. Most believed Brenner to be responsible. Others thought Helen had angered the delegation and that they had subsequently broken off communication. A few even suggested that Helen had kidnapped them herself, in order to consolidate her power through fear-mongering.

"No word," I said. "I think Brenner has them, and that he's playing cat and mouse with us. The longer Helen has to stew, the more likely she is to feel pressured into doing something desperate."

Caleb nodded. "Even more incentive to find his hiding place."

"Keep me informed of every change. Every single one."

"I will." In the ensuing silence, he drummed his fingers lightly on the table top—a sign that he wanted to offer me a piece of advice but was concerned about how well I would take a suggestion that hadn't originated with me.

"Out with it," I said, and his smile was rueful when he realized that he had betrayed his tell.

"Are you planning to go to Foster or Summers with this information?"

I considered the question. By all rights, Leon Summers should be my first call and Devon Foster my second. They were officially in charge of Consortium law enforcement, and each had made it their personal mission to capture Brenner. They had far more resources at their disposal than I did, but if I turned over this information, they would take charge.

"Why do you think I shouldn't?" I asked Caleb.

"I didn't say that."

"You didn't have to."

He blew out a sigh. "Foster and Summers will want to add their people, and that might spook Brenner. The coverage we have right now is working."

"I'll wait to call them until we have more information," I said. "Preferably when he's in a stable location. Not a restaurant—some kind of base."

"Fair enough." Caleb got to his feet, but when he headed for the door, I stopped him with one last question—about the one thing I was never quite able to banish from my mind, regardless of what else was happening.

"In all this chaos, have you heard anything about Alexa?"

"Not a thing. But the minute she gets on any plane larger than a crop duster, I'll know."

When he left, I returned to my desk and sipped lightly at my scotch—not to celebrate, now, but to settle my nerves. So much could go wrong with this operation—Brenner could realize he was being followed, or Caleb's team could lose him. My mind raced as I considered and rejected possibilities, and I soon found myself pacing the length of my office.

I finally returned to my desk, determined to read through a stack of paper work that had been piling up since the beginning of the week. But instead of serving as a welcome distraction, the work bored me and my mind began to wander, as always, to Alexa. She had been gone for a full week now, and I was starting to regret my order not to have her followed outside the country. My lack of knowledge was a distraction; I needed to know what she was doing, and with whom.

Thankfully, Caleb called a few minutes later with an update on Brenner: he and Blaine had moved to a club for drinks, and Caleb had replaced their shadows to cut down on the risk of suspicion. His contacts hadn't gotten close enough to overhear conversation, but they had witnessed the exchange of a thin envelope from Brenner to Blaine.

It was just shy of midnight—still early, by vampire standards—but I was too preoccupied to get anything done and would be more comfortable in my apartment. When Caleb's next call came through, I was lounging in my hot tub and wishing I could be one of the operatives tailing Brenner instead of someone who had to sit on the sidelines getting intermittent updates. But even if I could have hopped on a plane to D.C., it would have been too risky. Brenner and I had never met face-to-face, but I had no doubt that he knew what I looked like; he'd tried to have me killed three times, after all.

I wasted no time on pleasantries. "Is he on the move?"

"He was just picked up from the club. The car windows were tinted, so my people couldn't make out the driver."

I sat up so quickly that water cascaded over the lip of the tub. "But you've got him covered?"

"Yes. I'll call back as soon as we have a fix on where he's going."

When he disconnected the call, I hastily dried off and threw on some clothing, wanting to be prepared for anything. A few minutes later, I received a text that Brenner appeared to be headed to a private airfield in Virginia and that Caleb was pulling strings to get the passenger manifests of every plane scheduled to leave within the next few hours. I checked my watch and muttered a curse; there was no way I could follow him with only two hours until dawn.

Finally, Caleb called back. "You're not going to believe this. The only plane scheduled to fly out before the morning is headed to Linden Airport."

Linden Airport was a tiny airfield across the Hudson River that catered to the rich and famous who didn't want to interact with the crowds at Newark International whenever they came to the city. The sudden rush of adrenaline made my ears ring.

"Holy shit. He's coming *here*."

"Apparently. Do you still want our people on him, or are you going to call it in?"

My head pounded with possibilities. "Both. We need a full court press. We can't lose him."

"I'm on it."

The first number I dialed was Leon Summers's, and after I had him on the line, I added Devon Foster to the call.

"This had better be good, Val," she said. "I'm up to my teeth, here."

"You and me both," said Summers.

They both sounded fatigued, and it wasn't difficult to guess why; with no news about the status of the delegation, they were exhausting every avenue of inquiry. I cut to the chase.

"Balthasar Brenner will be landing at Linden Airport in about two hours."

The conversation exploded, as I'd known it would. Once they'd had it out with their expressions of incredulity, I explained my orders to Caleb and what he had discovered.

"The ball's in your court now," I told them, "but I want to be a part of this. Start to finish."

"Then get your ass over here," Summers snapped. "We'll be in the War Room."

"And bring guns," Foster added. "Lots of guns."

Chapter Fifteen

I had a separate closet for my guns, the way other women had a closet for their shoes. My collection had come a long way in the year and a half since Penn, my father's head of security, had given me my first revolver—a Colt M1911. Now, I debated between a wide variety of handguns, most of which had been custom-made by a small company in Arkansas. Finally, I selected three: the CQB Tactical Light Rail, which was excellent in low-light conditions; the M-4T Tactical Carbine, which could shoot thirty rounds before it needed reloading and was especially good at close-range; and the easily-concealed Combat Sentinel. And a knife, as backup.

Gray predawn light was filtering through my car's windows by the time I reached Headquarters, and I ducked inside the doors with relief. Giselle's replacement at the front desk was even more beautiful than her predecessor, with exquisite ebony skin and large, almond-shaped eyes. On any other day, I would have paused to introduce myself, but instead, I hurried for the elevator.

If Consortium Headquarters was a fortress, then the War Room was its keep. Giant plasma screens plastered almost every available wall, some displaying live video feeds from around the world, while others projected data arranged in charts and graphs. When I entered, I was directed to a conference room in the back where Summers and Foster were monitoring the team that had been deployed to track Brenner's movements.

Like everyone else in the conference room, I was wearing a black sweater, black pants, and black boots. We had all come prepared for a raid. Caleb greeted me tersely, his attention clearly divided between the two screens in this room. One was a long-distance shot of the airfield, while the other camera was inside the hangar. Our hackers had made quick work of the airport's security protocols.

I clapped Caleb on the shoulder. "Nice job picking up Brenner."

He only grunted in reply. Foster hailed me from across the room and I went to join her and Summers where they were examining schematics of the airport and hangar.

"I'm not going to believe you actually found him until I see the fucker with my own eyes," Summers said.

"Patience, Leon," I replied, though truthfully, I was just as impatient as he was. "What's the plan once he's on the ground?"

"We've got people on the tarmac, in the hangar, and in the airport," said Foster. "As well as two teams waiting in cars and a few extras on motorcycles. Anyone likely to get close to him is a human, to avoid suspicion. We'll be on him like crazy glue."

"As soon as we track him to his base, we'll mount a raid." Summers turned his full attention to me for the first time. "I take it you'll be coming along?"

I hefted the small duffle that held the M-4T and spare rounds. The Light Rail was already strapped to my waist, and the Sentinel pressed comfortingly against my lower back, fully concealed by my shirt. "Locked and loaded. Try and stop me."

"Plane's coming in," someone called, and all attention turned to the screen monitoring the runway. A few seconds later, a small silver airplane came into view and touched down smoothly before taxiing to the hangar. The minutes dragged by as we waited for its passengers to disembark.

Several armed men in dark suits walked down the stairway first and inspected the hangar and its personnel. One of them spoke into a wrist mic, and a few moments later, another figure appeared at the airlock. During the flight, Brenner had transformed from a business executive into a militia leader. Dressed in gray cable-knit sweater, camo pants, and military-issue boots, he looked ready for a fight.

"I'll be damned," Leon muttered.

Brenner bypassed the entrance to the small building that housed the airport's offices, walking toward the hangar doors and then out of the camera's field of view.

"Report," Foster ordered, sounding much more calm than I would have under the circumstances.

The speaker on the table crackled into life. "He's getting into a black Suburban parked around the corner. We'll pick him up."

For the next fifteen minutes, we listened to the operatives report in as they followed Brenner in a dizzying series of coordinated maneuvers designed not to arouse the suspicions of his driver or guards. Finally, the car turned into a derelict storage lot that, one of Leon's agents informed us, used to be an offshoot of the New York/New Jersey Port Authority before business had waned. Unfortunately, its security cameras had been disabled, so we had no way of seeing inside short of physically entering the yard.

"Watch the perimeter," Foster was instructing her team. "Every square inch, including the waterfront. Commandeer a boat if we can't scramble one fast enough. Nobody comes or goes without your knowledge. We'll be there as soon as it's dark again."

Once the operatives' affirmative replies had come through the speaker, Summers ended the transmission and whistled shrilly to call the room to attention.

"We have eleven hours to come up with an ironclad plan, people," he barked. "Failure is not an option. Let's get to work."

❖

As the van exited the Holland Tunnel, Foster called her team leader at the lot. "Status?"

"No change." If the man was getting tired of Foster's frequent requests for reports, his voice didn't reveal it. Before we left Headquarters, we had all been outfitted with earbuds and mics, and I could hear Foster's lieutenant as clearly as if he were sitting next to me.

"ETA twenty minutes," she said.

I stretched my legs into the space between the van's benches and mentally prepared myself for the skirmish to come. We had the element of surprise along with three different attack plans based on what we found when we arrived at the yard. Satellite photographs had helped us identify a cluster of three warehouses near the center of the complex where movement had been seen earlier in the day, and each plan focused on surrounding and securing the area with minimal chaos. The last thing we needed was to alert any human authorities.

We had fed before leaving Headquarters, and my senses were so amplified that I could hear every minor imperfection in the car; its front tires needed rotation and its back axle was a tiny bit crooked. When I closed my eyes, the sounds and scents jumped into even sharper relief: the low buzz of our electronic equipment, the acrid odor of gunpowder, the persistent grinding of Caleb's teeth as he guided the van in and out of traffic.

Summers studied the GPS closely. "Let's ditch the car up here," he said, indicating the parking lot of an abandoned grocery superstore. Caleb pulled over and maneuvered the van behind a large pile of dirty snow, concealing it from the casual view of passersby. I unzipped my duffle and pulled out a ski mask, then slung the M-4T across my shoulders and clipped the spare rounds to my belt.

"How far are we from this place?" I asked as I followed Foster out the sliding door.

"Just over half a mile." After radioing the team leader that we were approaching on foot, she led the way down the road at a jog.

The chill air sluiced down my lungs and my breath steamed into the night. It felt good to be on the move, and I allowed myself a brief moment simply to appreciate the crisp starlit evening before shifting my attention to the mission ahead. As the storage lot came into view around a bend in the road, Summers held up a hand to slow our pace.

I peered into the shadows ahead, straining with my other senses as well. There were humans not too far away—at least two of them. Weres had been here recently, but their scent was dull, like the stale smell of beer in an abandoned fraternity basement.

"Dobson, Harris," Foster murmured. "Show yourselves."

Two humans materialized out of the darkness. "Their perimeter is a hundred yards away," whispered the taller of the two. "Sentries still positioned at twenty-yard intervals."

"Stick to the plan, then," said Summers.

We fanned out at the fifty-yard point, a steel trap poised to close on Brenner's guards. In an effort to infiltrate the lot without alerting him, Summers and Foster had assigned two team members to each of his sentries. We were to avoid shooting our guns unless absolutely necessary. Unfortunately, using silencers wouldn't help; with their keen hearing, the shifters would still be able to hear a silenced shot.

Foster and I paired off, Caleb and Summers to our right. We moved like ghosts, sprinting silently between patches of shadow. As we crested a small rise in the terrain, we dropped to our stomachs. The chain link fence surrounding the yard was topped with rolls of barbed wire. A large gate bisected the road, flanked by two human-shaped figures. I was fairly confident they hadn't seen our approach, but the twenty yards between us and them was completely devoid of cover. We would have to make a dash for it. I hoped our team's human pairs were luckier in terms of their geography. Having fed so recently, I could cover the distance in only a few seconds, but they would be much slower.

"Ready?" Foster said under her breath. While the other pairs reported in, I disengaged my gun safeties and loosened the strap of the M-4T. When she glanced at me, I nodded.

"Go go go!"

I pushed hard off the frozen ground and raced across the intervening space, milking every ounce of superhuman speed from my legs. With no time to shift, the sentries snarled and reached for their weapons, but I pistol-whipped the first before he could fire. Distracted by me, the second guard fell to Foster who put him in a chokehold.

"Not bad," I said, my breaths still coming steadily. And then machine gun fire erupted off to our left like popcorn in a kettle drum.

Foster cursed but didn't take her focus off the gate. As we broke the chain and yanked it open, Caleb and Summers rejoined us. A moment later, Harris reported that one of his fellow operatives had been wounded but the others would join us shortly.

"Let's get in there while Brenner's troops are mustering," said Summers.

"We're going in," Foster said into her mic. "Assemble the rest of the team and then come and back us up."

We ran into the yard and immediately took cover behind the nearest shipping container. With our backs to the fence, we made our way toward the center of the compound. All my senses were on high alert, but the prevailing scent was a composite of salt water and rotting fish from the nearby bay, and the only sounds I heard were the ones our small party made as we traversed the broken asphalt.

"Where the hell are his goons?" Summers growled as we approached the cluster of warehouses that had appeared—from the sky, anyway—to be Brenner's base camp. Each of us in turn peered around the corner of the container we were currently using for cover. The warehouse buildings formed three legs of a square with a large empty space in the middle.

"Trap." Caleb sounded like he had no doubt, and neither did I.

"We need to spring it somehow," I said. "We're just giving them more time to get ready, otherwise."

Foster knelt and began to scratch patterns in the gravel. "Why don't we—"

From the bay, a nearby barge sounded its horn in a long, booming note, almost drowning out the scrape of a boot on metal above us. As the sound reached my hypersensitive ears, I dove into the corridor between our container and the next, rolled onto my back, and fired almost straight up into the air. Moments later, a twitching canine body dropped to my feet. I'd missed a killing blow and now had a fully shifted wolf on my hands.

"Ambush from above!" I hissed just before all hell broke loose.

The massive wolf lunged for my throat, but Foster shot it in the head before it touched me. Bullets pinged the metal walls all around us, ricocheting dangerously. One thudded into the earth just past my feet, and I scrambled up to find new cover. I sprinted around the back of the container and vaulted onto its ladder, sticking my head up above the walls just long enough to pick off one of Brenner's thugs. Bullets sprayed above my head as I dropped back to the ground.

"I'll cherry pick," I said into the mic. "You guys find a defensible spot."

I darted from container to container, shooting off as many rounds as I could and then zigzagging unpredictably so Brenner's mercenaries couldn't be certain of where I would pop up next. Meanwhile, Foster, Summers, and Caleb deployed most of the team to flanking positions near the central warehouses and instructed the rest to keep our path of retreat open.

But almost immediately, the first group ran into trouble. Brenner's men atop the shipping containers were joined by shooters on the second level of the nearest warehouses. The group was pinned in a no man's land. Instead of picking off one shooter at a time, I climbed out onto the container's roof and ran toward the warehouse. The M-4T felt alive in my hands, and I used it to nail both of the gunmen who were out in the open. As soon as the ones in the warehouse realized what was happening, they turned their rifles toward me, but I shot one of them as I continued to run toward Foster's beleaguered team.

I didn't slow as I reached the far edge of the container, and instead propelled myself into the air even as I continued to fire into the warehouse windows. When I hit the ground, I rolled right into the remnants of the team. One was dead and another wounded, and the metallic aroma of fresh blood filled my mouth with moisture.

Before I could speak, a deep voice rang out into the night.

"Cease and desist, or I will start killing your precious Sunrunners, one by one."

"Brenner!" Foster's whisper echoed through my ears.

I beckoned for the two remaining humans to join me and we edged forward until we had a clear line of sight into the courtyard. Balthasar Brenner stood near the entrance to the warehouse that sat along the waterline. He was flanked by two large black wolves, and Bai knelt before him, face bloodied and hands tied behind his back.

"This has gone on long enough," Brenner said, his voice echoing throughout the lot. "Leave at once, or you will have to explain this one's death to your bloodsucking bitch mistress." He tangled his fingers in Bai's hair and tugged, exposing his throat. "When I am feeling disposed to negotiate terms for her surrender, she will be the first to know."

I raised the M-4T to my shoulder and sighted along the barrel, not wanting to risk tipping off Brenner by using the laser sight. Even so, he seemed to know exactly what I was doing.

"And if you kill me now," he continued, "my soldiers have orders to end the pathetic lives of every single vampire in my custody."

Swearing quietly, I lowered the gun to my side. Foster and Summers were talking over each other, but their lines of reasoning seemed to be in agreement: under no circumstances could we risk Brenner killing his hostages. We needed to get out, inform Helen of the situation, and regroup.

"You've made your point," Summers shouted from their hiding place. "We will retreat."

I could only imagine how bitter those words tasted in his mouth. "Watch your backs," I murmured, even as I gestured for the humans to follow me back to the gate. "He didn't guarantee safe passage."

That became all too clear when the stillness of the night gave way to menacing snarls. Brenner had let his dogs out. We raced for the gate, and as it came into view, I heard Foster announce that her small group was through. But the growling behind us was growing louder. The wolves were going to overtake us.

I stopped and pulled the gun from my belt. I yelled at the humans to keep going, then planted my feet and faced back the way we had come. The two black wolves were covering the distance between us in ground-eating strides, their fearsome teeth bared beneath crimson gums. They would reach me in seconds, but I was still strong, still fast. Letting instinct guide my movements, I raised my gun and squeezed the trigger twice in rapid succession.

The first wolf fell like a stone, a bloodstain blooming across its barrel chest. But my second shot went wide, and I had only a heartbeat before those jaws would close around my throat. In one smooth movement, I dropped into a crouch, pulled my knife from its ankle sheath, and flung it into the chest of the beast just as it leapt for me. Its momentum knocked me to the ground, but the spasmodic twitching of its muscles signaled that my blade had found its mark.

I rolled out from under its weight and hurried to rejoin the others. Since we couldn't lock the gate, we raced back to the van, lest Brenner deploy more of his wolves. Caleb pealed out of the parking lot like a man possessed, and only then did I dare to take a deep breath.

"What a clusterfuck," I said, finally allowing myself to feel the full measure of disgust at our impotence. Perhaps I should have disobeyed orders and pulled the trigger when I had the chance. Those wolves would have instantly turned on Bai, but we might have been able to get rid of them before—

When I realized where my thoughts had gone, I almost laughed. Before what? Before they crushed his jugular? Before they ripped open his guts? Bai was second in command to one of the most powerful vampires in the world. Brenner had all the chips, and he knew it. I glanced at Summers's stony expression and wondered what he would advise Helen to do once we returned to Headquarters.

"He's toying with us." Foster sounded just as pained as Summers looked and I felt. "The bastard."

As we sped back toward Manhattan, my adrenaline rush and blood high began to fade simultaneously. Combined with my disappointment, it felt as though all color was rapidly being leeched from the world. I leaned my head against the cold glass of the window and closed my eyes, glad I didn't have to be the one to take charge of the report to Helen. She was going to grill Foster and Summers, but I could probably escape to my apartment. Or perhaps Tartarus, where I reigned like a god and could leave the memory of Brenner's taunts behind.

It seemed insane to be thinking about going back to my daily business as though I hadn't just seen his face in my gun sights. But what else could I do? The Consortium was hamstrung. Even with the element of surprise on our side, Brenner had easily neutralized our raid. A second extraction mission would be far more difficult to plan—it would take weeks, if not months, to execute properly.

Brenner seemed bent on making us wait, but I doubted he'd delay taking action for that long. And what was he waiting *for*, anyway? Was he playing mind games, or was he deliberately holding off until a certain date had passed or goal had been accomplished?

Unsettled, I disembarked with the team in the Consortium's garage and rode up to the seventh floor where we would be debriefed in the War Room. Before I could join them inside, however, Caleb pulled me into a corner. His expression was guarded.

"I just checked my voice mail," he said. "One of my FAA contacts left me a message while we were…preoccupied."

Alexa. The thought was involuntary, but despite the surge in my pulse, I forced my expression to remain neutral. "Oh?"

"An hour ago, Alexa boarded a flight from a regional airport in western Argentina, bound for Buenos Aires. Her name also appears on the manifest of a flight scheduled to depart early tomorrow morning for JFK Airport."

Every sense leapt into high alert as the memory of her incomparable taste flooded my mouth. A fine shiver swept me, but if he noticed, Caleb said nothing. The urgency and helplessness I'd felt over Brenner's plans receded to the back of my mind, banished like morning mist before the sun.

Alexa was coming home.

alexa

CHAPTER SIXTEEN

I set my teeth against a gasp of pain as the airplane hit another pocket of turbulence, jostling my left arm against the wall. Sensing a threat, my panther tried to ascend and I shut my eyes, turning all my attention inward to keep her under wraps. When Olivia reached for my hand, I squeezed hard enough to feel her wince. Her injury seemed not to be bothering her much at all, but then again, she didn't have a living organism trying to colonize one of her limbs.

As the panther finally retreated from the fore of my mind, I released my grip on Olivia and glanced out the window. Below, the land was growing larger, its features becoming more distinct. In the seat across the aisle, Solana gave me a sympathetic look.

"It won't be long now," she murmured.

The area around my scar had been red and puffy before we boarded the airplane, but in the hours since, my entire forearm had swelled significantly. I didn't know whether that was linked to the shifts in cabin pressure or whether it would have happened even had I stayed on the ground. Regardless, I was in constant pain. The wound throbbed dully and even the gentlest touch on any part of that arm was excruciating.

"Do you think ice will be safe?" I asked Solana. We had discussed whether I should go on broad-spectrum antibiotics to decrease the risk of infection, but since we had no way of knowing whether that kind of medication would affect the viability of the flower's root, I had decided to stay off all pills except painkillers.

"I should think so," she said, and I consoled myself by imagining how good it would feel to plunge my burning arm into a huge bucket of ice cubes once I was home.

When the plane finally touched down, I held my arm well away from my body to minimize the discomfort of the landing. Mercifully, the foot traffic through Passport Control moved quickly, and we claimed our bags within an hour. As we waited in the line to clear Customs, I couldn't help but flash back to the last time I'd returned to the States from abroad—back in the summer, when Constantine and I had used forged documents to avoid Brenner's detection after escaping from his outpost in Morocco.

This time I had my proper passport, but transporting a rare and potent flower inside my body was in flagrant violation of the injunctions—posted on the walls at regular intervals throughout baggage claim—against bringing foreign fruit, plants, and seeds into the country. Fortunately, the Customs official took my stamped paperwork and waved me through without any questions.

I searched the crowd for Karma and found her waiting next to a newsstand, but she was on the phone and didn't see us right away. A frown furrowed her brow as she spoke, and she looked as though she had lost some weight in the past week. But when she did catch sight of us, she smiled and waved and ended her call. I embraced her awkwardly with one arm, shielding the entire left side of my body.

"What happened?" she asked, the smile leaving her face as quickly as it had come. "Are you injured?"

"In a matter of speaking." I hadn't filled her in when I'd called from the airport in Buenos Aires asking her to meet us at JFK. Secrecy was paramount if this plan had any chance of working, and I had no idea who might be listening in to her phone calls.

"You remember Olivia," I continued. "And this is Solana Carrizo, who has been a huge help to us. She's an acquaintance of Helen's from, ah, several years ago."

Karma's thin eyebrows shot up. "Really. It's a true pleasure to meet you." She cut her gaze to the window, where the sun was just beginning to set, then back to Solana.

"We'll explain everything," I said, "but we need a secure place to talk."

Karma nodded. "You must be hungry. Let's chat over dinner. I know just the place."

We discussed only trivialities in the Consortium car that drove us into downtown Manhattan, and as an added precaution, Karma had the driver drop us off several blocks from our intended destination. Rabbit in the Moon was a cozy gastropub in Greenwich Village that specialized in updated British comfort foods, and they were happy to seat us at a secluded table in an alcove near the back.

"First of all," I said as the waitress left with our drinks order, "how is Malcolm?"

"He regained consciousness yesterday." Karma held up a hand to forestall my exclamation. "But he shifted immediately and hasn't yet transformed back."

"You don't think he's gone feral, do you?" I couldn't imagine that. Malcolm's will was strong and his control nearly perfect. Then again, his brain injury could have changed all that.

"Gone feral?" Olivia looked alarmed. "What does that mean?"

"Under certain circumstances, a Were can lose himself in his beast," said Karma. "When that happens, the Were becomes unable to shift and lives out the natural life of his other half."

"What are the physicians saying about Malcolm's condition?" I asked.

"The optimists among them believe this to be a necessary stage in his healing process. They have him under observation in the arena and are holding off on any action for now." Karma lapsed into silence when our drinks arrived, but focused back on me once the waitress had left. "There's something else you should know. Balthasar Brenner is here."

"Here? In New York?" The revelation triggered a surge of anxiety and I pressed the heel of my right hand to the space between my breasts, as though doing so might calm my pounding heart. Alarm skittered down my spine, and I took deep, even breaths to calm my panther. Karma was gripping the table hard, her jackal reacting to my volatility. For an instant, I was back in the prison

Brenner had arranged for me and Constantine, overwhelmed by the acrid scent of urine and wet fur, fighting off despair that I would ever see Val again. I closed my eyes and breathed in deeply, inhaling the aroma of pine wood and candle wax. I was free. I was safe. I was among friends.

"He's just across the river, actually." Karma's voice was tight with strain. "He arrived yesterday to join his soldiers. They've set up a makeshift base at a storage lot in Elizabeth."

I couldn't believe what I was hearing. "How did you discover this? And if you know where they are, then why hasn't he been captured? Or better yet, killed?"

I glanced at Olivia, wondering whether she found the harshness of my words to be disturbing, but she looked as grim as I felt. I shouldn't have been surprised. Brenner was the one responsible for Abby's illness, and she would want to make him pay.

"Valentine discovered his whereabouts," Karma said, watching me closely. "After Brenner's people captured the members of a delegation from the Sunrunner vampire clan. Last night, a team attempted a raid on Brenner's facility, but they had to turn back when he threatened to kill his hostages."

I took a long sip of my cocktail, hoping it would help to steady my nerves. "What's the plan, then? What does he want?"

"No one knows. He sent a message back with the Consortium operatives that he would open negotiations at some future time."

Olivia made a sound of disgust. "He's playing with you."

Solana, who had been following our conversation with interest, finally spoke. "I do not know Brenner, but I have known many men like him. He will make negotiation impossible. He'll take whatever he wants."

"What he wants is the dissolution of the Consortium."

"With Malcolm out of commission, Helen is the only one who can stand in his way," Karma said. "And she's shut us out. She mistrusts all Weres categorically, now—even Constantine."

"Perhaps she will listen to me," Solana said into the silence. At Karma's curious look, she elaborated. "We were lovers long ago."

I could tell that Karma wanted more details, but she didn't press for them. Instead, she turned to me. "Despite everything that's happened, I've been burning with curiosity to hear how your search went. Did you find it?"

"Miraculously, we did." I launched into the story of how we had traced the legend of the flower from documents in the National Library to the mountains of western Argentina. When I reached the part about Miguel's plan for the flower, I let Solana take over the narration since she knew far more about the flower's properties. By the time she drew to a close, Karma was leaning forward incredulously.

"The roots are literally inside you?" she asked me.

I checked to ensure that no other pub patrons were watching before I gingerly pushed up my sleeve.

"Dear God," Karma murmured in horror.

It was a ghastly sight, like something out of *Frankenstein*. The skin of my forearm was mottled red and stretched tightly over the bulge that rose around the site of the wound. My scar was so taut that it looked as though it might fly apart in the next second. When my fingertip accidentally brushed the fiery, swollen skin, I bit my lower lip to keep from crying out. Again, the panther battered at the walls of my psyche, and again I held her back. Pain blossomed at my temples from the strain.

"I need your help," I said once the sharp spike of agony had faded into the ever-present ache that refused to dissipate. "I have to convince Valentine to drink from me. We believe that if she does, she'll absorb enough of the flower's essence to reverse the transition."

"Convince?" Karma squeezed my right hand. "Sweetie, listen to me. That night, last month, when I convinced you to come to Luna? When she surprised us there? She may have come to the club to raise hell, but her entire demeanor changed when she saw you. She wants you. Badly."

Olivia seemed uncomfortable with this shift in conversation, and I wondered what she had thought would have to happen for Valentine to be saved. Perhaps she had deluded herself into thinking that my blood could be mixed with Val's morning coffee, but that wasn't how this worked. Val would have to part my skin with her teeth and drink deeply. At the prospect of her bite, arousal blossomed deep in my stomach, and I took another long sip of my drink to disguise my reaction.

"Although," Karma continued, leaning back in her chair, "She may be more suspicious now, after the most recent attempt."

"Attempt?"

"On her life. Brenner sent an assassin to the club last week—his third in as many months. According to the rumor mill, she closely resembled you as a human."

I growled, and Olivia instinctively jerked away. A haze of red filmed over my vision at the news that Brenner had used me to get to Valentine. In the process, he had made my task significantly harder.

"In other words," Solana said as I struggled to calm myself, "you will, in fact, have to 'convince her.'" One corner of her mouth quirked in a mirthless smile. "You will have to mount a seduction worthy of an epic."

Olivia visibly squirmed in her seat, but Karma's eyes glinted at the prospect.

"All's fair in love and war, and every war needs a staging ground. Come to my apartment tomorrow night, and from there we'll all go to Tartarus together." She focused in on me. "I have the perfect dress for you to wear."

I wanted to demand that we not waste even a second—that we ambush Valentine tonight. But I needed to sleep, especially if I was going to look my best and feel my sharpest. The fate of her soul rested on my ability to be both seductive and disarming—to convince her of my attraction without making my own capitulation unbelievable. To convince her that I still desired her now with a ferocity equal to the emotions I'd felt...before.

As we gathered our belongings, I found myself wondering how much of the charades to come would actually be an act.

CHAPTER SEVENTEEN

"Close your eyes."

I sat on one of Karma's bar stools that we had placed before her bathroom mirror. Her reflection looked insistent as she brandished her eye shadow brush as though it were some kind of weapon.

"I've always been a very light makeup user," I reminded her. "If you go crazy with this, Val will know something's off."

At Karma's exasperated sigh, I relented and let my eyes fall shut. For a moment, the scene felt eerily normal—as though we were simply a group of attractive, single women preparing for a night on the town. So much had never before been at stake on the outcome of a girls' night out.

As the brush fluttered across my eyelids, I tried to relax. The pain in my arm had temporarily receded after I'd submerged it in a bucket full of ice for the second time today. I didn't want to keep it there for too long, lest the cold somehow damage the root, but I needed to reduce some of the swelling.

"She's doing a great job," Olivia reassured me after a moment. She had arrived a few minutes ago with our ride for the evening—a Bentley four-seater sports car. I was glad to hear her speak up. After our conversation at the pub last night, she had seemed aloof and preoccupied. We had parted ways after dinner, Olivia and Karma heading uptown, while Solana and I walked to my Lower East Side apartment. I'd been surprised that Solana hadn't taken the opportunity to see Helen. She had claimed to want to stay with me because of the flower, but I thought she might actually be nervous.

Karma patted me on the shoulder. "Take a look."

I was impressed. Karma had used a delicate gray-green shading to bring out the color of my eyes, and a subtle touch of eyeliner to make them look bigger and darker. I didn't look exhausted or in pain—I looked elegant.

"Wow. You missed your true calling."

She handed me lipstick the color of a dusky red rose, and I applied it lightly. At that moment, Solana, who had been perusing Karma's collection of books in her living room, joined us. In a silver spaghetti-strap dress, she looked a far cry from the woman who had surprised Olivia and me at Shadow Ranch.

"You look beautiful," she said, then gestured toward the ice bucket. "You've probably done that for long enough."

I removed my arm, but when Solana approached me with a towel, I waved her away. "Let's just let it air dry. Putting the glove on is going to be agonizing enough."

Olivia's mouth tightened at my reference to just how much pain I was in. Despite her professed desire to help Valentine, I had a feeling that she was starting to wonder whether Val was truly worth this level of effort. The only questions on my mind, however, were the ones that would make this mission more likely to succeed.

"While we're all here, let's figure out the specifics." I glanced at Karma. "Have you been to Tartarus? What's the layout?"

Karma perched on the edge of her Jacuzzi-style tub. "There are three entrances: the main entrance, a VIP entrance, and Valentine's private entrance. Each has its own elevator that goes down to the dance floor. Security was tight when I was last there, and I imagine it will be even tighter after the most recent assassination attempt." She shuddered. "The club is deep underground—very deep. I've been there only once, and I don't relish going back."

I sighed. Not only would I be suffering from chronic pain and performance anxiety, but also claustrophobia. Wonderful. Hopefully, I could minimize my time underground by convincing Val to take me back to her apartment.

"Do you know where Val lives in Soho? Just in case you aren't able to follow us there?"

"I do. But I don't think her first inclination will be to take you home. She'll probably just take you to her office."

"Well, that's not going to work," said Olivia, sounding agitated. "How are we going to be able to get to Alexa if we have to fight through security in an underground fucking fortress?"

I leaned over and briefly rested one palm on her knee. "I'll just have to convince Val to take me back to her apartment somehow." A sudden thought made my gut twist. "Unless she shares it with Sebastian?"

"Don't worry," Karma said. "Sebastian lives on the Upper East Side. Val's apartment will suit our purposes well. Her penthouse has its own entrance. Once she is…incapacitated…you can let us up and we'll be able to avoid suspicion entirely."

"The only flaw in that plan is that I might not be able to stop myself from shifting," I pointed out.

Karma pondered for a moment. "If that happens, you could try to lock yourself out on the roof where the pool is."

I couldn't help but feel incredulous. "So that rumor is true? She actually has her own pool?"

"We need to establish a timeline," Solana broke in. "There needs to be a cut-off point after which we find a way inside, in case Alexa is not able to communicate with us."

Karma gave me a questioning look and I cleared my throat, unable to escape feeling self-conscious. Essentially, Solana was asking me how long I thought it would take me to seduce Valentine into biting me.

"Ah, let's say two hours. Just to be safe."

"Two hours without any backup?" Olivia said.

I held her bright, angry gaze. "Val will want to feed from me, not hurt me. I'll be fine."

Olivia spun away and left the room, but I didn't go after her. There was nothing I could say that she wanted to hear, and the clock was ticking. It was time to put on my gloves.

❖

Olivia maneuvered the Bentley into a spot across the street from the club's nondescript entrance. When she cut the engine, I brushed my palm across her shoulder.

"Thanks for driving. Hopefully, you won't have to wait long."

She kept a white-knuckled grip on the steering wheel and didn't meet my eyes. "Be careful."

I got out of the car, smoothed the folds of my strapless black dress, and turned to Karma. "Any final touches?"

She looked me up and down, then smiled and shook her head. "You're perfect."

"Sweet-talker." Squaring my shoulders, I took her arm. "Shall we?"

Karma led the way, circumventing the line to approach the bouncer—a clean-shaven male vampire who would have looked more at home behind a desk than in front of a door. He recognized her on sight and waved us inside.

"Enjoy your evening, Ms. Rao."

Once inside the door, we found ourselves in a Romanesque atrium. Tall, white pillars connected the black mosaic floor to an identically tiled ceiling. The effect was disorienting. I felt as though I had fallen through the rabbit hole and no longer had a clear sense of what was right-side up. Across the chamber, a bank of elevators waited to take us down into the club, but we had to pass through a metal detector first. I wondered how old the detector was—whether it had been put into place recently, or whether Valentine's would-be assassins had found ways of circumventing it. Fortunately, my weapons weren't made of steel.

I walked through it to join Karma and Solana on the other side and together, we stepped into an elevator. No other patrons had been admitted despite the length of the line. As the doors closed, I inspected my appearance in the mirrored walls. My black hair cascaded in glossy waves over my shoulders to brush against my collarbone, and the dress hugged my body like a sheath, accentuating the fullness of my breasts. I had elected not to wear any jewelry, in hopes that the pale expanse of my neck would prove irresistible.

The elevator whirred into motion, its descent rapid enough to make my ears pop. My panther paced behind my eyes, discomfited by the walls that had closed around us.

"How is your arm?" Solana asked.

I glanced down at the long black satin formal gloves Karma had given me to hide the gruesome scar. The swollen skin throbbed against the fabric, and I couldn't wait to be rid of them.

"Painful but not unbearable."

The elevator slid to a stop, and we disembarked into a marble-tiled corridor. The DJ's beat was strong enough to cause the walls to pulse, as though we had walked into the heart of a massive stone beast. No guards were stationed here, but I had no doubt that we were under video surveillance.

The hallway curved left and then right before ending at a set of marble doors. The flickering lamps highlighted veins of silver and gold within the milky rock. As we drew closer, the doors slid open to reveal a crowded dance floor in full frenzy.

I took a deep, steadying breath. "Do you think she knows I'm here?"

Karma led us just inside and pointed up at the glass cube that projected diagonally out into the airspace above the dance floor. Its surfaces reflected the lights and movements of the dancers, and I had to look away or risk becoming dizzy.

"That's Valentine's office. If she didn't know already, she does now."

"Let's give ourselves a tour," I suggested, wanting to canvass the perimeter of the dance floor in case we had to make some kind of hasty exit. Together, we moved around the periphery, taking note of security personnel stationed at regular intervals. But there was no visible back door—not even an emergency exit. My panther growled in protest and Karma and I shared a strained look. We were well and truly trapped.

As we returned full circle to the doors, Solana grasped my right shoulder. "Look," she said, gesturing back the way we had come.

An elevator was sliding down the elaborate network of cables along the side of the room that extended all the way up into a narrow passage cut into the vaulted ceiling. Made of the same material as the cube, it glittered like a gigantic strobe as it descended to the dance floor.

Karma shot me a wry smile. "You've called the goddess down from Olympus."

My heart was galloping, but the rest of me was frozen. Even my panther held perfectly still, waiting. Waiting for our mate.

The doors opened to reveal Valentine looking for all the world like a fallen angel. She was dressed in black from head to toe: a collared shirt perfectly tailored to the contours of her torso, and button-fly leather pants that clung to her muscular legs like a second skin. Heavy motorcycle boots completed the outfit, and I felt my mouth go dry at the aura of power and confidence that filled the air around her.

She headed directly for us, her gaze homing in on mine as though I was the only person in the room. Her golden hair was not set in spikes tonight, but fell in feathered waves across her forehead, and I longed to let the soft strands run through my fingers while I kissed her. Just a few short weeks ago, I would have tried to talk myself out of such thoughts—to impress upon my heart the need to be hard and unyielding. But not now, when her eyes were glittering with lust and thirst only for me. Not now, when I was poised to restore compassion and empathy to her handsome features.

"Alexa." She spoke my name like a magic word, but then a shutter fell over her expression, as though she realized her voice had betrayed too much. "Welcome to Tartarus."

I had to swallow before I could reply, and I wondered if she had noticed. The absurdity of making small talk in this situation made me feel as though I were having an out-of-body experience. "Thank you."

The world narrowed, telescoping down until it contained only us. I had forgotten how blue her eyes were—the deep, clear blue of a sunlit summer sky she could no longer see. But after tonight, she would no longer be bound to the darkness.

"Why have you come?" Her tone was curious, but suspicion showed in the rigidity of her stance.

I had prepared an answer and gestured toward Solana. "Karma and I are entertaining a visitor from abroad. Solana Carrizo showed me great hospitality on a recent trip to South America, and I wanted to return the favor."

Val glanced between Solana and me, her expression wary. Did she think we were involved? Was she jealous? The idea pleased me, and I took a step closer. When she focused back in on me, a rush of heat surged down my spine at the possessiveness that sharpened the planes of her face.

"I hope you enjoy your night," she said, the words intended for Solana but her gaze never leaving mine. "Your drinks are on the house." She took a step backward and extended one hand. "Dance with me."

Once again, the rest of the world receded. "Right now?"

"Right now."

I let my gloved fingertips skim her palm as I took her hand and was gratified to feel a subtle shiver course beneath her skin. I was affecting her strongly. Good.

Despite the strength of that brief contact, we didn't touch at first. She danced better than I remembered, her body an extension of the beat. Her focus never wavered, and I felt as though we had somehow traveled back in time—back to the early days of our courtship when we had wanted each other with a shared ferocity so unexpected, so unique, that we had forced ourselves to move slowly.

But tonight, slow wasn't going to work. After a while, I turned my back to her. She took the invitation to cup my waist and pull me close, and I sighed as she wrapped her arms around me. I had to remind myself then that this wasn't my Valentine. She felt the same—the same taut muscles, the same coiled strength, the same cool scent that inflamed my desire while promising to soothe it. And yet, for all the passion I'd seen in her eyes, there was none of the warmth I had loved.

Her mouth brushed first my temple, then my ear lobe. "Where's Olivia?"

"Olivia?" Confused, I tried to face her, but her grip was firm.

"You've been practically inseparable for weeks, and then you took that trip together. Why isn't she here with you?"

Surprise trumped my indignation. Valentine thought Olivia and I might be a couple. She had been spying on me. Perhaps I should have felt violated, but her obsession only increased my confidence.

"She said she wasn't feeling well." The white lie was easy. "But maybe she didn't want to see me with you."

"With me." Val grew silent then, and I was just about to break free of her hold when her breath once again cascaded over the sensitive shell of my ear. "Why did you really come here tonight?"

My heart careened wildly in my chest until I reminded myself that there was no way she could know our plan. She did, however, know me better than anyone else in the world, and she could tell when I was holding back. So I didn't.

"I missed you. I couldn't stay away any longer."

She pulled me closer, her hands tracing spirals on my stomach. "That's not what you said the last time we saw each other." She sucked my ear lobe between her lips, then grazed it lightly with her teeth. My knees quaked, and she felt it. "What's changed?"

"I have." Somehow, I managed not to stammer. As my pulse accelerated, so did the throbbing in my arm, but my panther seemed as enthralled by Val's seduction as I was. Our mate's proximity had soothed her panic into a state of high alertness.

Val's hands edged higher until her thumbs were ever so lightly brushing the undersides of my breasts. I couldn't contain a tiny gasp, and as the sound left my throat, I knew it was time to surrender. I turned, melding my thighs to hers and threading my good arm around her neck. And then I confessed.

"I need you, Valentine."

Triumph flared in her face before thirst trumped it. "I have a room up—"

I pressed two fingers to her mouth, silencing her. "Not here. I want to be in your bed."

She searched my gaze and found whatever she was looking for, because she leaned down and kissed me slow and deep. Her lips stole my reason and her tongue stole my breath, and by the time she pulled away to whisper that a car would be waiting for us upstairs, I would have followed her anywhere.

❖

By the time we reached the black Rolls Royce, my head had cleared a little. I needed to take some power back, and as soon as Val had settled herself on the leather seat bench, I climbed on top of her and proceeded to lavish her neck with long kisses and tiny bites. Every time I set my teeth in her skin, she released a guttural groan. Her sounds of abandon inflamed me, and I bit down hard enough to mark her.

"Did you ever touch Olivia like this?" she gasped harshly. When I didn't answer right away, she caught my breasts in her palms and ran her thumbs across my nipples, wringing a cry from my throat. "Did you?"

"Never. Not once." My words were breathless. "Not even a kiss. There hasn't been anyone since you."

She growled her satisfaction, and before I could protest, I found our positions reversed. For one breathtaking moment, she loomed over me, sensually menacing, before dipping her head to trace the pulsing veins in my neck and throat with her tongue. Teasing me, even as she teased herself.

Her driver had us in Soho inside of ten minutes. He pulled over at the side entrance of a tall brick structure boasting elaborate wrought iron balconies and large windows on every floor. The penthouse level was set off by a gleaming white cornice illuminated by the waning moon. For a moment, I felt a wave of nostalgia for the days early in our relationship when Valentine and I had spent Saturdays roaming lower Manhattan visiting luxury real estate open houses. The apartments we'd seen then had inspired dreams for the future. Perhaps some of those dreams would now come true. If this worked.

She held me close while guiding us to the door. As she fished out her key chain, I worked my hand beneath the hem of her pants, sweeping my fingers back and forth across her lower abdomen. She groaned and dropped her keys.

"What are you doing to me," she breathed, hands shaking as she crouched to retrieve them.

"Showing you how much I want you," I said, molding myself to the length of her back as I followed her inside.

Once the doors of her elevator had closed, she pushed me up against the back wall and devoured my mouth. If not for the spike of agony that seared down my left arm as she held me pinned, I would have lost control of myself completely. But the pain reminded me that I had a job to do, and that I needed to do it before she decided to undress me. If my wound was revealed, the gruesome sight would freeze the ardor between us, especially since it would rouse her suspicions about why I hadn't simply shifted and healed.

She kept a firm grip on the key this time, turning the lock with superhuman speed. I was aware only of an oak-paneled foyer and the faint scent of salt water before she had me pressed up against the inside of the door, one leg between mine. Hands braced on either side of my head, she thrust with short, sharp movements that rocketed me toward ecstasy. She was wild for me, a creature possessed by a hunger beyond the physical. I could see it in the ferocity of her eyes, in the tautness of her lips, and I threaded my hands in her hair to pull her mouth to mine.

In that moment, I realized that despite the emotional distance that had grown between us, our bodies were reacting on a wholly instinctual level. The chemistry between us was a law of nature that could not be denied. We would always be attracted to one another, always attuned, but I was about to use that power to make a choice for Val. She had been turned involuntarily, transfused involuntarily, and she had certainly never wanted to become a full vampire. Now I was poised to take another decision from her, and I couldn't. I refused to join the ranks of people like Helen and Clavier and the Missionary—people who had made life-altering choices for Valentine to serve their own ends. If I was going to go through with this, I needed to know that somewhere, deep down in her essential self, Val still needed me just as much as I did her.

I wrenched her head back and stared up into her dark, fathomless eyes. "What do you want, Valentine?"

Confusion momentarily eclipsed her frenzied desire. "You. I want you. All of you."

She moved to bridged the gap between us, but I held her back. "How badly do you want to taste me?"

Her eyes grew darker and the muscles in her jaw tightened spasmodically. "More than you can possibly imagine."

Again, she tried to lunge forward, and again, I stopped her. The tendons in her neck strained as she pushed against me.

"Let me have you!"

Drunk on the power I held over her, I only tightened my grip. "I'm the one you crave, Val. I'm the one you need. I'm the one you can't be without. What would you give to drink from me forever?"

She growled possessively and bared her sharpened teeth. "Anything. Anything you want."

"Just you," I whispered, finally releasing my grasp.

The force of her kiss slammed me against the wall, but I felt no pain. Exhilaration swept me at her confession, and my lingering doubts fell away. When she reached down to stroke my inner thigh, I gasped my assent. But when her teeth scraped along my jaw line, I begged. "Please, Val!"

Despite my ulterior motives, my plea was the truth. Beyond her touch, I needed her teeth in my throat and my blood running down hers. The ultimate connection. I tugged urgently at the nape of her neck.

"Do it. Touch me. Bite me. I need to feel you everywhere."

Triumph sang through me at the welcome flash of pain, at the hollowing sensation of my blood being drawn between her lips. At her broken moan that belied the potency of my taste. And as she drank, she filled me with her fingers, my body stretching to welcome her home.

Ecstasy crashed over me then, tearing a scream from my vocal cords, and the climax battered me like ocean waves against the shore. I clutched at her shoulders, desperate to keep her inside of me.

Please, I thought dimly. *Please let this bring her back.*

A moment later, her body went suddenly stiff. I looked down to see panic in her eyes, but her throat continued to spasm. Something was happening, but she couldn't make herself stop drinking.

Finally, she wrenched herself away, my blood trickling over her chin and onto the wooden floor as she stumbled backward. I sagged against the wall, wanting to move but not trusting my strength.

"Val," I managed to whisper, every other word beyond me.

Confusion and fear warred on her face, and she held up a hand as though to fend me off.

"What—" she choked out. "What did you—"

And then she collapsed to the floor.

Chapter Eighteen

M oments later, she began to convulse. I rushed across the hall and nearly panicked at the sight of the red-flecked foam that had collected at the corners of her mouth. As quickly as the spasms had come, they abated. Her body was still.

"Oh God, Val."

Hastily, I felt for breathing and a pulse before turning her onto her side so she wouldn't choke. Her vital signs seemed strong, but Solana had never mentioned anything about going into seizures. Then again, she had probably been unconscious for this part, too.

I scrambled for my phone and punched speed dial for Karma. "It's done. She passed out, but she had some sort of seizure."

The sounds of the street filtered through the receiver as Karma updated the others. In another moment, Solana had taken her place. "Is she breathing?"

"Yes. Are you at the door?"

"We are."

"I'll let you in as soon as I figure out how it works." I hung up and scanned the wall for some kind of intercom, finally finding one just off the kitchen. After buzzing them inside, I knelt beside Val and ran my fingers lightly through her hair, my heart throbbing rapidly in time with my arm.

"Your last thought was that I'd betrayed you," I murmured. "But you're going to wake up from this, and when you do, I hope you can see things differently. I hope you can understand why I did it."

A tear fell from the corner of my eye onto her cheek, and I smoothed the tiny drop into her skin. "There was a time when you wanted me, and only me, for eternity. And I let you down by going away and putting your soul in jeopardy. So this is my chance, sweetheart—my chance to give you back the only thing you've actively chosen since you were turned. Me. Us. Ever after."

The front door chimed and I reluctantly left Val's side long enough to answer it. Solana went to Val immediately.

"How is she?" Karma asked.

But Olivia was staring at me in horror. "Christ, Alexa, you look like you've been mauled! What did she do to you?"

Her reaction wasn't exactly unfounded. I was a mess. My dress was in disarray and a stream of blood had caked on my neck and collarbone. My eyes were probably red and puffy. I raised one hand, hoping to calm her down, only to notice that my fingers were trembling.

Karma was now looking at me in concern. "Alexa, how much did she take?"

"Not very much," I said, then winced as a streak of shooting pain traveled along my arm. "The scar is starting to feel worse, though. And I'm very thirsty."

Olivia stalked to the kitchen, and a moment later I heard the tap running. Karma laid the back of her hand to my forehead. "You're warm."

I craned my neck to catch a glimpse of Val. "Once I shift, I'll be fine. How is she, Solana?"

"As well as can be expected. I am not worried."

"That makes one of us," I said before gratefully accepting the glass of water Olivia held out to me. "How long were you unconscious when you went through this?"

"Several days," Solana said. "But remember: I ate the flower's roots. Valentine has consumed its essence in your blood, and the blood of a Were is the greatest healing elixir I know."

"So she might wake sooner."

Solana shrugged. "We'll see."

Fire seared up my arm, a sudden blaze so intense I couldn't hold back a gasp. My panther shoved hard, wanting her claws and teeth instead of this fragile human body. As the pain worsened, her strength grew and mine weakened.

"Alexa?" Karma was kneeling beside me now, one hand on my knee. Olivia stood over us, her anger displaced by alarm.

"Need to shift." I forced the words out between gritted teeth.

"Can you make it to the Consortium?" she asked.

"I'll drive you," Olivia added.

I nodded, then cut my gaze to Val. "Please don't leave her alone."

"Of course not." Karma gently took my right hand and helped me up. "Go. We'll call you with any updates."

Fortunately, Olivia's car was parked nearby. I focused on breathing deeply and putting one foot in front of the other as the periodic flashes of agony continued. When I slid into the passenger seat, my left arm brushed against the seat back and the resulting spike of pain was so intense that tears leaked down my cheeks.

Olivia got into the driver's side, and I braced my good arm against the glove box to hold myself steady as she peeled away from the curb.

"I'll try to make this a smooth ride," she said.

"Thanks." I didn't know what else to say, especially given her mercurial moods ever since we'd gotten home. "I mean it, Liv. Thank you. For everything."

For a long time, she didn't reply. I examined her profile as she expertly navigated the late night streets of the East Side—the delicate sweep of her cheekbones, the elegant strength of her jaw. She was beautiful, and in a parallel universe, I could have fallen in love with her. But in this reality, I was claimed. And it didn't matter that my soul mate was a vampire, or that she was lying on the floor of her apartment a broken, bloody mess. She was mine. I was hers. I would fight for us as long as I had to.

Olivia pulled up at Consortium Headquarters in record time, and I sighed in relief. But just as I was about to thank her yet again, she spoke.

"Have dinner with me."

Taken aback, I didn't respond right away. I had just taken extraordinary measures—even for a shifter—to save Valentine. I was bloodied and feverish and my panther was a hairsbreadth away from emerging. And this was the moment she had chosen to ask me on a date?

"I can't, Olivia."

"Breakfast, then." She sounded almost desperate. "If Val hasn't woken up. We can go somewhere near her apartment. I just…I just need to talk to you. Alone."

The pain in my arm flared again, and I exhaled sharply. "Okay. Breakfast." I never would have acquiesced if I hadn't been in her debt, and my frustration at her insistence only fueled the panther's urgency. "I'm sorry, but I really have to go now."

I didn't look back as I jogged up the steps and into the building. The receptionist was new, and I had to pause to show her my identification before catching an elevator down to the hunting arena. Once I reached the foyer, I took off my borrowed dress and the right glove. My left arm was so swollen that the other glove was almost cutting into the engorged skin. There was no salvaging it.

I stepped up to one of the doors and keyed in the code that would unlock it. As it opened, I was greeted by a warm breeze and the scent of flowering grass. For the first time since the full moon, I relaxed my grip on my panther. And I smiled.

"Uje!"

Eager to escape the incessant pain, she was upon me in a flash, and I imagined I could feel the flower's roots disintegrating in the whirlwind of my transformation. As my paws made contact with the springy, moss-covered earth, I crouched low, tail lashing. A jumble of scents quickly resolved: the rich, verdant aroma of growing things; the faint musk of a lynx who had passed this way a few hours ago; the tang of blood from someone's recent kill.

A flash of motion to my right caught and held my focus. When I spun toward it, I scented prey—a deer. I leapt into motion, earth churning beneath the pads of my feet. After a zigzagging chase through the forest fringe, the deer bounded into a small clearing. I extended my body in ground-eating strides, determined to use the open space to narrow the gap between us. And then I caught the other scent: a wolf off my left flank, also in pursuit. When I turned my head slightly, a blur of brindle fur was visible though the tall stalks of grass.

Two predators, one prey. I was not in the mood to share—especially not with a wolf. When Sebastian's face flickered before my mind's eye, I snarled and pushed harder.

The doe reentered the woods and began a dizzying series of cuts back and forth between the closely-knit trees. I followed her, reveling in my ability to mimic her movements, but the wolf, too, was agile and had managed to keep pace. And then, without any warning, the doe faltered. In that barest of pauses, I leapt, claws unsheathing instinctively. They caught and held in the deer's hindquarters, and I dragged her down thrashing into the underbrush. Narrowly avoiding her flailing hooves, I sank my teeth into her throat. She twitched once and was still.

I looked up to see the wolf only a few yards away, saliva dripping from his jaws. When he snarled, daring to assert a claim over my kill, I lashed out. He barely dodged my swipe, and I settled back onto my haunches to wait for him to try again. Hunger cramps were twisting my belly into knots, but the moment my concentration slipped would be the moment the wolf made his play.

Thankfully, his will was weaker than mine. The instant I saw him focus on the kill instead of me, I sprang forward again, this time scoring a hit across his shoulder. The three-point scratch was starkly visible for an instant before blood welled up to cascade down his front leg. Growling, he finally beat a retreat into the underbrush.

As soon as he was gone, I gorged myself on my kill. After such a harrowing week, I was even hungrier than usual, and I caught myself purring even as I ripped at the sinews of the corpse beneath my paws. Strength and vitality returned to my muscles, and with them came clarity of thought. Valentine could wake up at any moment. My feline half wanted to doze in the artificial sun, but I would have to wait to indulge her.

Leaves rustled in the direction the wolf had gone, and I growled a warning. If he wanted to pick over whatever bones I left, he would have to wait a little longer. But when a large golden lion padded into view, the snarl choked in my throat. I had never seen Malcolm four-footed, but I had no doubt that he was standing before me now.

Slowly, I backed away from my kill. It was both an instinctual and calculated move. I wanted to give the lion a wide berth, and I wanted Malcolm to feed on what meat remained. He loomed over the carcass, his red-gold mane framing liquid brown eyes above a long, thick muzzle. Tail lashing, he regarded me silently before finally bending to eat. It was impossible to tell whether he had recognized me in any meaningful way, but I wanted to believe it. We needed him back. He was our general and our rallying point in the stand against Brenner. Without him, others would lose hope. They might even defect.

Reflecting on his inability—or unwillingness—to shift made me suddenly eager for my human form. I returned to the door and let my desire to check in with Solana propel me into a painless transformation. After Valentine recovered, there would be plenty of time for me to indulge my inner feline. Maybe we could even return to the cabin we'd rented last year in the Catskills for a much-needed getaway. Val and I had found balance and harmony there before, and perhaps some time away from the political chaos of the city would help us as we reforged our relationship.

But I was getting ahead of myself. Solana seemed confident that our plan had succeeded, but we couldn't know for sure until Val woke. My phone display indicated no missed calls or messages, but I threw my clothes on hastily. I wanted to be back at her side. I wanted her to feel loved, even if she couldn't consciously perceive it. I wanted to think of all the right things to say when she finally opened her eyes. I wanted her to make me whole by awakening healed.

As I walked toward the elevator, some impulse made me look over my shoulder. Malcolm was padding into the small clearing in front of the door, and I wondered if he had followed me deliberately. I wanted to take it as a good omen and waited to see what he would do. Had he witnessed my transformation? Was there any impulse in him that wanted to take human form again? I waited for a few minutes, daring to hope that having seen me might trigger his shift, but he only nosed around the door before returning to the shelter of the trees.

I pressed my palm to the cool glass as he walked away. Malcolm Blakeslee was so much more than a noble beast, but only time could tell whether he would ever fully recover. In a way, his predicament was similar to Valentine's. She, too, had been separated from her humanity—trapped by her physiological needs in a mentality that rewarded dominance without compassion.

Right now, there was nothing I could do for Malcolm. But if Solana was right and we had succeeded, Val's body was even now reverting back to its former state. Not wanting to spend another moment separated from her, I turned back toward the exit.

❖

When Val's status hadn't changed by the following morning, I grudgingly met Olivia at a French café around the corner from Valentine's apartment.

"How is Val?" she asked as I sat opposite her.

"Still unconscious."

I looked down at the menu, wanting to order quickly so I could get back. After I'd returned last night, Karma had left to check in with Constantine, and Solana and I had moved Val to her bed. I'd napped fitfully next to her, waking often to check that she was still breathing.

Olivia cleared her throat into the awkward silence. "And how about you? How's your arm?"

"It's fine." I heard the note of incredulity in my own voice. This latest display of my regenerative capabilities still felt miraculous. I pushed up my sleeve and showed her the unbroken skin of my forearm. "Better than fine."

"Amazing." Olivia lightly traced the spot where my scar had been. "Like it never happened."

Uncomfortable with her touch, I pulled away. "Any idea what's good here?"

"Not a one." She leaned over to point at the menu. "Though the French toast is probably a sure thing."

"I am hungry," I conceded.

"You're thinner than I've ever seen you. You should eat more."

My temper flared at her presumption. "Excuse me?"

She had the decency to look ashamed. "I shouldn't have said that. I'm sorry."

Despite her apology, I might have left if the waitress hadn't arrived at that moment. After we ordered, Olivia leaned forward. "I'm doing this all wrong. Every time I try to tell you that I care about you, the sentiment comes out horribly twisted."

"I know you care about me. You've gone so far above and beyond the call of duty for a friend, it's absolutely mind-boggling."

She sat back in her chair and crossed her arms. "But?"

"But you know what I'm going to say. I belong to Val, Olivia. And if that offends your twenty-first century, liberated woman's sensibilities, then fine. But that's how it is. She's who I want—who I need. And I need you to respect that."

To her credit, she met my gaze squarely. "I understand," she said after a long moment's pause. Her smile was a little sad, a little wistful. "It's not easy to compete with Valentine Darrow."

"Funny. She once said almost exactly the same thing about you."

Our food arrived then, and the French toast was indeed delicious. I ate more quickly than I should have, and when Olivia very deliberately turned the conversation to human politics, I was happy to follow her lead. Until my phone rang. Solana.

"What's happened?"

"She's not awake yet, but she's stirring."

I reached for my wallet, ignoring Olivia's vigorous head shaking. "What does 'stirring' mean?"

"Mumbling incoherently. Twitching. REM."

Rapid-eye movement? "So she's asleep now, instead of unconscious?"

"No," said Solana. "I can't wake her. But I think she's dreaming."

"I'll be there in two minutes. Maybe less."

When I hung up, Olivia forestalled my speech. "Go. If I can help, you'll tell me?"

"Yes. Of course."

I raced from the restaurant back to Valentine's apartment. When I burst through the door, I rushed immediately to the bedroom. Solana was sitting in a chair near Val's head, and she stood as I approached.

"Sweetheart," I murmured, dropping to my knees and twining my fingers with Val's. "Can you hear me?"

Her eyes were moving beneath the thin lids as though she was searching for something. I leaned in to press my lips to hers.

"Wake up, Val. Come back to me."

For a long moment, nothing happened. And then, as though we were living a fairy tale, Valentine opened her eyes.

CHAPTER NINETEEN

A lexa?"

She spoke with a wistful uncertainty, as though she didn't know whether I was real. My vision swam, and I dashed away the tears impatiently. I had to be strong.

"Hi, love." I kissed her cheek and rubbed my thumb across her knuckles. "How do you feel?"

Her brow furrowed as she considered the question. "Weak. Thirsty. What hap—" She caught sight of Solana, then, and suddenly a gun was in her hand. I jerked backward in shock, my panther clamoring to shift. Despair threatened to overwhelm the hope that had just begun to take root in my soul. Had I failed? Was she still a full vampire?

"Who the fuck are you?" Val's eyes had never left Solana, but her voice held no fear. Miraculously, Solana also seemed calm.

"This is normal," she said, her gaze not on Val's weapon but on me. "You don't need to worry. Her body is in conflict and her memories do not match her emotions. She's disoriented."

"The hell I am." Val cocked the trigger. "Explain yourself. Now."

"My name is Solana Carrizo, and I'm a friend of Helen Lambros. We met yesterday at your club." When Val's frowned deepened, I knew the memories had not yet fully returned to her.

"Your confusion is a normal reaction to the flower," Solana continued.

The pistol trembled ever so slightly. "What flower?"

"It's a long story," I said, daring to rest my hand on her thigh. "Solana's no threat to you or to us. Put down the gun, and I'll tell you everything."

Slowly, Val lowered her weapon, and I sighed in relief as she reengaged the safety. She rested her hand atop mine and turned to face me. "You were in the club last night. I remember that much."

"That's a good sign." I worked to keep my voice calm. "Try to think back. What else?"

Several fraught seconds passed. "I remember dancing with you."

I dared to lightly brush my lips over hers. "Yes, we danced for a long time. I love being in your arms that way."

Val was shaking her head. "I wanted you so badly, but I couldn't have you. Why does it feel like I couldn't have you?"

The anxiety in her voice tore at me. "I'm yours, love. I'll always be yours. Now and forever." I took a deep, steadying breath. "Can you remember a little further back? What brought you to the club last night?"

Val squinted down at the tangled sheets. "I was there because... because I needed to introduce Giselle to—" What little color had been in her cheeks abruptly disappeared, and I clutched her hand tightly.

"What just happened, sweetheart?" I asked, trying to keep my tone soothing. For a moment there, she had seemed to be back on the edge of unconsciousness. "You just got as pale as a ghost."

She swallowed hard, looking everywhere but at me. "I turned Giselle," she finally whispered. "She wanted it, and I...I think I might be sick."

Even as my stomach tied itself into knots at the thought of Valentine deliberately turning anyone, I felt a glimmer of relief. She wouldn't be contrite if she was still a full vampire, would she? I traced the veins that swirled beneath the back of her hand. "You're okay. You're going to be okay."

She met my gaze, then, misery and confusion warring on her face. "How can you say that? You, of all people?"

"I'll get some water," Solana said, clearly wanting to give us time to talk privately.

As she left the room, I rose from the floor and sat next to Val on the bed. She propped herself up on the pillows and I rested my hand on her thigh, needing the contact. "Tell me what you're thinking," I said. "What you're feeling. I can't even begin to guess."

She picked at a thread on the coverlet, her face a study in confusion. "I don't know where to start. I have all these memories, but the emotions that go with them don't fit. I transitioned, didn't I? Why am I feeling this way?"

"You did become a full vampire," I said, struggling not to betray the pain her question had caused me. Had I misinterpreted her answer last night? A knot of dread rose into my throat at the thought. "Last night, I brought you back. You have your soul again. I thought that's what you wanted."

Finally, Val raised her head. Her eyes looked like bruises, dark and anguished. "I never wanted to lose it in the first place. But I don't know what to do with these feelings."

Solana must have been able to hear us, because she took that as a cue to enter. After placing a tall glass of water on the nightstand, she rested her palm briefly on Val's shoulder. "Your mind is more resilient than you think. Give yourself time to assimilate the past with the present."

Val nodded warily but didn't reply. She reached for the glass and drained it in a matter of seconds, but the tension didn't ease from her face, and I knew the water hadn't done much good. She didn't need water; she needed more blood.

"I'll be in the sitting room," Solana said. She flashed me an encouraging smile before leaving us alone, and I took heart in her confidence. As she closed the door behind her, I leaned in to press gentle kisses to each corner of Val's mouth. Her distraught expression was breaking my heart, and I wanted to do something that would reassure her.

"I want you to drink from me."

"Why?" she whispered, even as thirst flared in her eyes. "Why do you want that? Do you have any idea what I've done?"

I shifted on the bed until I had one hand braced on either side of her waist, effectively trapping her. "I know enough. We'll talk about all that later. Right now, I want to be close to you and I want for you to get well."

When she still didn't move, I cupped the back of her neck and pulled her in to the juncture of my neck and shoulder. "Taste me, Val. Please."

With a muffled groan, she slid her teeth into me. At the jolt of pleasure-pain, I tugged at the short golden hairs beneath my fingers and she gasped against my skin. My desire for her only grew the longer she drank, but I forced myself to keep my touch platonic. We couldn't make love until we had at least begun to clear the air between us. Tenderly, I stroked her shoulders and scalp, wanting her to feel the lack of recrimination in my touch.

She withdrew sooner than I would have liked, but she didn't pull away. Instead, she kissed the tiny wounds until they closed, then blazed a path to my ear with her mouth. "Thank you," she said, her breath tickling my sensitive lobe.

I tugged at her shirt collar until she put enough space between us for me to see her eyes. They were clearer now, but still sorrowful.

"I'm married," she said suddenly. "To Sebastian."

My stomach soured and I let my hands fall away. "Believe me, I know."

"You saw the announcement?"

I nodded, deciding to hold off on telling her just how strongly it had affected me. Now was not the time to add to her guilt. Instead, I asked the question that had plagued me since reading that headline in the *Times*.

"Do you love him?"

Val shook her head like a dog shaking off water. "What? No! He came to me suggesting marriage as a business proposition. I did it to get my inheritance."

"Did you have sex with him?"

My heart thudded painfully when Val looked away, taking a white-knuckled grip on the blanket. "Not the way you're thinking."

Rage tinged my vision red, and I watched my own hands tremble as I struggled to hold both it and my panther at bay. "What does that mean?"

Val blew out a long sigh, and I fought to remain patient. "I fucked him," she said finally.

For a moment, surprise trumped my jealousy. "What?"

"He was the one who suggested the whole marriage thing, and he pitched it to me as a business proposal. But a few weeks after I went along with it, he started badgering me. For intimacy. I kept putting him off and putting him off until I got tired of listening to him whine." She paused to scrub at her eyes with the heels of her palms. "So I gave him a choice between...ah, that way and nothing."

My emotions were in turmoil. A part of me was still jealous, because even Val topping Sebastian—as unorthodox as it might have seemed—was still a violation of my claim on her. But I was also intrigued, and more than a little impressed. He must have been so angry. And yet...

"Did he like it?"

Shock again crossed her handsome features. "What? Alexa—"

"It's a simple question, Val."

She held my gaze this time, jaw clenching spasmodically. "He liked it, yes. And he hated it at the same time."

"Do you want to stay married to him?"

"No!" She took my hands and cradled them in her own. "I don't want anyone but you."

Satisfied that she meant every word, I curled up along her side, tucking my head beneath her chin. When her arms came around me, I relaxed into her.

"Marrying Sebastian isn't all I've done," she said fretfully.

"I know. But I don't want to hear any more just now. Let's sleep for a while."

"All right," she whispered, daring to dip her hands beneath the hem of my sweater to caress the skin of my lower back. "All right."

❖

When I woke an hour later, Valentine was still sleeping soundly. It was a testament to her exhaustion that I was able to disentangle myself without waking her. I stepped into the bathroom to check my phone messages. Karma had texted asking for an update, and I typed out a quick answer before calling Olivia.

"Hi," she said tentatively. "What's up? How's Val?"

"She's having a bit of a hard time adjusting," I said. "There's a lot to discuss."

"Anything I can do?"

"Actually, yes. She needs a divorce lawyer. A good one, equipped to handle large sums of money and who can work fast. Can you recommend anyone?"

If Olivia was surprised, she didn't let on. "Of course. If I e-mail the names, will that be okay?"

"Perfect. Thank you, Liv. I owe you."

After ending the call, I found Solana in the living room, sitting on the loveseat and reading. I collapsed into a nearby armchair.

"How is she?"

"Still confused. There's a lot she still needs to work through, but she's strong. We both are."

"You both are." She smiled ruefully. "The kind of love you share happens only once in a lifetime. Don't let it slip away—especially not now."

I wondered if she was thinking of Helen, and it suddenly struck me that I had never seen Solana feed. Perhaps she had found a willing human at the club last night. "How are you? Do you have everything you need?"

But before she could answer, Val entered the room wearing NYU sweats and a faded gray T-shirt. She looked soft and vulnerable, and it struck home that against all odds, I had gotten her back. This was my Valentine—the one who was sweet as well as sexy, rumpled as well as rapacious.

When she saw me, relief softened her features. Somehow, I was going to have to convince her that I was not going to leave—no matter what she told me next.

"Hi," she said, looking around uncertainly. "Ah. Can I offer anyone a drink?"

I rose from the chair and went to her, resting my hand on her sternum as I leaned up to kiss her. "It's a little early for a drink, unless you want to make mimosas."

As I spoke, Solana got to her feet and went to the window. The room brightened only infinitesimally as she drew back the curtains to a reveal dark clouds above the cityscape. An unrealized tightness eased in my chest as the sky was unveiled and my panther purred in approval.

"I have no idea what time it is," Val was saying. "The bank must be frantic by now."

"Do you need to go in?"

She kissed my forehead before stepping away to grab her laptop from the counter. "Let me just check my inbox. I'll go in later." She sat on the vacated couch. "Will you come with me? I'd like to show it to you."

"I'd like to see it."

I joined Solana at the window, where she was examining the impressive view. Val had a clear line of sight from the Empire State Building to the spires of Wall Street—a breathtaking panorama of steel and sky.

"I can't thank you enough," I told Solana quietly. "Your generosity made this possible."

She smiled. "I'm only paying forward the generosity that was shown to me so many years ago."

We stood in silence for a few more moments, watching the clouds swirl over the rooftops of Manhattan. They seemed to be breaking up. Slim shafts of sunlight fell at various points throughout the city, as though heaven was shining down a spotlight.

"Have you considered going to see Helen?" I asked. I didn't want to pry, but I also didn't want her to feel as though she had to stay here with us.

"I have." For once, she seemed uncertain, casting a sidelong glance at me as if unsure of how much she should say. "Truthfully, I'm concerned she might not want to see me."

"How do you know her?" Val asked. She had closed her laptop and was looking at us curiously.

"We were lovers briefly at the turn of the twentieth century," said Solana. "In Argentina, where she was consolidating power at the time."

Val didn't outwardly react, but I could tell she was surprised. "I agree with Alexa," she said. "Helen is under a great deal of stress at the moment, and she needs every ally she can get. You should go to her."

Solana's expression turned wistful. "Perhaps."

At that moment, the clouds broke above us, and a wide swath of sunshine streamed into the room. Val's face registered horror as she instinctively raised her arm against the light. Even across the room, I could hear the thunder of her panicked heartbeat. In another second, I was at her side, triumph singing through my veins even as I tried to comfort her. She wasn't burning. The flower had fully worked its miraculous transformation.

"You're okay, sweetheart. Remember?" I stroked her arm, then gently pushed it away from her eyes. "The sun won't hurt you now."

Gradually, her pulse slowed and the harsh gasps of her breaths quieted. Wonder replaced the fear on her face. She grasped my hand tightly, then stood and led me back to the window.

"God," she breathed, closing her eyes and turning her face fully into the light. "I hadn't realized just how much I missed it."

I slid my arms around her and rested my head over her heart. "Welcome back, love."

We stood there for several minutes, simply appreciating the warmth and the brightness, until Solana turned away. "I'll do it," she said, and I wondered if watching Val's return to the light had somehow inspired her. "Right now. I'll go to see her."

"If you need any help getting access to her, call us," Val said as Solana collected her belongings, and I felt a small thrill at her use of the plural pronoun.

"I will. But I think, despite the dire situation, that she will see me once she hears my name." We followed her into the foyer, where she paused to inspect her reflection. "You see, she still believes me to be dead."

"I wouldn't mind being a fly on that wall," said Val as we returned to the living room. "Do you know her story?"

She propped herself against the armrest of the couch and I settled between her legs with her arms around me. It was such a familiar configuration for us, but I knew I'd never take it for granted. When I turned to meet her eyes, I could tell she was thinking the same thing.

"You feel so good," I admitted. "There were times when I lost hope of ever having you back."

"I'm right here. Thanks to you." She stroked my stomach and kissed the top of my head. "I'll never be able to thank you enough. You saved me again, baby."

"Solana played a significant role," I said, launching into the story of our trip to South America. By the time I had finished, Val and I were stretched out on our sides facing each other and she was looking at me incredulously.

"How long do the effects of the flower last?"

I stroked her face lightly, craving the physical contact with her. "No one knows. Up until now, Solana has eaten the roots monthly. She's not sure what will happen to her now that she's skipped a month."

"And I didn't eat the roots at all," Val mused. "Both of us need answers, and soon. I'll go to Headquarters and run some blood tests to see if I can figure out what's going on."

"Right now?" I tried to keep the dismay out of my voice. I didn't want to move. Ever.

Val laughed. "No way. I'm not letting you up."

I nipped at her chin. "Oh? You think you're in charge, here?" I wriggled closer and slipped one leg between hers. "You know, we're finally alone now."

But instead of inspiring a kiss as I'd hoped, my words made her look away, over my shoulder. I swallowed down a surge of dread.

"What is it?"

"Something else I need to tell you." She rubbed a strand of my hair between her thumb and forefinger. "Over the past few months, I've turned three people."

"Who else besides Kyle and Giselle?"

"Tonya. She worked in the Consortium's medical wing."

Her confession rattled me more than I would have liked. I closed my eyes briefly, as though I could somehow escape the visions of her drinking from them. Touching them. "Did you sleep with them, too?"

"Not with Kyle. But I...with the women, yes."

"You made them come?" I asked, unable to keep the harshness from my voice.

"Yes."

"Did they make you come?"

"No. I didn't let them touch me. That's not what turning them was about."

I sat up, and when she tentatively rested her hand on my shoulder, I stood. "I need a minute."

Sensing my discomfort, the panther had become agitated. I went to the window and rested my palms against the sill, watching the wind drive the clouds across the sky. Her news didn't come as a surprise, but hearing my suspicions confirmed was a blow nonetheless. I hurt, and I didn't know how to stop.

"Alexa," she called softly. When I turned, I found her curled into corner of the couch, arms encircling her knees. "Talk to me."

"I know I have to accept that you...what you did," I said, fumbling for the right words. "But I can't help but feel betrayed, even though it's irrational."

Val looked stricken, and silence reigned between us until she visibly pulled herself together. "I'm only going to say this once," she said, "because otherwise I'll never say anything else. I'm sorry for all the ways in which I hurt you over the past few months. Most of all, I'm sorry that I ever turned to anyone else for my needs. You're the one I *really* need. The only one. You always have been."

The earnestness in her voice and the determination that suffused her face made it impossible for me to stay away any longer. I returned to the couch and held out my hand, wanting nothing more than to move past this moment.

"I'll do everything in my power to make sure I never hurt you like that again," she said as she slid her palm against mine. "You'll never, ever have to doubt how much I love you. How much I need you."

I didn't reply, only tugged at her hand. When she stood, I led her back into the bedroom. Jealousy still roiled in my chest, stoking my desire to claim her. I pointed to the bed.

"Sit down."

Her unquestioning obedience ratcheted up my pulse. Feet dangling, her chiseled arms braced against the mattress, she awaited my next command with a painfully eager expression.

"No touching," I said as I approached, before proceeding to divest her of the T-shirt and sweats.

"Please," she said once she was naked, "let me undress you."

"I said no touching." I pulled off my shirt and slid out of my jeans, revealing a simple black bra and matching panties.

"So beautiful," Val whispered.

"And you are still the hottest woman I've ever seen." I pushed her legs apart so I could stand between them. "You're also mine. I'm going to remind you of that."

When she cupped my waist, I reached down and firmly moved her hands back onto the bed. "What part of 'no touching' don't you understand?"

"Please." Her eyes were feverish. "Please let me."

"No. Keep your hands on the mattress, or I'll stop."

I leaned in to kiss her, then, and took my time of it—a whisper-soft brush of my lips against hers, over and over until she lost control and her tongue flicked out to tease me. I allowed it, allowed her in, and paid her back in kind. Clutching her head between my palms, I feasted on her mouth, then trailed my lips across her jaw and down the column of her neck.

I bit her where she'd bitten me this morning, not hard enough to draw blood, but enough to leave a mark. When she cried out, I did it again. And then I stepped back.

"No, please," she breathed. "Where are you—"

I cut her off by grasping one rose-colored nipple between my thumb and forefinger. "I'm not going anywhere, Val. Not without you, not ever again. I promise."

I twisted lightly and her eyes fluttered shut. When I brought my other hand into play, she groaned. I teased her for minutes, alternating the pressure of my fingers until her lips were parted and her face was flushed and her hips were rocking against the comforter.

I dropped to my knees and replaced my fingers with my mouth, swirling my tongue around her while stroking the taut skin of her stomach. As I moved closer to the juncture of her thighs, she began to beg.

"I love how you want me," I said, massaging the tight ridge of muscle framing her abdomen.

"Need you," she corrected me, panting. "So bad. You're the only one I need."

"That's right."

I slid my fingers home to find her hot and wet and tight. She cried out as I entered her and collapsed back on her elbows. When I dipped my head to taste her, she screamed my name.

Another time, I would tease her. We would go slowly and gently with each other. I would cherish her for hours and we would slip effortlessly between laughing and kissing, claiming and cuddling. Another time. Not now, when I so desperately had to prove to her that we belonged together despite all of the many obstacles that had come between us. The politics, the distance, her descent into darkness—none of it mattered. None of it would ever matter. I reminded her of our truth as I murmured my love against her most sensitive skin.

When I finally allowed the ecstasy to find her, she whispered my name over and over, trembling. Her body clenched around me, pulling me even deeper inside, and tears spilled down her face to anoint the bed covers.

After her body quieted, I stretched out next to her and tenderly wiped away the tear tracks from her cheeks. She opened her eyes and her smile was brilliant, without any hint of guilt.

"I love you, Valentine," I said, claiming a gentle kiss.

"And I love you. More than anything." She propped herself up on one arm and traced the skin just above my breasts. "Do I get to touch you now?"

I rolled onto my back, urging her on top of me. "As much as you want, for as long as you want."

Her smile turned dangerous. "Good. Because I *want*."

Despite the ferocity of her expression, she made love to me in a slow, reverent exploration that set my every nerve aflame. Her mouth and her hands moved in counterpoint across the planes of my skin, rekindling the passion at the very heart of us. She teased me with soft strokes of her hands and mouth for what felt like hours, until I was incandescent with the need for her to fill me. And when she did, her teeth and her touch conspired to finally make me whole again.

Afterward, we lounged like cats on a sun-warmed rock. Eventually, she turned me over and gave me a long massage, working the knots out of my back and shoulders with practiced hands. When she began to pepper my back with kisses, I purred, feeling content for the first time in months.

"I love that sound," she said. And then, after a beat, "I love you."

Her fingers wandered down the slope of my back until I felt myself go liquid beneath her teasing touch. "I love you. And I want you again."

"That's good," she said, shifting my left knee up on the bed to grant herself better access. "Because I'm going to take you again, right now."

With excruciating slowness, she pushed two fingers into my body. By the time she was buried as deep as she could go, I was keening into her pillow.

"Feel me, Alexa," she murmured as she thrust. "Feel me inside you. One with you."

I turned my head and gasped for air just in time to shout her name as she brought me over the edge into ecstasy.

CHAPTER TWENTY

We dozed. We made love again. Finally, as the late afternoon light began to wane, we wandered into the kitchen in search of food. While I scavenged, Val checked her phone messages and placed a few calls.

Her fridge didn't yield much, but I was able to find eggs and a small wedge of cheese that could serve as the basis for omelets. In her pantry I scrounged up an onion, then moved on to the fruit bowl where I found an avocado and a tomato. And an extravagant diamond ring. Its large, square-cut diamond was set into a platinum band that was itself partially encrusted with smaller diamonds. When I held it up to the overhead light, it sparkled like a crown jewel. My temper flared and the panther snarled as I realized who this must have come from.

"What is this?"

Val looked sheepish. "Sebastian gave it to me. He insisted on taking some pictures while I was wearing it."

"Why is it in your fruit bowl?"

She got up and cautiously slid her arms around my waist. "I don't know. I remember taking it off as soon as his damn photo op was over, and I guess that's where it ended up."

"Is it real?"

"I assume so." She kissed the nape of my neck, then rested her chin on my shoulder. "Want to come with me when I give it back to him?"

"Oh yes. Yes. When?"

Val spun me to face her. "Right now."

I studied her face, seeing nothing but sincerity. "What will you say to him?"

"That this so-called marriage is over and he'll soon be paid a visit from my divorce attorney."

My anger began to melt away, and I leaned up to kiss her. "I've already asked Olivia for recommendations. Her list is probably in my e-mail."

"Good. Let's pick one out together and see if we can get a meeting tonight."

Just as I was about to claim another kiss, the intercom buzzed. Val looked over at the microwave clock and pulled away reluctantly. "Those will be the dogs."

"Dogs? You own dogs?"

She held up one hand as she had a brief conversation with the person at the door—a man whom she referred to as Brandt. "Two Dobermans," she said after buzzing him in. She turned back to me with a grin. "My head of security at the club suggested them after Brenner's first assassination attempt. But mostly, I got them because Sebastian hated the idea."

"I like them already."

The man who stood at the front door holding the leashes of two black and tan Dobermans was tall and lanky with a patchy beard. He handed the dogs over to Val with a promise to be looking out for her call about when he could next pick them up. The dogs entered the apartment eagerly, but halted as soon as they saw me. As one, they began to growl.

"Edward. Jacob. Settle." The dogs stopped making noise immediately, but they didn't relax their wary stances.

"You named your dogs Edward and Jacob?" I asked, feeling the last remnants of my jealousy fade.

Val's smile grew wider. "Well, yeah."

I crouched down to be at their level and released my grip on the panther just enough to let them see exactly what was lurking behind my eyes. Immediately, they dove onto their bellies, whimpering softly.

"That's right, dogs," I said conversationally, holding my hand out for them to sniff. "I'm in charge." As they slunk closer and began to lick my fingers, I looked up at Val. "Ah...you do know that 'Edward' is female, right?"

"Mm. She's very pretty, isn't she?"

Laughing, I stood and threw my arms around her neck. "I think I just fell more in love with you."

Val reached down to scratch between the dogs' ears. "I never thought I'd say this, but, Edward, I am in your debt."

She kissed me, then—a series of soft, lingering kisses that made me melt against her. "I love you," she murmured. "Let's look through that list of attorneys, and then go pay Sebastian a visit. Afterward, I can show you my bank."

Exhilaration rushed through me at the prospect of taking such important steps forward already. This was how things would be from now on: Val and I, rebuilding our life together, creating even stronger foundations than we'd had before. I pressed a kiss to the soft fabric over her heart and nodded my assent.

❖

Night had fallen by the time we arrived at Luna, but it was still too early for the club to be open. Val led us to the business entrance, where we were admitted without search or question. After tonight, I imagined, that would change.

As we rode the elevator up to the second floor, Val squeezed my hand in reassurance. I had expected her to be the anxious one, but she had remained calm—even while selecting a gun from her extensive collection. When I'd asked why she wanted to bring one at all, she had said only, "Insurance."

The doors opened and we stepped out into a luxurious waiting area. The ornate wall panels were fashioned out of some kind of dark wood—mahogany, I thought—and the chairs were upholstered in a sapphire-colored fabric. Sebastian's secretary was a young, blond werewolf who looked like she had just stepped out of a Victoria's Secret catalogue. She greeted Val with a long-suffering air and informed her that she could see Sebastian whenever she liked.

"What was that about?" I whispered as we walked down the hall toward his office.

"Christina has the hots for Sebastian," Val said. "She doesn't approve of me."

"Today will be a happy one for her, then."

When Val halted in front of the door to the corner suite, I squared my shoulders and took a deep breath. My panther, already on edge amongst so many unknown Weres, snarled at the scent of Sebastian behind the doors.

Val bent to kiss me. "I love you," she said, and the words sounded confident and strong. After knocking and receiving the go-ahead to enter, she pushed open the doors and I followed her inside.

Sebastian's office had only one opaque wall. The rest were made of glass to show off his view and, I suspected, to mollify his wolf's need for space. His profile was masculine and striking: dark, wavy hair; thick eyelashes; strong chin. For a moment, I pictured him as he must have looked at Valentine's mercy: defiant yet submissive, furious but aroused. Desire for her spiraled down my spine, momentarily displacing my jealousy. Val would be tentative with me for a while as we reestablished our dynamic. But someday soon, I wanted her to take *me* with the same take-no-prisoners attitude she had shown him.

As we entered the room, Sebastian looked up from his desk, his mouth thinning in displeasure when he noticed me at Valentine's side. He pushed his chair back and crossed one leg over the other.

"Last I heard, you two weren't speaking. What's the occasion?"

"The situation has changed." Val withdrew the ring from her pocket and tossed it to him. He automatically reached up to catch it. "You and I are getting a divorce."

His jaw dropped. "What the fuck?"

"You heard me." Her tone was conversational, but steel undergirded her words. "You can keep the half of my money to which you're entitled. Those were the terms of your business proposition, and those will be my terms to end it. My attorney will bring you the paperwork tomorrow."

He leaned back in his chair, lacing his hands behind his head. "And if I refuse to sign?"

My panther hissed and spat, pushing hard for control. She wanted to teach him a lesson—preferably a mortal one. But as much as I wanted my teeth in his throat, I held her back. This was Valentine's fight. Faster than even my eyes could follow, she had drawn her gun and was pointing it at his crotch.

"Here's a curious question. If I shoot them off now, do you think they'll grow back after you shift?"

I almost laughed. Sebastian's eyes widened. "You wouldn't."

Val smiled sweetly as she cocked her pistol. "You sure?"

I watched Sebastian battle down his wolf as he held Val's gaze. It didn't take long for him to end their silent standoff. "Fine. I'll sign the fucking papers."

"A wise decision." Val put up her gun and pulled out her keychain. She removed one of the keys and tossed that to him as well. "I won't be needing this either. See you around."

She turned to go, but I wasn't about to leave without saying my piece.

"Stay away from her, Sebastian. If you personally need to get in touch with her for any reason, you come through me. Are we clear?"

His lip curled in a silent snarl. "Crystal. Now run along, kitty, and enjoy your ball of string."

"Oh, I plan to. You have a good night."

As we walked back to the elevator, I remained on high alert, but we left the building without incident. The night was warmer than I'd anticipated—merely cool instead of bitingly cold—and the reminder that spring was just around the corner made me smile. Soon, the wintry bonds that had imprisoned the earth would dissolve completely, and the air would be redolent with the green scent of growing things. Now that Val was mine again, I could welcome the spring without resentment.

Val linked her arm through mine as we made our way back to her car. "That went pretty well, I thought. You?"

"It could have been much worse," I acknowledged.

The buzz of my phone interrupted our conversation, and I looked down at the screen where Karma's photograph was flashing.

"Hi, you."

"Even your monosyllables sound happy," she said, sounding bemused. Val, whose keen ears had heard the words, caught my free hand and squeezed gently.

"Thanks in large part to you," I said. "What's up?"

"I just wanted to see how you're doing."

"We're good. Really good." I wrapped Val's arm around me and leaned back against her chest. "I can't thank you enough for all your help. How are you holding up?"

"Brenner has Headquarters in chaos." Tension crackled beneath her words, and I felt a frisson of guilt. I'd been so preoccupied with Val that I'd almost forgotten about Brenner and the hostage Sunrunners.

"There's no new word on his movements?"

"Exactly the opposite. His people haven't *stopped* moving. We think they're trying to mask where they're taking the prisoners. The security teams are going out of their minds."

"You sound exhausted. What can I do to help?"

"Nothing, short of finding a way to bring Malcolm back," she said wistfully. "We need him more than ever."

"You know, I saw him yesterday."

As I told her about my encounter in the arena, Val's cell rang. She dropped my hand and moved away a few paces. I heard her murmuring into her phone but couldn't make out the words. After a few moments, she returned, sliding her arms around my waist. Her embrace was at once comforting in its familiarity and exhilarating in its newness. My breath caught and I covered her hands with my own, slipping my fingers between hers.

"Hey," she whispered against my ear. The sensation of her lips against my earlobe sent tiny shivers coursing beneath my skin. I knew she could feel them.

"I need to go, Karma." Miraculously, my voice remained steady as I told her not to hesitate to call if she needed anything. After disconnecting, I leaned my head back against Val's shoulder and smiled as she kissed my neck.

"How's Karma?"

"Burned out. This waiting game is really getting to her. Who were you talking to?"

"The divorce attorney. She'll have the paperwork to Sebastian tomorrow." She guided me into the car and gave the driver an address on the west side. "Ready to see my bank?"

"Mm." I leaned into her and exhaled deeply in an effort to ease the knots that had gathered between my shoulders, but I couldn't quite dispel my anxiety about Sebastian. "How do you feel about getting a divorce?"

She seemed confused by the question. "I feel great. Relieved. Free." She pulled away enough to meet my gaze. "Did you think I was going to feel sad?"

"I don't know. You were married to him, after all."

She grasped my chin gently. "Alexa, I need you to believe me when I tell you that this thing with Sebastian…for me, it really was all business. For him, I guess it wasn't. But I don't want him and I never loved him. Marrying him was expedient so I could have access to the kinds of capital I needed to get the bank on its feet."

"I understand," I said. "Really, I do. Thank you for being honest with me."

"I will always be honest with you. I swear it." She pulled me closer, and I watched the city roll by with my head cushioned on her chest.

"Speaking of money," she said a few minutes later, "I'd like to hear your thoughts on what we should do with it."

"Yours or mine?" When she regarded me quizzically, I told her about Constantine's generous gift. "I don't have nearly as much as you do, but I'm no longer in debt and my financial outlook is good."

"That's wonderful, baby." Val's mouth suddenly tightened in determination. "Move in with me. Into my apartment in Soho, into our apartment in the Village, into any place you want."

I thrilled at the confidence in her request. "Of course I'll move in with you. And your new place is exquisite." A sudden thought made my eyes narrow. "Have you ever brought anyone there? Tonya? Giselle?"

Panic rose in her eyes. "No. No one. Ever."

"So I'm the only one you've ever made love to in that bed."

"The only one."

"Good." I considered our options as she combed her fingers through my hair. "Let's stay in your current apartment for now. We can find a new place together later if we want to."

Her radiant smile was contagious, and for the first time in months, I found myself excited about what the future would hold. The car pulled up at the Bank of Mithras a few moments later, where Val gave me the access code for the side entrance used by the vampires and few shifters who needed to access the bank at night.

"Kyle will probably be here," she said as we went down to the nocturnal lobby. "He works here as one of my assistants. Is that okay?"

"I'll manage." I didn't relish seeing Kyle. The last time we'd been in the same place, I had lost control of my panther. But at least Val hadn't slept with him.

When we entered the bustling lobby, all eyes turned to Val, who slipped her arm around my waist. I struggled with self-consciousness, but Val seemed relaxed despite being the object of so many curious stares. Then again, she had grown up under this kind of scrutiny.

"Good evening, everyone," she said, raising her voice so the entire room could hear her. "Employees and guests alike. I want to be certain that you've all been introduced to my partner, Alexa Newland. Please ensure that she is afforded the same courtesy and respect you show to me."

As we walked across the floor, I finally understood what Homecoming queens felt like. Touched as I was by Valentine's need to make a grand gesture, I was ready to be out of the spotlight. "What prompted the speech?" I whispered.

"Something I remembered from my teenage years about how to spread news quickly: tell just enough of the right people, and everyone will know within hours." She rested her hand at the small of my back. "And I need everyone to know I'm yours again."

I leaned into her as we walked, momentarily overcome by the passion behind her words. *Yours again.* In the darkest times, I had given up all hope of ever wresting her back over what had seemed an impassable divide, and now she was making public proclamations about belonging to me. I could look into the future without feeling fear or loneliness. Valentine was my eternity, and we could embark on our shared life together knowing we'd been made all the stronger by the crucible we'd had to endure.

When Kyle met us at the entrance to Val's office and began talking a mile a minute, my nerves were soothed by his obvious anxiety.

"Kyle," Val said, cutting off his babbling. "There are some additional details I want you to know. Alexa found a way to reverse my transition to full vampire. And Sebastian and I are getting a divorce, at my instigation."

Kyle blinked, too shocked to speak, and Val clapped him on the shoulder. "Spread the word for me, will you? Things are going to work a little differently around here now. I'll call a staff meeting for the beginning of next week."

She turned and led me past Kyle's desk, through a waiting area, and into her office. When the door closed behind us, she immediately shrugged out of her suit jacket. "I'm glad that's over with."

Too busy taking in the décor of Val's office, I didn't reply. She had furnished the room with pieces that combined an old-world consciousness with modern materials. Her desk was a steampunk masterpiece: shaped like a bent airplane wing, its distressed aluminum surface gleamed under the lamplight. The conference table was made of salvaged wood that fit together without any screw or bolt, and the chairs around it were upholstered in supple, chocolate-colored leather.

"What do you think?" she asked as she sat in the chair behind her desk.

"Comfortable yet distinguished. I like it very much. It suits you."

She grinned, a hungry glint in her eyes, and gestured for me to come closer. I was just about to ask whether she had locked the door, when her phone rang. With a sigh, she lifted the receiver.

"Oh? Yes, I did see them. Well, ah, send him in then."

After replacing the phone, she got up and joined me near the table. "I'm about to be paid a visit by a very angry Pritchard," she said. "Will you stay?"

"Are you sure I shouldn't go?"

"Please don't," she answered quickly. "This won't take long. I promise."

A moment later, Pritchard stormed in. He had dressed well for this meeting in a black suit and striped tie, but the polished effect was spoiled by the weight he'd put on since last I'd seen him.

"Pritchard," Val greeted him before he could open his mouth. "You remember Alexa, I'm sure. Please have a seat. Would you like a scotch?"

"I sure as fuck will have some of your fucking scotch," he growled. "It's the least you can do."

"I understand that you're angry," Val said as she poured the rich liquid into a snifter.

"Angry?" He shook his head. "You made me believe you were going to help me, and then you went behind my back and poisoned my investors against me!"

He took a long drink from the glass Val handed him. She sat next to me and leaned back in her chair, seeming unfazed by Pritchard's rant. As I took in the strong, elegant lines of her stretched legs, I felt my desire reawaken. Val may have formerly eschewed this life, but it was already clear to me that she had the instincts for it.

"You're right. That's exactly what I did."

Clearly, Pritchard hadn't expected her to own up to her actions, and he sat gaping like a fish for several seconds. "So what are you going to do about it?" he asked belligerently.

Val rested her hands on the table, and I was momentarily distracted by the memory of exactly what her talented fingers could do. "Here's what I propose," she said. "Given that I now have your investors' confidence, I'll take over management of the fund. But I want you to be BlueFin's president."

He scowled. "What will my responsibilities be?"

"You'll be the face of the fund. You'll take all of the press calls and you'll manage the relationships with BlueFin's investors."

He shot the rest of the glass back in one gulp, and my throat burned in empathy. "So basically, I'm your monkey with no real power."

Val's eyes glittered, and for a moment, I thought she might rise to his baiting. Instead, she folded her hands on the tabletop. "Yes. But you'll be a very, very well paid monkey."

Pritchard's lip curled, but he held his temper in check. "Fine. What's the next step?"

Val leaned back in her chair, and I could tell she was pleased. "My assistant will draw up the paperwork. It'll be finalized by next week."

He stood and reluctantly held out his hand. "I'll wait for your call, then."

Once Val had ushered him out, she returned to find me lounging in her desk chair. "You make a very sexy banker," I told her as I propped my feet up onto her desk. I was gratified to see her eyes darken.

"Do I?" She stalked toward me, but stopped when I held out one hand.

"Don't come any closer. And yes, you do. Who would have thought?"

Her smile was rueful. "I fit in well with the rest of my family when I'm behaving like a soulless vampire."

"Come here," I said, torn by the distress in her voice. When she was close enough, I slid one hand beneath her oxford shirt and rubbed the taut muscles of her abdomen. "I saw what you just did for Pritchard. You can be good at this without being ruthless."

Val dropped to one knee and leaned in for a kiss. "Only when you're with me, baby. Only then."

The kiss deepened quickly, and we might have finally made love in her office if her phone hadn't rung again. When she answered, I could hear the breathlessness in her voice, and I felt smug until alarm registered on her face. At that moment, my cell buzzed and I fished it out of my pocket to the sight of Solana's new number.

"Solana," I said, retreating to the other side of the room. With a twinge of shame, I found myself hoping to hear details about her rendezvous with Helen. "How are you?"

"I need your help," Solana said, sounding disturbingly close to tears. "Helen just received a message from Brenner. She is planning to sacrifice herself to save the Sunrunner delegation, and I can't talk her out of it. Will you come to the Headquarters building as soon as you can?"

I owed Solana more than my own life; I owed her Val's. "Of course. I'll be there right away." Val set down her phone then, and I could tell from her shell-shocked expression that she had just heard the same news. A sense of dread tightened my throat. "We both will. Sit tight, okay? Don't let her do anything drastic."

"Hurry," was all Solana said before disconnecting the call.

"That was Devon Foster," Val said as I returned to her side. She looked dazed—as though she'd just weathered a nasty blow to the head. "Helen is going to walk into a death trap set by Brenner, and Foster wants me to talk her out of it. She thinks Helen might listen to me, since I'm a member of the Order."

"My call was from Solana. Same message." I ran my fingers through Val's hair, needing the connection. "Not that Helen would listen to me in a million years, but Solana wants reinforcements."

Val caught my free hand and pressed it to her lips. "I was hoping we'd have more time. This is going to get very ugly, very fast."

She was right. This kind of power play could only end badly. Brenner had sidelined Malcolm, perhaps permanently. If he managed to remove Helen from the picture, he would create a power vacuum at the highest level of the Consortium. But despite the grim outlook, I felt hopeful. Val and I had already proven that we could survive anything as long as we were together. This would be no different.

"Oh, my love." I leaned down to kiss her forehead. "We'll get through this, I promise. And then we'll have plenty of time just for us. I'm not accepting anything less than forever with you."

Chapter Twenty-one

The new receptionist was clearly frightened, but she managed to hold herself together long enough to tell us that Helen was taking meetings in her office. We found ourselves alone in the elevator, and I went into Val's arms willingly.

"Helen and I have had our differences," she said as she stroked my hair. "Big ones. But I don't want her to die, and definitely not like this."

I slipped my hand beneath her shirt and lightly massaged the tight muscles of her lower back. I could feel her getting riled up, and I wanted to have all the information before we did anything rash. "Let's just wait and hear what she has to say before we make any decisions."

Devon Foster was standing guard outside Helen's office, looking sick with anger. When she saw us approaching, relief momentarily eclipsed the rage clearly written on her face. Once, her attention would have been riveted to me, but now she was staring hard at Val.

"I've been hearing insane rumors about you."

"For once, they might actually be true." Val looked past Foster to the door. "We can talk about that later. Can I see her now?"

"She's in with Constantine. She won't be long. No one has lasted past ten minutes."

"What do you mean?" I asked.

"She's made up her mind to meet Brenner's demands and won't hear any criticism."

Val frowned. "What are his demands, exactly?"

"You haven't seen it yet?" Foster pulled out her phone. "He released this message two hours ago using the same distribution channels as when he delivered that proclamation about the virus last summer. Leon and I have been over it twenty times already, trying to figure out what we can do."

She passed the phone to Val, who angled it so we could both see the screen. The video revealed a male figure, his face cast in shadow, seated behind a desk set in an alcove. Behind him, bay windows with a view of the surrounding nighttime cityscape stretched from the floor to the ceiling. When the figure switched on the desk lamp, my panther tried to lash out. She wanted Balthasar Brenner's heart between her teeth.

"Easy, sweetheart," Val murmured. When she began to rub my back, I realized I was trembling.

As I pulled deep, even breaths into my lungs, Brenner smiled into the camera. He wore a simple blue oxford shirt and his dark hair was pulled back into a long ponytail, just as I remembered. His smile reminded me of Sebastian's—charming and charismatic. He looked normal, and that was the most frightening part of all.

"Good evening, Helen. I'd like to extend an invitation to you to join me here, at my suite in the Four Seasons, at midnight tomorrow." He unclasped his hands and rested his muscular arms on the desk. "There is, you see, an experiment I've always wished to try. I'm deathly curious about how much time it takes for one of you Sunrunner vampires to immolate."

Foster looked murderous, and Val was grinding her teeth. I leaned against her, needing to reassure her just as she had done for me a moment ago.

"If you come alone and unarmed as my test subject in this matter, the Sunrunners who are currently my guests will be released. However, if you do not abide by my precise terms, I'm afraid I will have to use all of the delegation members in my research." He smiled again. "I very much look forward to hearing from you by daybreak regarding your intentions."

When the video went dark, Val shoved the phone back at Foster. "Damn it!"

Foster was livid. "That rat bastard shot this video in the Ty Warner Penthouse of the Four Seasons—the most expensive hotel room in the city."

"And he did his filming in front of the window with eastern exposure," I added.

Foster gripped the door jamb so hard I thought it might crack. "Leon and I came up with some thoughts about how to extract the delegation right away, but Helen wouldn't hear of it. She insists that meeting Brenner's demands is the only way."

"She can't risk the delegates," Val countered. "Bai is the second-in-command of the most powerful vampire in Asia and possibly the world. The rest of the group is comprised of more of Tian's trusted lieutenants. Letting them die at Brenner's hands would mean the end of Sunrunner support for the Consortium."

"But wouldn't the Consortium also suffer a deathblow if Helen were to die?" Foster asked. "Especially since Malcolm is still... recovering?"

Val shook her head. "The infrastructure of the Consortium will still exist if Helen were to die. She has no clear successor, but one could be put in her place."

Foster opened her mouth to reply, but at that moment the door opened and Constantine emerged, his panther close to the surface. When he saw Valentine and me standing together, surprise eclipsed his internal struggle.

"You've returned." He glanced from Val to me, his expression wary. "With success, I take it?"

I stepped forward to embrace him. "With great success. Can we talk soon?"

He nodded. "Come find me in the War Room."

As we watched him walk way, Val looked troubled. "I need to apologize to him."

"You don't. He's always understood the situation."

"Even so." She took my hand and rubbed her thumb in soothing circles over my skin. "I hurt you, and he feels protective of you. He should have my apology."

Foster, who had ducked inside Helen's office, returned to her post. "She's ready for you. Both of you," she amended when I hung back. That was strange. Helen had never particularly liked me, and I assumed she would have private matters to discuss with Val about the Order of Mithras.

Helen's secretary barely even acknowledged us. She was simultaneously talking on the phone and typing furiously. When Val opened the door, I was even more surprised to see Solana seated next to Helen at the small conference table. Sorrow suffused her face, making her even lovelier.

"Solana tells me you have done the impossible," Helen said to me as Val and I sat in the remaining chairs.

"Thanks entirely to her generosity."

Pride flickered in the brief curve to her lips, coupled with some other, softer emotion. But then it was gone, and she turned her attention to Valentine. "How do you feel?"

Val reached for my hand. "Wonderful. As though the past several months never happened."

Helen's eyes narrowed. "Although, of course, they did."

"I'm not about to neglect my responsibilities, if that's what concerns you," Val said firmly. I found myself impressed. I'd never heard her use such an assertive tone with Helen before. "But from now on, I'll attend to them in ways that won't jeopardize my relationship with Alexa."

Helen leaned back, seemingly mollified. She stroked Solana's arm, and I wondered again how they had spent their brief time together. "I presume you've heard Balthasar's ultimatum."

Val nodded. "Is there no other way?"

"Leon, Devon, and I discussed my options. Accepting Balthasar's terms is the only course of action for which the risk level is acceptable." She glanced at Solana, then me. "If you would be so kind as to step out, there are a few matters I must discuss with Valentine in private."

"I'll be waiting," I told Val, leaning in for a quick kiss before Solana and I returned to the corridor.

Once we were outside, I embraced her. Despite Foster's inquisitive gaze, Solana sagged against me, clearly distraught.

"I don't know what to do, what to think," she said, her voice snarled by unshed tears. "We had only hours together, before that monster sent out his despicable threat. It flicked some sort of switch in her, and nothing I could say made any difference."

I grasped her shoulders and held her at arm's length. "So you think she's wrong? That there are options she's choosing not to explore?"

Solana's eyes were wild with grief. "I think she believes that giving up her life is her only proactive option against him. She is burdened by the weight of constantly being on the defensive, and she hasn't been able to adequately protect her constituents. Until now."

"She probably thinks we'd be better off with someone else." I released Solana and began to pace, my panther urging motion in the face of frustration.

"You're right," Foster said into the silence. "Me."

"You?" Solana echoed in confusion.

"An hour ago, she told me that I'll be named her successor in the Order of Mithras."

I stopped in my tracks. "Doesn't her successor also have to be a Sunrunner?"

"Yes, I am. Helen was the one who turned me."

I flashed back almost a year ago to the sight of Foster lying motionless on the floor of the Missionary's warehouse. We'd surprised him as he fed, and I knew I would always remember the sound of Foster's blood trickling from his chin onto the floor.

"The Missionary fed from you. I saw it."

"So I've been told." She shrugged, no longer fazed by such matters. "But Helen was the one who ultimately turned me."

I began pacing again in an effort to digest this new information. It seemed folly for Helen to appoint Foster, who had been a vampire only a year, to a post of such importance. If the rest of Val's clan hadn't been dead, she would never have been made Missionary so soon after being turned. Had Helen been grooming Foster for this purpose all along?

Solana slumped to the floor, her back to the wall. "Then she truly has given up all hope. No wonder she can't be persuaded to take any other course of action."

"Wait," I said, suddenly inspired. "What if we let her do what she wants, but we do what *we* want?"

When they both stared at me blankly, I forced myself to stand still. "We let her walk into the hotel. But we have a plan—or several—to get her and the delegation out safely."

Foster's eyebrows shot up. "You want to countermand her orders."

For the first time since Solana's frantic call, I smiled. "Of course I do."

The door opened, then, and Valentine emerged. She looked weary, as though the weight of the world had been placed on her shoulders. With all three of us looking at her expectantly, she suddenly bared her teeth.

"I'll be damned if I just sit idly by while she lets Brenner get the upper hand."

Foster barked out a laugh. Solana smiled tremulously. Val looked very confused until I threaded my arms around her neck and leaned in for a kiss.

"Great minds think alike, love."

"I want to help," Solana began, "but I don't want to leave her alone."

"Go. We'll fill you in later." I looked to Foster. "Who else?"

"Leon Summers. Constantine."

Val was nodding and her eyes were bright again. She looked at her watch and her jaw tightened. "We have just over twenty-four hours. We're going to have to move fast."

"We can assemble in the War Room," said Foster. "Once I arrange for additional security up here, I'll join you."

She disappeared back into the antechamber, leaving Val and me alone. Val held me tightly, sliding her hands along my ribs as she stared into my eyes.

"We might not be able to pull this off," she said.

"I know."

"We might start an all-out war."

I thought about that for a few seconds. "Also true."

"I love you." She tucked a stray strand of hair behind my right ear. "Thank you for saving me."

"You're mine. I'm always going to save you." I thought back to the summer, when she had discovered the cure for the deadly virus that Brenner had unleashed during his first power play against the Consortium. "Just like you're always going to save me."

She smiled at me, a bright, uncensored, fully human smile. The smile that was mine and only mine. The smile only I would ever see. And then she pulled back, but only far enough to take my hand.

"Let's go be superheroes, baby."

"Yes," I said as we walked toward the elevator. "Let's."

Epilogue

valentine

The rifle grip had long since warmed from the heat of my palm. My skin was normally cool to the touch, but just before we'd parted ways two hours ago, Alexa had pulled me close and brushed the hair back from her neck. The gesture had been a clear invitation. If Foster and Constantine hadn't been watching, I would have pushed my hand down the front of her tight black jeans and taken her where we stood. Instead, I had swirled my tongue against her skin as I claimed her with my teeth. Desire swept over me at the remembered sensation of her fingertips massaging my scalp while I drank. Arousal pulsed in time with the beat of her blood in my veins, but I refused to allow my breathing to accelerate. Helen's fate might depend on the steadiness of my hands.

The carpeting beneath me was comfortable in its lushness, but I wished for hardwood. This luxurious corner office in the Seagram building had only a small angle of correspondence with the eastern window of the Ty Warner suite, but it had been the best of our viable choices. My grip on the sniper rifle was firm and my body immobile, but the slight give to the carpet fibers had the potential to sidetrack my shot.

I peered through the scope, listening intently for any word from the extraction team. They had gone dark half an hour ago, and I told myself that their silence was a good sign. At the first hint of trouble, they would reopen communications, and that would be my signal. I was the insurance. Either I'd manage to create enough chaos to help them free Helen, or I'd have to perform a mercy killing as the sun rose.

The suite's lights were on, and I could see her clearly through the scope. She sat regally, as though she hadn't been bound to a chair and forced to stare at the gradually brightening sky. Her expression was serene. Peaceful. She had given up.

Anger washed over me and I focused on maintaining even breaths. Helen wanted to die a martyr, a choice I would have respected only if it had been her last possible recourse. In refusing to fight, what did she hope to gain? Especially now that Solana was back in the picture. They looked at each other as though they could fall in love all over again, and yet Helen had insisted on walking directly into the jaws of death. I had been that stupid once, and Alexa had talked me down from the ledge. Since Helen wouldn't listen to reason, we were poised to forcibly drag her off her own metaphorical cliff.

A flicker of motion drew my attention back to the tableau visible through my scope, and not for the first time, I wished I could hear what was going on inside the room. I'd been in position for almost two hours, but Balthasar Brenner had yet to cross into my field of vision. If he did, I would take the shot without hesitation, but I doubted he would make that kind of mistake. He hadn't lived almost five centuries by being reckless about his personal safety.

My breath caught as a familiar figure moved into the space between Helen and the window. Sebastian.

Mind racing, I struggled to keep my body under control. Why on earth would Sebastian show up at his father's suite now? He stopped with his back to the gray sky and crossed his arms over his chest. His lips moved, but I couldn't read the words. Was he in collusion with his father after all? Or had he come to try to bargain for Helen's life?

And then my earbud crackled to life in a cacophony of snarls and the staccato of gunfire.

"Val, do you read?" Foster sounded breathless.

"Yes. What the hell's going on?"

"Game's up. We're cornered."

A low, animal groan followed on the heels of her words, galvanizing my heart into overdrive. Was that Alexa? Had she been wounded? A fresh salvo of gunfire erupted even closer to Foster, and I fought the impulse to cover my ears. Foster was cursing colorfully, and I could hear the slap of her boots against the floor as she ran— whether toward or away from the spray of bullets, it was impossible to say.

"We're out of time," she rasped. "Take your shot, Val!"

The connection snapped, cutting off an eerie canine howl and plunging me back into silence. My heart thudded painfully against my ribs as the image of Alexa, wounded or worse, haunted my mind's eye.

No. No distractions. I had no margin for error. She was alive. I had to believe it. The sooner I fulfilled my mission, the sooner I would be able to join her. And if Brenner's mangy curs had so much as laid a claw on her, I would tear them apart beyond any hope of regeneration.

I took in a deep breath and expelled it. Another. Then another, and another, until my body was steady and my mind was empty and all I could see was Sebastian and Helen. Helen's expression had not changed, but Sebastian's neck was flushed and his jawline sharp as a knife. He was furious.

In that moment, the sun broke free of the horizon. Beams of light streamed into the suite and scattered as they hit the crystal chandelier. Tiny rainbows blossomed on the wall and floor, scintillating like ethereal flowers.

I did not wince. I did not blink. No apology rose to my lips, nor tears to my eyes. Beyond thought or emotion, I pulled the trigger.

The End

About the Authors

Nell Stark is an Assistant Professor of English and the Director of the Writing Center at a college in the SUNY system. **Trinity Tam** is a marketing executive in the music industry and an award-winning writer/producer of film and television. They live, write, and parent a rambunctious toddler just a stone's throw from the historic Stonewall Inn in New York City. For more information about the *everafter* series, visit www.everafterseries.com.

Books Available From Bold Strokes Books

Harmony by Karis Walsh. When Brook Stanton meets a beautiful musician who threatens the security of her conventional, predetermined future, will she take a chance on finding the harmony only love creates? (978-1-60282-237-5)

nightrise by Nell Stark and Trinity Tam. In the third book in the everafter series, when Valentine Darrow loses her soul, Alexa must cross continents to find a way to save her. (978-1-60282-238-2)

Crush by Lea Santos. Winemaker Beck Montalvo loves a good challenge, but could wildly anti-alcohol, ex-cop Tierney Diaz prove to be the first obstacle Beck can't overcome? (978-1-60282-239-9)

Men of the Mean Streets: Gay Noir edited by Greg Herren and J.M. Redmann. Dark tales of amorality and criminality by some of the top authors of gay mysteries. (978-1-60282-240-5)

Women of the Mean Streets: Lesbian Noir edited by J.M. Redmann and Greg Herren. Murder, mayhem, sex, and danger—these are the stories of the women who dare to tackle the mean streets. (978-1-60282-241-2)

Cool Side of the Pillow by Gill McKnight. Bebe Franklin falls for funeral director Clara Dearheart, but how can she compete with the ghost of Clara's lover—and a love that transcends death and knows no rest? (978-1-60282-633-5)

Firestorm by Radclyffe. Firefighter paramedic Mallory "Ice" James isn't happy when the undisciplined Jac Russo joins her command, but lust isn't something either can control—and they soon discover ice burns as fiercely as flame. (978-1-60282-232-0)

The Best Defense by Carsen Taite. When socialite Aimee Howard hires former homicide detective Skye Keaton to find her missing niece, she vows not to mix business with pleasure, but she soon finds Skye hard to resist. (978-1-60282-233-7)

After the Fall by Robin Summers. When the plague destroys most of humanity, Taylor Stone thinks there's nothing left to live for, until she meets Kate, a woman who makes her realize love is still alive and makes her dream of a future she thought was no longer possible. (978-1-60282-234-4)

Accidents Never Happen by David-Matthew Barnes. From the moment Albert and Joey meet by chance beneath a train track on a street in Chicago, a domino effect is triggered, setting off a chain reaction of murder and tragedy. (978-1-60282-235-1)

In Plain View by Shane Allison. Best-selling gay erotica authors create the stories of sex and desire modern readers crave. (978-1-60282-236-8)

Wild by Meghan O'Brien. Shapeshifter Selene Rhodes dreads the full moon and the loss of control it brings, but when she rescues forensic pathologist Eve Thomas from a vicious attack by a masked man, she discovers she isn't the scariest monster in San Francisco. (978-1-60282-227-6)

Reluctant Hope by Erin Dutton. Cancer survivor Addison Hunt knows she can't offer any guarantees, in love or in life, and after experiencing a loss of her own, Brooke Donahue isn't willing to risk her heart. (978-1-60282-228-3)

Conquest by Ronica Black. When Mary Brunelle stumbles into the arms of Jude Jaeger, a gorgeous dominatrix at a private nightclub, she is smitten, but she soon finds out Jude is her professor, and Professor Jaeger doesn't date her students…or her conquests. (978-1-60282-229-0)

The Affair of the Porcelain Dog by Jess Faraday. What darkness stalks the London streets at night? Ira Adler, present plaything of crime lord Cain Goddard, will soon find out. (978-1-60282-230-6)

365 Days by K.E. Payne. Life sucks when you're seventeen years old and confused about your sexuality, and the girl of your dreams doesn't even know you exist. Then in walks sexy new emo girl, Hannah Harrison. Clemmie Atkins has exactly 365 days to discover herself, and she's going to have a blast doing it! (978-1-60282-540-6)

Darkness Embraced by Winter Pennington. Surrounded by harsh vampire politics and secret ambitions, Epiphany learns that an old enemy is plotting treason against the woman she once loved, and to save all she holds dear, she must embrace and form an alliance with the dark. (978-1-60282-221-4)

78 Keys by Kristin Marra. When the cosmic powers choose Devorah Rosten to be their next gladiator, she must use her unique skills to try to save her lover, herself, and even humankind. (978-1-60282-222-1)

Playing Passion's Game by Lesley Davis. Trent Williams's only passion in life is gaming—until Juliet Sullivan makes her realize that love can be a whole different game to play. (978-1-60282-223-8)

Retirement Plan by Martha Miller. A modern morality tale of justice, retribution, and women who refuse to be politely invisible. (978-1-60282-224-5)

Who Dat Whodunnit by Greg Herren. Popular New Orleans detective Scotty Bradley investigates the murder of a dethroned beauty queen to clear the name of his pro football–playing cousin. (978-1-60282-225-2)

The Company He Keeps by Dale Chase. A riotously erotic collection of stories set in the sexually repressed and therefore sexually rampant Victorian era. (978-1-60282-226-9)

Cursebusters! by Julie Smith. Budding-psychic Reeno is the most accomplished teenage burglar in California, but one tiny screw-up and poof!—she's sentenced to Bad Girl School. And that isn't even her worst problem. Her sister Haley's dying of an illness no one can diagnose, and now she can't even help. (978-1-60282-559-8)

True Confessions by PJ Trebelhorn. Lynn Patrick finally has a chance with the only woman she's ever loved, her lifelong friend Jessica Greenfield, but Jessie is still tormented by an abusive past. (978-1-60282-216-0)

Ghosts of Winter by Rebecca S. Buck. Can Ros Wynne, who has lost everything she thought defined her, find her true life—and her true love—surrounded by the lingering history of the once-grand Winter Manor? (978-1-60282-219-1)

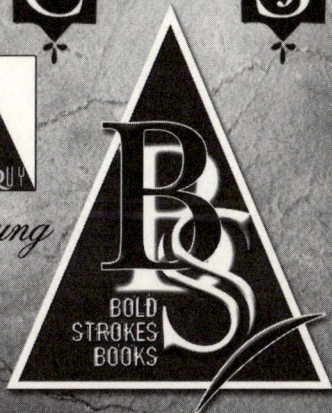